Willow

Willow

TONYA CHERIE HEGAMIN

CANDLEWICK PRESS

Copyright © 2014 by Tonya Cherie Hegamin

First edition 2014

Library of Congress Catalog Card Number 2013946610
ISBN 978-0-7636-5769-7

13 14 15 16 17 18 BVG 10 9 8 7 6 5 4 3 2 1

Printed in Berryville, VA, U.S.A.

This book was typeset in Garamond 3.

Candlewick Press
99 Dover Street
Somerville, Massachusetts 02144

visit us at www.candlewick.com

Dedicated to Trayvon Martin
and Kelley Williams-Bolar,
to remind us just how much history repeats herself

Part

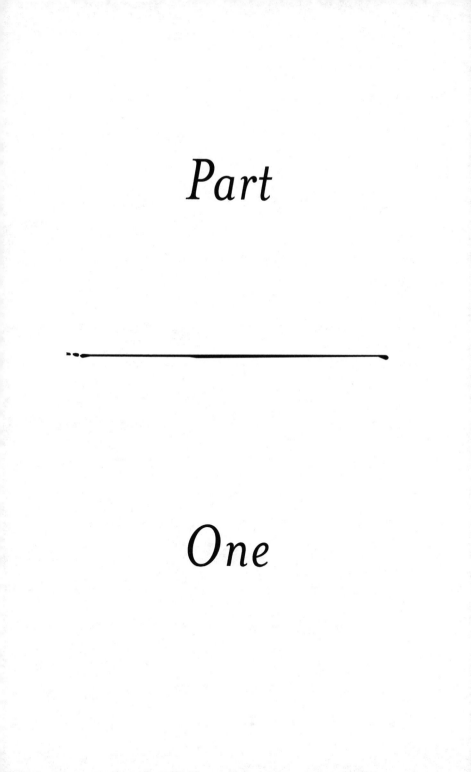

One

September 10, 1848
Knotwild Plantation, Maryland

Dear Mama

    I know you rest in heven in Gods cradle arms. Here,
I am cradle by the twisted bow of yor healing tree, one
you name me for and birth me under fifteen years ago
today at the bank of this sweet river. The sun shine itself
down on the mountains like it cradle there too, in so
much comfort it turn the whole sky pink. It get harder
to find such comfort in this world without you, Mama.
And since Granmam pass last year, make it harder still.
Now I only get held soft by this old tree.

Mama, I dremt it once that you was right here in this tree telling me my mind is my nest and the thoughts my eggs. How very P-E-C-U-L-I-A-R. That mean strange. Mama, you the bird who built this nest and lay these eggs I think.

Granmam used to say that this here tree be the last of many to be holding up the banks of this river. Chop a willow branch, she say, then boil down the bark to ease all pains. She always say I pay more attention to her medcine recipes than her food recipes.

Mama, I know you miss living here on the prettyest and most prosprous piece of land in all Frederick County maybe even all Maryland, specially since we got me the onlyest colurd girl who can read and write and ride a horse like shes the wind.

Granmam would wash my mouth to humble me. . . .

No matter how good this type of free, no black girl meant to be so much of herself they say.

I hope Rev dont miss this bit of grafite pencil and copybook I found in his old schoolboy box in the attik. I was getting ink stains in my nails and fingers and it do cost to replenish Revs supply. Papa wouldve seen red to know.

Granmam would be shame to see the shabby state Rev house in. To tell truth, now with her gone I read bold as I please even whilst doing the chores specially when Rev Jeff be gone almost six month straight! There be nothing in me to help it. The stories, they drunken me. I mus try an be more careful — that be why now I only write way out here. Papa dont mind me takeing Mayapple out so early, long as I bring back willow bark and herbs for his sleeping tea, jus like you used to. He miss you so, he barely breathe your name.

Dearest Mama, goodby for now. I only remember your face full, so full of light.

> *We are such stuff*
> *As dreams are made on; and our little life*
> *Is rounded with a sleep.*

Prospero says in Mr. Shakespeares Tempest. *I memorize the most beautiful bits I read, tho sometimes the words be slick and stick to my tongue like okra, just how they come slow as molassas out the pen.*

Your most loving daughter
Willow

Carefully, I wrapped the copybook and pencil together in a bit of thick cloth and placed them in a worn leather pouch. I always sat down low in the riverbank when I wrote so nobody could see me plainly, down where the roots of the huge tree jutted out of the earth then plunged back in like crooked fingers testing the soil.

I breathed in deep the fresh, musky air of early autumn, watched my breath plume back out of me, disappearing into the mist of the crisp morning. The chill was sharp and my lungs tightened, racked with cough. I adjusted my knitted shawl and tried to recall if I'd ever had any other birthdays with such an early frost, but the memories turned my heart to missing Granmam and Mama again. A breeze lifted a few of the lifeless leaves from Mama's tree; they scattered and floated clumsily along with the river current. The tree bowed to the edge of the river in such a polite way that it looked as though the tree were asking the river for a waltz. . . . I almost took out my copybook again to write down that pretty thought, but I knew I needed to go.

I moved some leaves and twigs from my hiding nook inside the tree trunk, where I always kept my writing tools. I covered them up again and climbed up the sloping bank, brushing my hands on the back of my riding clothes—a patched and repatched pair of Papa's pants cinched with rope, worn under a plain old smock. I looked over at Mama's grave again; a large mound of faded whitewashed stones marked it. Mason and Dixon had left a granite marker showing the difference betwixt the Maryland and Pennsylvania sides, not too far off. I could see it gleaming white, but never went close. Can't say it looked much different over there than over here. I wondered if I'd feel any different if I stepped over Mama's grave and sunk my big toe deep into that free soil. . . . The thought gave me another chill, but this one went from inside my head down to my heart.

Mayapple greeted me from behind with a snort and a shake of her glossy copper mane.

"Sometimes I do believe you're vainer than any human I know," I told her, turning to stroke her muzzle. Mayapple was indeed the prettiest horse in all of Frederick County, but more importantly, the fastest. Papa and Rev Jeff once timed me riding her out here and compared it to the times of other horses who won at them British *darbys*. They had nothing on us. 'Course, we never raced anyone for real, since I was the only one who rode her. Mayapple don't take so well to everybody. While she tolerated Papa, more than once she threw Cholly Dee off her back when he tried. He would have liked to make her into glue, I'm sure — Rev, Papa, and I still get a good laugh out of that story! Me and Mayapple both stay out of Cholly's way on purpose. He don't like me, either, though I never threw him off any-thing. Papa say Mayapple can tell a bad one from a mile away. Papa say Cholly Dee's mad at us 'cause he's only num-ber three at Knotwild, after Rev Jeff and Papa. Rev Jeff would say Cholly's number four, 'cause though Rev's the master of the plantation, he himself must answer to God.

Mayapple gave a whinny to let me know she was done dawdling, and ready for her breakfast, too. We raced back home just so to feel the wind in our faces.

Back in the stable, I brushed Mayapple twice, 'cause she just wasn't satisfied with a once-over, and I put on her feed bag. When she looked so forlorn that I was leaving her, I promised to braid her mane later. But as I left the stable, I could see the sun sitting right atop the mountains, so I knew Papa would be waiting. When I rushed into our cabin, Papa was already seated at his place and had a steaming plate of grits in front of him.

"Papa, I—"

"Girl, you're lucky it's your birthday," he cut me off sternly, chopping at the lumpy mound he'd made for himself. "A man could starve around here waiting on you. How you supposed to keep a husband happy if you can't even take care of your own pa?"

My heart felt all crooked, like it sat in my elbows instead of my chest. Papa was always a bit cranky when he was hungry, but it was his talk about husbands that hurt the most. I whispered I was sorry and began cleaning up the pot he'd cooked in. The grits were burnt and clung to the bottom of the pan like they were afraid to come out. I knew how they felt.

For the past few months, Papa had been bringing up this husband business. It wasn't that I didn't want a family of my own one day, but right now I wanted to think about finishing all the Greek myths this winter and to ponder Mr. Shakespeare's word puzzles. There was no husband I knew in these parts who I could tell that to, much less Papa. He seemed fine with me reading the Bible if nobody else knew, but I don't think he know I can and do read so much more.

"Aww, now, don't sulk," Papa said gently when he'd finished his food, handing me the dish to wash. "I didn't mean to hurt your feelings, 'specially not today. I know you'll make a mighty fine wife for a nice man. You know I don't mind you spending time at your mother's grave, darlin', but I just want to make sure you remember your place, your duty."

His hand felt real heavy on my shoulder. I nodded and smiled up at him. Papa's favorite talk was about "duty" and "responsibility." You couldn't argue or tell him different; it just wasn't done. Cholly Dee was the only one who dared disagree with Papa, and even that wasn't too often.

"Now, then." Papa's voice brightened. "It's your birthday, and let's have it right. Go get yourself seated."

"Papa, I'd like to go wash up and change. . . ." I was still in my riding clothes.

"Naw, you're just fine. Sit." There was a little twinkle in his eye as he went back to his room. I went and sat down carefully at Granmam's old rocking chair. She would've made me scrub till I shined before letting me perch. I looked down at my cracked fingernails and tried to coax some of the dirt out from underneath. I caught a glimpse of myself in the copper kettle hanging in the hearth—a luxury Rev brought back 'specially for us from Paris. I had a dirty face and an old rag on my head, unruly braids poking out in all directions, wearing men's clothes to go riding out into the wood to read and write. Who'd want such a wife?

Papa came back with a box tied with a white ribbon. He was grinning from ear to ear. "I know things are different this year, with Granmam gone and all. . . ." His face twisted a bit, fighting back his grief. He swallowed hard and continued.

"I'm sure Rev Jeff wanted to be here, but he'll be back soon to wish you a happy birthday himself. So it's just us, Mite. We all each other's got."

Mite is my old pet name from when I was a tiny baby, born early and sick, and it softened my sadness a bit. My scalp tingled as Papa put his hand atop my head and carried out our usual birthday custom.

"God, thank you for giving us this fine day. We ask you

in your infinite wisdom to bless this girl another year of life. We pray that you find it in your plans to keep her here on earth with us, and that you don't need her in heaven with you just yet."

Papa paused at the end of the prayer. It was the same one that was said over my head every year of my life. Granmam said they never thought I'd survive that first year. And the following years I was never all too strong, especially when I was just barely two, Mama died, from that bad pox was going around. From Papa's silence, I reckoned he was thinking of Granmam just then. Usually she and then Rev Jeff would've put their hands on my head all together and said the same prayer, a triple blessing. Finally Papa added, "And merciful God, we have a special request this year. . . . We pray that you see fit to find the right man to make our dear Willow his wife."

I almost forgot to say "Amen." When I looked up, the tears in Papa's eyes matched mine. Papa patted my face tenderly and turned to wipe his. I busied myself by opening the box he'd set on my lap. As I opened it, a familiar scent found its way to my nose. I couldn't place it, though. I looked up at Papa, who was sitting on the edge of his seat. Carefully, I unfolded the thin paper inside. There was a yellow vest embroidered with tiny delicate green vines of pink flowers over the heart. Under that, there was a sky-blue dress. Papa stood and pulled the dress from the box, holding it up proudly for me to see. It was lovely — simple, with a modest ruffle around the bottom, at the neck collar, and on the sleeves. The buttons were little carved wooden shells.

"It was your mama's, Willow, though she didn't get to wear it much." Papa's voice quivered a bit in his throat. "See here? I carved these buttons for her myself, and the vest — I had Tiny do that embroidery just for you."

"Papa," I nearly whispered, "it's beautiful. Thank you."

"It's about time you start dressing like a grown woman. Now, go wash up and put it on."

I climbed up the narrow, twisting stairs to the loft where I slept and laid the dress out on the bed while I cleaned myself up in the washbowl. The dress and vest fit me almost perfectly; my cheeks heated to find that I still needed to grow quite a bit into the chest area. Luckily, the vest would cover that. I was small for my age, people always told me. Granmam said it was because of my weak constitution. But the dress wasn't too long; I suppose my mother was small, too. Or maybe Tiny just hemmed up the bottom of the skirt to fit me. I'd grown out of my everyday dress and my Sunday dress, so for the past few months, with Rev Jeff gone, I'd taken to wearing Papa's shirts and Granmam's skirts, both were too big.

I admired the threadwork Tiny had done — she was known throughout the county for her fine stitching. Rev

Jeff had bartered her from our neighbor Master Rawlins a little over three years ago. I heard Papa and Rev Jeff talking about how Rawlins had used her for breeding more slaves, putting her with whatever man he thought she'd make strong children with, like she was a dog. Granmam said Tiny got the illness that withered her lady parts from being passed around so much. Then once she couldn't have more children for him to sell and she was too weak to do fieldwork, Master Rawlins was set to sell her, too. One of our horses had just birthed a foal Rawlins wanted so Rev Jeff made the trade. Rev told Papa he felt bad knowing she'd already had all of her children sold from her, and then she'd probably be sold who knows where. Rev Jeff did kind things like that often. Papa says he's the gentlest, kindest white man on earth, and he would know, as they grew up together at Knotwild, Papa just six weeks older than the Reverend.

Rev had hoped Tiny would be able to help Granmam and me doing light housework, but Tiny ended up being a disaster around the house. Rawlins had kept her busy giving birth almost every year. She could cook all right, but in the big house, she was as clumsy as an ox. Once she even caught her bottom on fire in the hearth! I think it was Granmam's solemn and quiet ways made Tiny nervous. The only thing we could find for her to do where she could sit quietly and not get in the way was sewing. We were all surprised to see how neat and small Tiny's stitches were, even when she was just mending moth holes in the table linens. Granmam began to give her more and more delicate work to do, since I'd always ruin it. Tiny even taught herself how to embroider, and she found joy in that. I showed Rev Jeff how good her work was and he began to let her hire out, saying she had "true artistry." Now women came from as far away as Baltimore for Tiny's handiwork. Rawlins was still sour over that—especially when the foal he'd gotten in trade for her broke its ankle and had to be put down. Rev Jeff made a nice profit off his own kindness. I helped Tiny count her earnings so far—almost seventy dollars.

I took off my raggedy bonnet, then oiled, parted, and finger-combed my thick black hair, making two neater braids. I tucked the braids up under my Sunday bonnet; they were getting long and as stiff as hemp rope. By the time I was ready, Papa had already gone down to the meeting-house. I gathered the Bible Rev Jeff gave me and my white lace Sunday shawl, then hurried out to meet Papa and the others. Papa says most slaves don't even have their own proper place to meet for Sunday prayers and communion— down south it was against the law. Rev Jeff wanted us to have pride in our plantation being the best in the county, and he said he wanted us to be grateful not to him, but to God. Rev Jeff studied religion at the college in Princeton, New Jersey, and he believed in "public religion." He passed on his learning to Papa. I read in one of Rev's newspapers that two years ago New Jersey had abolished slavery. But they were keeping all the blacks in "indentured servitude" for life. I still don't understand how that was different, but I tried not to think about white men's laws too much. They were even harder than Shakespeare to decipher.

There were nearly eighty hands working our land. Most were families who'd been at Knotwild for many years, most for at least two generations. My great-great-grandmother was one of the first slaves here. Rev Jeff's grandfather Zacharias bought this land in 1760, Rev would tell us. Rev's grandmother had been from Germany, of the peaceful Mennonite tradition, but his father was from a wealthy old South Carolina family who owned a plantation with at least two hundred slaves. Papa said Zacharias never needed to use force to get a body to do something. He'd been a strict but fair master who, just to please his wife, would sell a slave rather than beat him. I never been whupped, but I'd still say I'd rather take the rawhide than get sold away to who knows what or where.

Rev Jeff was a kind master, like his granddad. As the foreman, Papa managed the whole plantation—livestock, stables, and ironworks included, and Papa's father had done the same for Rev's grandfather. Cholly Dee was the driver of the field hands, making sure everyone worked hard and fast. He answered to Papa. Cholly came to the plantation when he was in his teens, Papa told me, having been bought and sold several times for his sour and spiteful ways; he settled down at Knotwild, tired of getting beaten and sold. I reckon he was always jealous of Papa's standing with Rev Jeff—they were like two peas in a pod, after all, having grown up so close.

Our cabin was only a few paces from the main house. I walked down the tree-lined path to where the slave cabins and meetinghouse stood. Everyone was greeting one another outside. A few of the women commented on my dress and how much I looked like my mother. I sat down next to Tiny when I got inside. She grabbed me up in a hug.

"Well, I hope it made a happy birthday, Willow! Lookin' like a grown *lady*," Tiny said after I told her how much I appreciated her work on the vest. "You look 'bout ready to catch yourself a good man!"

My cheeks burned from the attention as others sitting around us turned to giggle or agree. I just lowered my head and studied my hands. I knew Tiny was teasing, but I did feel a slight bit out of place with my clothes being so much finer than anyone else's. I wondered how my mother felt when she wore them.

Papa didn't make it easy for me to socialize much. Used to be I'd have to sit next to Granmam, who held a place of honor at the front, since she was the eldest and had the most respect. At first Papa wanted me to take her chair, but I insisted that Old Samuel, the shepherd, was rightfully next in line. Now I got to sit next to Tiny, with Papa's approval. He thought Tiny was too big and too loud, but he didn't mind her outside of that since she was so profitable. Tiny fell on Papa's every word like they were feather pillows.

There were no girls my age at Knotwild; Tiny guessed she was nearly twenty. The closest boy my age was just ten. Rachel was the only other one close to my age, but she was nineteen and had a family. For two sad winters in a row, a bad pox took the lives of most of the young children in Knotwild, as well as a few adults — my mama included. Granmam had tried every remedy she knew, Papa told me, but the fever was an ugly and merciless one. So many of the women were so heartbroke over losing their children in such a horrible way that they couldn't bear to have more for a few years after. Several women who survived having the pox found that it had taken their fertility.

Before she died, Granmam told me the secret of how to make an herb tea to slow down a woman's moon cycle. Granmam said it was a dangerous thing to use too much, but it was a useful thing to know during those years of the winter pox.

"Those were the worst years I remember here at Knotwild," she told me once. "I was glad to offer the women of Knotwild some peace."

Since I was such a weakling, Rev and Papa were so

afraid for me that they had me kept up in the house most of that time. Granmam didn't even get to see me much. My mama was already dead, and Rev's own baby daughter and wife had died in a terrible fire when they were visiting family in Pennsylvania, less than a year before I was born.

The other women regarded me kindly but were always distant . . . maybe because I had been spared back then. Tiny's the closest thing I ever had to a friend. I often felt that most folks felt sorry for me, not just lately 'cause of Granmam's death, or even for my own mama's passing when I was so young. It was more than that, something I didn't really understand.

"Now, if everyone gets seated, we can begin." Papa's voice boomed around the room. He stood at the pulpit he'd made himself; the cross on the front was fashioned out of twisted cypress branches. The light filtered in brightly from the large picture window at Papa's back. Folks immediately hastened their step to find a seat. Everyone came to Sunday meetings except Cholly Dee. Sometimes I believe I'd forget how many of us there were if it weren't for Sunday. All in all, among the working-age men, women, and children (and three on the way), there were eight families, including me and Papa.

"Let's begin with 'Amazing Grace,'" Papa said, and everyone joined their voices together with his. Tiny's voice was high and thin, and it seemed to rise up and disappear into the air as she sat next to me. I didn't feel much like singing, so mostly I just hummed along. Something about this dress felt comforting, but at the same time, it put my mind in a buzz. All my thoughts whirled around Mama's face as I last remembered her. She was about my age when she and Papa wed, Granmam told me. 'Course, many slaves don't know their true age. Most folks at Knotwild only knew 'cause they'd been lucky enough to grow up here with their families. Some like Tiny and Cholly Dee, who were bought from somewhere else, didn't know for sure. Papa said it was surely something to be proud of, knowing one's age and family line. I even had a birth record in the big family Bible that Rev Jeff kept with other important papers, locked away somewhere in the house. He'd shown it to me once when I was a girl. I was the only slave here documented in such a way. Papers, Papa says, are the most important thing a slave could have. Everyone else, including Papa, was just logged in a big book that tallied all of the rest of the family's ownings. My birth record was really the first gift Rev Jeff ever gave me.

The singing stopped, and Papa was now talking about our duty and responsibility to God and to Knotwild.

"We were all given a station in life, our own crosses to bear. . . ." Papa looked out over us all, his eyes stopped on me.

"Some got lighter crosses than others, don't forget,"

a voice called out from the back. Everyone turned to see Cholly Dee with a fishing pole slung over his shoulder standing at the door, which was open to let in the fresh air. He was a big man, solid and dark like an old walnut tree, where my Papa was built like the branches of my namesake. Cholly's mouth was twisted, fixing to laugh when he looked right at me, like something had sucked his breath away. He shook his head and walked away, whistling.

Cholly Dee never came into the meetinghouse. He spent most of his Sundays lying about somewhere in the woods, Papa said, probably making moonshine. I couldn't remember him ever disrupting us like that, though. I don't know why Rev Jeff tolerated him, much less let him oversee the field hands. I knew Rev thought that white overseers were too harsh, and Cholly Dee was surly enough to get folks to do their work without question. Folks were always trying to run away from Merriend so as not to feel Boss H's evil horsewhip, but we never had anyone run from Knotwild.

Papa was quick to get the attention back up front. "That may be," he said, trying not to show his anger at being disrupted, but even from where I sat, I could see the vein on his neck popping out. "But it is not our place to question or judge! We are but lowly servants of the Lord and will be rewarded for our burdens and toil in heaven!"

There were several "Amens" called out around the

room, including a loud "And don't let the devil tell you different!" from Tiny. Papa took it as an opportunity to tell the story of Jesus being tempted in the desert.

I tried not to think so much of Cholly's foolishness and put all my attention into Papa's sermon, but I couldn't help but wish I was back at my tree.

After the meeting, when we'd finished chatting and shaking everybody's hand, I was looking forward to the rest of the afternoon. Generally I had plenty of time to go back up to our cabin and read before starting on supper. When Rev Jeff was away, Papa went over to see Master Rawlins at Merriend on Sundays to dictate the week's happenings so Rawlins could send it in a letter to Rev. It usually took him most of the afternoon. When Rawlins had found out that Rev was leaving Papa in charge of the plantation alone for long periods of time, he called the law on Rev, saying he was putting Merriend at danger. 'Course, the law couldn't do much about how Rev ran his own place, but they made Rev agree to Rawlins taking down accounts and collecting the mail, and to let Boss H patrol our land from time to time. After all the bloody, murderous riots and revolts in the past years, white men were always worrying about another one.

"Willow," Papa said, his hand on the back of my neck, "I want you to ride to Merriend with me."

I looked up at him; the pressure of his thumb under my jawline ached a bit as I turned my head sharply. He loosed his grip when I winced.

"All right, Papa," I said slowly. "But I won't have much time to cook a decent supper when we get back."

"Not to worry. You can pack a lunch to hold us. Tiny will have a meat pie ready for when we get back."

I had to fake a smile, and not just because I hated Tiny's meat pies. "That'll be nice."

While Papa hitched the mules to the rig, I braided Mayapple's mane as we stood in her stall. She kept turning, nudging me, maybe knowing I was doing it sloppy.

"I know it's not perfect, May, but I'm just not in the mood, I guess," I apologized. She was the most particular horse I knew. The other horses barely cared how they were brushed, just so it was done to soothe their skin. But having their mane braided? I don't reckon they'd even let me. Papa always said I spoiled Mayapple, so that now she was more a human than a horse. Though Tiny was my closest human friend since Granmam died, Mayapple has always been my best friend. I was eight years old when she was born, and her mama, a sweet mare we called Babs, had to be put down when Mayapple was on the way; she was bleeding too much. Papa, Rev, and even Granmam said Mayapple would never make it, but I made sure she did. Her eyes were big as saucers, and when she looked into mine, we felt each other's pain.

At first, I even slept in the stable with her some nights, no matter how much Granmam would scold me. I was the only one to care for her from then on. Granmam would say I cared for Mayapple's looks more than my own. I knew it was true. I'd rather have my face in a book than a mirror.

Maybe that was what made me so restless in Mama's old dress — I felt a bit too gussied up, like I was putting on a show for an audience I couldn't see.

"Time to go," Papa called.

"Yes, sir." I pulled my bonnet on and dragged my feet to climb up next to Papa. The buckboard jolted and bounced as we left Knotwild property. I couldn't help looking back over my shoulder as we passed the fence. I always felt uneasy leaving my world.

"What you frowning so hard for, Willow?" Papa asked. He turned the horses east on the main road toward Merriend.

"Just . . ." There was so much I was frowning about, I didn't know where to begin. "I just was thinking."

Papa said, "That's what I wanted to talk about — part of it, at least."

I studied Papa's profile; he was fixing to talk about

something I could tell had been on his mind for a while. I noticed, too, that he had a few more lines around his striking green eyes, and his fine, close-cut curls were receding and more peppered with gray.

"You a grown girl now, Willow," he began. My stomach soured. "You don't have time for riding wild all over creation no more. You've got to be putting your mind to getting a husband and having children — the future. Don't think I don't notice your chores being half done 'cause you been daydreaming rather than doing things right. I'd like to think you been daydreaming about your future as a mother and a wife, but I'm no fool. I know you been taking books out the Rev's library. Next you be wanting more, and no good can come of it, child."

"But you read, too, Papa! And Rev's the one who taught me to read!" I was so hurt by his words, and humiliated for being caught. I was relieved, though, that he didn't know I was already writing.

"Don't back talk to me, girl!" Papa roared so loud, it startled not only me but the mules plodding along the road.

"Rev thought it was fine to teach you to read bits of the Bible, but that's where it was supposed to end," he said after a moment. "I should've never let you learn your letters. I feared it would come to this! I only learned to read and write a bit 'cause Jeff and I spent all our time together. Now, what it done for me? If the wrong folk found out,

I could be hanged for it! And they'd do the same to you. Poor Rev would pay for it dearly, too.

"You got to know your place, Willow," Papa continued, even though I wished he'd stop. I lowered my head to watch the road roll underneath the wheels. "You got a responsibility to Knotwild and Rev Jeff—they been good to you. You a slave, just like me, and you always going to be. The world ain't like Knotwild, where you do as you please. If you was a boy, maybe you could learn a trade in Baltimore. But you ain't. It's time you get a hold a that in your head. Your duty as a woman is to take care of the home and have children. You not being in the best health, you 'specially need a man to look out for you."

"But, Papa, there's you! And Rev . . ."

"We ain't gonna live forever, girl," he reminded me gently. "All the more reason you need a husband now. . . . You got to be provided for. . . ." He finished his sentence in a whisper, to himself.

He must've had someone in mind. The only single man at Knotwild was Old Sam and—

"Papa, please," I blurted out. "You ain't thinking of me and Cholly Dee, is you? That mean old cur can't stand me a lick! And I can't stand him, neither!"

Papa looked at me with surprised eyes and let out a laugh like I'd just told the best joke in the county. I crossed my arms over my chest and turned away from him.

"Cholly?" He wiped his eyes when he finished laughing at me. "I wouldn't give nothing to that man but a piece of my mind, much less my only daughter! Besides, I don't reckon he'd even *want* you, much as he hate me!"

"Then who?" I asked, relieved.

"Well, now, ain't that the question" Papa seemed more relaxed; he nudged me in a kind way. "That's exactly what we doing today. I know you don't got too many quality options, but I was hoping maybe you already got anybody in mind. Somebody already caught your fancy? Somebody, say, at Merriend?"

My mind ran through everybody I knew there, and I didn't know many. I mostly only ever saw Rawlins's people at Christmastime, when we'd all get together for the annual party. There were a few boys my age, but they were just a blur to me. Rawlins had a habit of losing his slaves in poker games, Papa said, and almost everything else. Besides, his slaves was always looking so . . . *worn out.*

There weren't many who ever talked to me at the parties except a man called Raymond. He had a terrible scar on his face. Last Christmas, he asked me to dance and stepped all over my feet trying to pull me in closer. Tiny still tease me about how my toes was all swollen into the New Year. But worse than that, my dress got singed 'cause he kept whirling me too close to the bonfire. Tiny told me that before Raymond came to Merriend plantation, the last place he'd been down south had a practice of branding all their new slaves. Raymond struggled when it was his turn—he was just a boy—and the brander missed his shoulder and burned his face instead.

I didn't like him at all. Not 'cause of his face, but he was always talking something slick to me when Papa was around. Like telling me how nice I looked or how fine I talked. Tiny say that's how the men let you know they like you, but when Papa wasn't there, he looked at me in a way that made me feel uneasy.

"No, Papa. Nobody." I hoped that might be the end of the conversation.

"Well, what about that Raymond? He seems a likely fellow. You and him danced real nice last Christmas. And Boss Hendricks told me he's a good worker and trustworthy."

I certainly didn't want nobody Boss H thought trustworthy. Hendricks was Rawlins's overseer, the son of Rawlins's sister, who'd married a poor prospector over in Kentucky. Hendricks was exactly why Rev Jeff didn't want a white overseer. Four or five years ago, he whupped a pregnant woman for not working fast enough and she lost her baby. He drank too much and liked to hear himself talk. When Rev Jeff was away, it was Hendricks's duty to "look in on us" as he pleased. More like sneaking around, trying to see all what Rev Jeff had and Master Rawlins didn't. I swear, the two of them was more jealous than a pair of jaybirds in spring.

Boss H gave me a fright just last week when he looked in the open front window and saw me with my nose in a Shakespeare, sitting on the floor of the library, no less! God must've placed that forgotten rag in my apron pocket so that I could pretend to be dusting. He seemed to believe me when I said Rev liked every page of his books dusted. I don't think Boss H can read. He looked around at all of Rev's books, mumbling about "a waste of time and money."

If Raymond was a favorite of Boss H, then I was quite sure he was trouble.

"Well, I just danced with him that one time," I tried. "I don't really know him."

Papa looked at me and winked. "Like I said: *exactly* what we doing out here today."

"August 27, 1848
Boston, Mass.

Dear Ryder,

I trust that everything at Knotwild is as usual in my absence. Send my regards to all the people there. Let them know that they are in my prayers and thoughts every day. I am sure that you instill in them the pride of their noble home as I would. I have had a wonderful stay here in Boston, and my sermons seem to be well received. I have been invited back by many of the churches and have, in fact, been generously offered to speak in London by a parishioner who is well associated there. I am still only considering the idea, since it would take me away from Knotwild for a better part of next year.

I am sure that the fields will be bare by the time I return. I will be home by the eighteenth of September, so you do not need to send me a return letter with estimates for what will be sold. I will be home long enough to go to Baltimore with you for market, as I also have business there at that time. I remember fondly our boyhood days when we looked forward to that trip with excitement. It has been too long since we have done this task together. But as usual I put all faith in you, as you conduct this process now with more confidence than I. I hope that you and Cholly Dee can amicably decide on fair pricing in comparison to last year.

I have also sent along a present for our Willow's birthday. I will say a special prayer for her here. I shall be overjoyed to see you all when I return.

Yours Truly in the Spirit of the Lord,
Reverend Jeffries"

Papa and I looked up at Rawlins as he finished reading Rev's letter out loud while we stood near the foot of the broken porch steps. Unless you worked in the house, Rawlins didn't allow many "darkies," as he called us, to set foot in his home. I reckoned he hated having to talk to us at all, much less read to us in front of his house. Folks who did work in the house entered and left through the back. Tiny said most of the house servants had to wear white gloves all the time. There was a handful of half-naked brown children running around the side yard, and I could see some field hands, each toting a huge bale of hay on their backs. I still didn't understand how Rawlins could squander his money when his folks worked so hard. Everyone knew Rawlins thought Rev Jeff pampered us at Knotwild. Most of Rawlins's hands didn't even have warm clothes and shoes in winter, and they all lived shoved up in one big cabin all together. Plus, they had to work half days on Sunday, where we had the whole day and half of Saturday to ourselves, except during harvest. Rev Jeff and Papa was always quick to point out that Knotwild was more prosperous than Merriend 'cause we all was content enough to take pride in our work. 'Sides, we all was assured that every single body at Knotwild was tired and sore at the end of each working day, but those same bodies also slept good at night. At Knotwild, families worked together in groups or pairs, like when we would harvest wheat. The men would be working the scythe and cradling the stalks while the women would rake the wheat, binding it into sheaves. Then the children would come along after, gathering small bits and stacking it all together. It seemed like a better process than the one here at Merriend, where each slave was responsible for their own row, which was a considerable amount of work for one person.

"Thank yuh, Massa Rawlins, suh. I appreciates yuh collectin' Massa Jeffries mail from town an' readin' his lettas for me." Papa's talk was different at Merriend than at Knotwild—each time he said "Massa," it was like somebody working a slow drill in my chest. I noted that the way he stood was different, too. His shoulders were hunched and he clutched his hat in his hands, wringing it slightly in an embarrassed sort of way. At Knotwild he stood tall and easy and only took off his hat to greet a woman or to go indoors. This was why I hated leaving Knotwild. It rubbed it in hard what we were: property. I couldn't stand seeing Papa like this. I kept my eyes off of him as much as I could.

On the porch was a girl about my age, rubbing Rawlins's bare feet. I'd seen her last Christmas, standing off by herself; Tiny had pointed her out as Rawlins's "special gal," who'd already had a child by him. She was pretty, with rich-brown skin, almond-shaped green eyes, and a long, slender neck. I hadn't believed it to be true. How *could* she?

The girl kept her eyes downcast, but I could see she wasn't looking at Rawlins's bloated, scaly feet but off toward the children in the yard. Tiny said her pale baby was sold away just a few weeks old so it wouldn't shame Rawlins too much. Her eyes darted toward me; as soon as our gaze met, we both looked away quickly. It confused and horrified me to think of it.

"Jenny, give them this." Rawlins handed a package to the girl, and she brought it down to me. She didn't look me in the eye and all but ran back up the porch steps. "It baffles me why Jeffries gives his darkies gifts," he said out loud, but not so much to us. "A waste of money, I'd say."

"Yassuh. Thank yuh, suh." Papa bowed a bit to Rawlins. It was almost too much to bear. I blinked away threatening tears. "We gettin on our way, then, suh."

I wanted to run back to the rig.

"No, wait. Not yet." Rawlins lifted his nose in my direction. I looked up at Papa, pleading with my eyes, but he wouldn't look back. Rawlins called out, "Bring it here." I was surprised that he got himself up, slowly and with a cane.

I reluctantly pried open the box, not wanting to reveal anything to Rawlins, especially something as precious as a gift from Rev, which was sure to have a note. Inside, the box was carefully lined with newspaper. I was grateful just for that—something new to read. I wondered if Rev thought of that, too. Under the papers was a small velvet box, which I pulled out and opened. It was a gold locket pendant, etched with scrolls and flowers. It hung from a gold brooch pin in the shape of a bow-tied ribbon. Rev Jeff had given me lots of gifts over the years—fancy lace handkerchiefs, dainty glass ornaments, pretty trinkets that didn't have much use to a slave girl.

As I pushed my thumbnail in the side groove to open it, beads of sweat broke out on my forehead even though there was a cool breeze whipping around my new dress. I'd seen an envelope at the bottom of the box, which I didn't want Rawlins to notice in case it got Rev and me in trouble. I pushed the newspapers down and put the velvet box in my right hand, carrying the other box under the crook of my left arm, hoping it would go unnoticed. Taking slow steps up to the porch, I popped open the locket, determined to be the first to see what was inside. It was a clock. The numbers were painted upside down so that when I wore the pin on my clothes I could easily tell the time. I smiled at it briefly before Rawlins's shadow was over me, standing at the top of the porch steps; he reached out to take it from my hands.

"Huh," Rawlins huffed, handling my gift roughly. "Must've cost a good ten or fifteen dollars, maybe even more if it's real gold. . . ."

I could feel his eyes studying me, but I didn't dare look him in the face.

"You must be real special for him to give you that." His smile gave me a chill. "What you doing for him that's worth so much?"

His meaning brought bile to my mouth. I wanted to shout that Rev wasn't a filthy pig like him and snatch my present back.

The sound of Papa kicking at the dirt behind me brought me back to reality. "I wouldn't know, sir," I said through my teeth. "He's just real generous, I guess."

Rawlins threw his head back and laughed in an ugly way, almost dropping the box. "Listen, gal," he snorted. "White men don't just be generous for nothing in return. That's why we're the master race. We're shrewd. Jeffries might be a weak example, but he's a white man all the same."

My throat burned with all the things I wanted to say. I could only study the cracking whitewash of the porch steps. I heard a horse riding up behind me. I never thought I'd be so glad to see Boss H.

"How are you this fine day, Uncle?" Hendricks said, still perched on his saddle.

"Just fine, Nephew," Rawlins replied, waving my locket. I couldn't help following it with my eyes. "But I see the crew looks like they might be dragging their feet today. Can't you do something about that?"

"I'll get 'em right perked up, Uncle." Boss H patted his whip. "I have some news to tell you, though. Timmons caught up with me last night while I was on patrol."

Timmons was the owner of Rawlins's neighboring plantation Blue Bell, farther southeast. We didn't see them much. Our only close neighbor was Merriend, since our land went right up to the Catoctin Mountains to the west and Pennsylvania to the north. The plantation closest south of Knotwild was a good twenty miles away, and I'd never seen them. Often Boss H talked about how he "patrolled" our land, Rawlins's, and to the north, but I heard Rev complain once that he mainly stayed drunk in the woods with a few of the other low-class whites who were overseers.

"What'd that old barrel of pickles have to say besides how bad I beat him at cards last week?" Rawlins asked, laughing at his own joke. I looked over my shoulder at Papa; he was still studying his hat in his hands.

"Yeah, everybody knows you won the shirt off his back, Uncle! You on a winning streak for sure!" Hendricks said, pushing his wide-brim straw hat up on his brow. "But last night Timmons told me there's been word of some runaway slaves coming up from Virginnie, trying to cross the state border through the mountains," Hendricks said. "I told Timmons to just let me at 'em! We going riding tonight, see if we can rustle 'em up out the woods. Timmons said he'd bring his bloodhounds."

In Rawlins's hand, my brooch glinted in the sunlight. I wished Papa hadn't brought me here; I'd never had a birthday worse than this.

"Ryder," Hendricks called out, "you better keep all your people indoors tonight, else they might get a butt full of buckshot! Any darkies I see is dead!"

"Yassuh, Boss Hendricks," Papa said. "Ain't none a Knotwild folks be out after dark."

"You lying to me, boy!" Hendricks brought his horse closer to Papa and leaned down, towering over him. "You lying right in my face!"

"Nawsuh, Boss! I wouldn't do that!"

"Then why is it I've seen that rascal Cholly Dee creeping around some midnights? Or am I just seeing haints?"

"He what . . . ?" Papa looked up, obviously upset to be called out like that. He took great pride in having control of Knotwild, knowing every little thing that went on, especially when Rev Jeff was away. "I'm real sorry, Boss. I'll have to talk to him 'bout that, suh. He know he ain't 'lowed out roamin'. He won't be doin' that again."

"You better handle that, Ryder, or I'll have my nephew do it for you," Rawlins said.

"And I'd love to take a big piece out of that one, Uncle. Some darkies over to the west of us think they free like a white man."

I kept my eye on my brooch. Rawlins and Hendricks chatted a bit more about the price of this and the state of that before they noticed we were still standing there.

"Y'all go and get on back home, now," Rawlins said as though we'd rather be here with him. He turned toward the house, my box still in his hand.

"Uh, excuse me, sir?" I managed to get the words out politely.

"What?" He turned, annoyed. I lowered my eyes and pointed toward my box in his hands. "Humph," he huffed as he snapped the box shut and tossed it at me. I almost didn't catch it and stumbled over myself. The box holding Rev's letter tumbled out from under my arm. My heart skipped a beat. I quickly stuffed everything back inside and scrambled onto the rig. The girl on the porch watched us as we pulled away.

I was breathing regular again once we were on the road, but we hadn't even passed the fields of Merriend when Papa stopped the mules. "Jump out," he said.

"Why, Papa?" I whined. I just wanted to get back so I could read my letter and forget everything else about this day.

"Do what I say," he replied. "Go stand by the fence." He got down and started fiddling with the rig's wheels, though I could plainly see they were fine. I stood by the fence wondering what he was doing.

"Well, hey there, Miz Willow." I jumped and turned sharply to find Raymond behind me, sipping at a ladle of water from a bucket that was left in the shade of an old oak tree. "Lucky me to find you here just as I'm takin a li'l break. Hey there, Mr. Ryder. Everything just fine?"

"Why, hello there, Raymond," Papa said in a falsely surprised tone. "I think I might have just a small problem with the rig. Nothing much. You two young people continue your conversation." He smiled to himself and went around to the other side of the rig.

I couldn't believe Papa set this all up. I looked back at Raymond; he winked his good eye as though we were all in on it. On his cheek, the skin was uneven and colorless. The scar wasn't horrible, but it was hard not to stare at, and knowing how it happened made it even more pitiful.

"You sure looking real pretty today, Miz Willow. I reckon you must be the finest darkie gal between Knotwild and Baltymore." I flinched at him saying "darkie." He drew the ladle back to his mouth, studying me from head to toe. It all made me skittish like Mayapple in a thunderstorm. I pulled my shawl closer to my neck.

"Uh, thank you." I turned back to the rig, calling, "Papa, you fixed it yet?"

"Naw, not yet, honey. You go on and chat."

I looked back at Raymond, who wore a crooked smile. "Miz Willow, can I ask you something?"

"I suppose."

"You ain't afraid of me, is you? My scar, I mean. Am I too ugly for you to look on?"

I felt shameful; he couldn't help what had been done to him.

"No! Not at all," I said quickly. "I'm just . . . shy." It was true, but also the only thing I could think of as an excuse.

"That's what your daddy said," he told me with his crooked smile, stepping closer to the fence. "Just so long you ain't stuck up. I can't take no uppity womenfolk like the ones they got over here. I like girls nice and shy. That way I ain't got to worry none about you spendin' your affections on some other darkie."

I tried not to wince.

"I hopes you let me come callin' on you over at Knotwild sometime soon, Miz Willow. If your daddy don't mind, 'course. I kin get me a pass from Boss, maybe Sunday next."

Just then I saw Boss Hendricks over Raymond's shoulder, galloping up at a quick pace. I sucked in my breath and widened my eyes to alert Raymond, expecting he'd scramble back to work, but he just turned around and took another sip from the water bucket, as though nothing was amiss.

"What're y'all plottin' on?" Boss H demanded with

his hand on his braided leather whip, his eyebrows knitted under his sweat-soaked hat.

"Ain't nothin' like that, Massa Boss H, suh," Raymond replied. "I was just takin' a drink after I'd worked my row faster den everybody else, yuh see, when I saw these folks in some troubles. I just took a moment to ax if I could help. You knows I'm always just tryin' to be helpful. I's 'bout to go lookin' for yuh to approve my work."

Hendricks looked over his shoulder at the rows of corn. Sure enough, it seemed as though most of the other workers were two-thirds an acre or more behind, where Raymond's row was finished and neatly stacked in burlap bags.

"Why, you the quickest darkie I ever seen!" Hendricks exclaimed.

Papa appeared from the far side of the rig. "We just lost a bolt, Boss, but I got it fixed. We'll be on our way now. Thank you, Raymond, for offering your help," he said, reaching for my hand to help me up onto the rig. "Merriend's sure lucky to have a fine worker like you," he added, tipping his hat.

I almost grabbed the reins and kicked the mules myself.

Once we were well on our way, Papa said, "So what you think? He's real sweet on you."

"Papa, I don't know. . . ."

"Well, you listen here. You got to marry this spring, so if it's not him, we'll buy someone at auction."

We rode in silence for a while. I remembered one night long ago, when I was a child—Gran was alive and strong. Rev had come to visit us and we were all sitting on the porch. I had grown tired of hearing Papa and Rev's childhood remembrances of mischief together and longed for a friend of my own. I understood that slavery meant that Rev had the power to buy and sell workers, the people in the field. It never occurred to me that he could, or *would,* sell *us.*

I crawled up in Rev's lap and asked him to buy some more children my age for me to play with. Rev was clearly uncomfortable and laughed nervously. Granmam yanked me off Rev, saying it was my bedtime. When we got inside, she lit into me good—one of the few painful punishments I ever got as child—and she told me I should feel shamed for myself.

I cried and cried, not realizing what was so wrong with my request. I requested things often from Rev and usually got them.

"Don't you see," Gran hissed, "that if Rev were to buy you some other children, they would be taken away from they own family?"

Finally I broke the silence between Papa and me. "How'd Raymond finish his row so quick?"

Papa kept his eyes on the road. "Girl, don't you know that in this day and age, anything can be bought or bartered?"

"You mean, he paid someone to do it for him?"

"He's a resourceful fellow, that Raymond," Papa said admiringly. "That's why I like him. He arranged this whole thing just to talk to you."

I was a bit amazed. "How?"

"The last time I was over there, he waved me down on the road. Had somebody working for him then, too. Shame a clever fellow like him is wasted at Merriend."

"Do folks do that at home?"

"There's no need for the hands to be like that at Knotwild," Papa explained. "The workload is fair and everybody works together. Sometimes folks fill in for others, but it's usually out of kindness or a special need. Over there at Merriend, or at another place run like it, white folks only see what they want to see — or more like what the colored folks let them see. When white folks are devious, then everyone else acts the same to survive. You understand?"

Papa didn't wait for me to answer. "At a place like Knotwild, where the colored folks have dignity, only someone with a hard heart and a hard head would go against the grain." His forehead wrinkled tightly.

"You talking about Cholly Dee?"

"No-good rascal!" Papa spat. "Rev's a fool not to sell him down to some sugar plantation in Barbados!"

"You don't think he had a good reason to be out at night?" I asked. I didn't care for Cholly much, but I didn't want my worst enemy to be sold down there. Tiny told me they don't even let their slaves sleep—they make them work through the night—and it's so hot that even the darkest African would melt.

"I don't care what his reason was! He made me look bad in front of white folks, and I can't stand that."

The look on Papa's face told me not to ask any more questions, so I just listened to the road.

Soon as Papa unhitched the mules, he rang the call bell. The bell stood on a post outside the big house; it was used to call everyone to work, worship, eat, rest, and meet. Papa and Rev Jeff were the only ones to use it. Papa rung it at sunup to get everyone up, then a half hour later to get them started at their work, at noon for lunch, again at sunset for dinner break, then at nine thirty for lights-out. It was the way things always was at Knotwild. Rev Jeff's granddad planned the schedule and we still stuck to it. On Sundays it was only rung for worship, and on Saturdays the noon bell also meant the workday was over. If the bell was rung out of the usual time, like now, it meant everyone had to drop everything and get to the center of the quarters lickety-split to hear some important news. It was seldom rung this way.

I reckon if Papa was a cat, his back fur would've been all a-bristle. I followed behind him, almost at a run to keep up. It was only when he heard me cough from the growing congestion in my chest that he looked back at me and slowed his pace two steps. All the excitement of the afternoon had set my chest to tightening again. I worried the whole ride home about Raymond and the thought of marrying. I even worried about Cholly Dee rising Papa to anger. I worried over when and how I'd get to read Rev Jeff's letter, and more important, the bit of newspaper that came along with the package. I worried over everything I could think of, until my chest felt like a fist was squeezing on it. Then I worried about getting sick.

"Maybe you should go back home," Papa said. "Drink some hot tea. I don't want you getting sick."

I held in another cough as the thought made the fist in my chest squeeze my insides tighter.

"I'm fine," I told him.

Everyone was waiting at the fire pit for us, a fire already blazing. Some nights somebody would make a fire in the center of the quarters, and folks would gather to cook, talk, and sometimes to sing. I'd never been invited to any of those nights, and if I had, Papa probably wouldn't have allowed me to go. Sometimes I watched from my loft window, but not often, 'cause it made me feel lonely.

Papa looked around at all the faces. I did, too, and didn't see Cholly Dee. I found Tiny, though, and went to stand beside her.

"What got your papa so worked up to a lather for?" she whispered. But her whisper was loud enough for everyone to hear.

"I'm worked into a lather 'cause I got some disturbing news today over at the Merriend plantation," Papa said in his church voice. It boomed and echoed around the cabins and into woods behind.

"Seems like there's some no-good, no-account runaways back in the woods, coming out of the mountains from the southwest. You all know how I feel about that, but I'm telling it again."

Papa stood on an upright stump that was used for a seat, so that he towered over everyone, looking like a giant of a man.

"We were brought here out of dark Africa for a reason, and that reason was to be saved from heathenism."

There were some "Amens" called out from the crowd. Papa gave a pause before he continued.

"We should all be grateful just for that. Especially us at Knotwild, who have it so good. Last time I was in Baltimore, I heard they was trying to send the free colored back to Africa! Why, over at Merriend, they toil even on the Lord's day! And we know Boss H ain't stingy with his whip." More "Amens" scattered around, the loudest one from Tiny, who was whipped when she couldn't work the fields.

"Those that run from their assigned stations in life are trying to run from God himself. It'll just bring failure and regret! My father himself traveled to the North with old Master Jeffries and told me how the colored folks were worse off there than here! He told me how so many of them begged on the streets for food and died on the streets, too. In fact, even as far as New York City, the colored ain't any better off! Most spend their time gambling and drunk, fighting and rioting for lack of work.

"And if you think the white man will treat you any better up there, you're wrong. Sorely wrong. The Irish are just as bad off, and they blame the blacks for taking what little they have. Rev even told me they tried to burn a white woman's home for teaching colored children. I've even heard that in Canada, colored folks freeze in the winter 'cause the whites won't allow them to live in the towns; they have to live uncivilized in the woods, at nature's mercy!

"I'm here to tell you that's what running north will get you. You all remember how just three summers ago, we heard about that mob of armed slaves trying to get to Pennsylvania, and how they got stopped by the Rockville militia. Most of them got caught and sold. One of the leaders, Wheeler, got hung, and the other, Caesar, is rotting away in a cell as I speak."

Folks clucked their tongues and shook their heads,

even though most had heard this story a hundred times, like I had. Many of the little children clung to their mothers, eyes wide with confusion and fear. I felt the same way every time Papa told it. It used to give me nightmares of running through strange city streets, or sometimes snow-thick forests, naked, chased by white people and colored, too, all with my murder on their minds. I shivered remembering that dream.

"So it would be better for us to turn in any runaways, simply to save them from the ignorance of their fate," Papa told us. "If you see or hear anything out of turn, you be sure to let me know. And until those lost souls are caught and returned to their masters, we should all be in our cabins by eight o'clock, and every candle must snuffed by then as well. It's our duty, our responsibility. We owe it to Rev Jeff. Remember — if you see or hear anything out of the ordinary . . ."

Papa's voice trailed off as everyone's head turned toward the woods behind Tiny's cabin, where there was a crash. The evening was just closing in, and the sky was a heavy blue blanket tucking in the trees, making the woods a weary sight. I could hear every breath sucked in as the sounds of footsteps came toward the clearing. We all let out a sigh of relief as Cholly Dee emerged, singing the spiritual "Let My People Go." A rod slung with six fish was hanging over his shoulder. He laughed when he saw us all staring at him.

"Looks like I'm the fox in the henhouse!" He smiled deviously. "What's all the fuss and frowns for?"

Papa's chest heaved up and down with each breath as though he were fixing to leap onto Cholly and pummel him to pulp. Through his teeth, Papa said to everyone else, "Put out the pit fire and go 'head inside for the night."

The tension was so thick in the air that folks just milled around, murmuring and whispering to one another.

"What for, now?" Cholly stepped forward into the light of the fire. "It ain't barely moonrise and you tellin' folks on they day off they gotta retire? 'Specially when I gots all these fish and a story to tell?"

"Cholly, I want to see you in the hay house. Now." Papa turned on his heel and stalked off.

Cholly Dee handed his fish over to Tiny, who was standing closest to him. He looked me up and down again, almost as though a cloud passed over his face.

He furrowed his brow and mumbled, just loud enough for us all to hear, "Betta go see what *Li'l Massa* want from me."

Folks stood around and whispered for a bit while Old Samuel doused the flames with water. The rest went back into their homes.

Tiny nudged me with her elbow. "Go see what they sayin'!" she hissed.

I nodded and headed off toward the horse stalls, which stood next to the hay house. I figured I could hear what was going on without getting caught. I went back to Mayapple's stall; it wasn't the best place to hear, though. She and I greeted each other with a nuzzle. I could already hear Papa's loud but muffled voice as I started braiding May's mane again, just for something to busy my nervous hands.

". . . and I ain't going to be humiliated for you again, fool!"

"I reckon you already do a good job of it for yourself, Ryder," Cholly said, not at all ashamed.

"Cholly! If I wasn't a man of God, so help me . . ." Papa was yelling now. "This ain't like last time. You can't be acting like you can come and go as you please! You best believe Rev's going to hear about this mess. And don't be surprised if you find yourself shackled up in a boat floating south!"

"Since you a 'man of God,' like you say, I guess you won't take a wager on that, huh?" Cholly replied coolly.

I couldn't believe Cholly was mocking Papa to his face!

"Dammit, Cholly Dee!" Papa's voice was strained; he paused and lowered his voice. "I'm not playing this game with you. You best stay in and act right till they get caught and Rev comes home."

"Yassuh, Massa Boss, suh. I's gon' be a good darkie fo' yuh." Cholly must've walked out on Papa, who was saying something I couldn't quite hear. I crept out of Mayapple's stall, tiptoeing toward the door, trying to stay hidden behind it, but I reckon Cholly Dee must've seen me as I crossed the stable, 'cause he stopped in his tracks.

"And I see you done dressed up Adlile's daughter to look just like her," Cholly said in front of the open stable door. "Hope you treat her better than her mother — like a woman, not a prize."

Before I knew what was going on, Papa was lunging at Cholly Dee, throwing him to the ground; one hand was on his throat, and the other cocked back in a fist.

I screamed and ran forward, out of the darkness of the stalls into the waning twilight. Papa looked at me and blinked three times before he returned to himself. He got up and brushed off.

"Get inside, Willow," Papa said quietly. I tucked myself under his outstretched arm. My lungs heaved and shuddered as I coughed. I stifled it best I could, but it felt like some old mountain lion had sat on my chest and dug his nails in me good. I was still trembling from the fright of seeing Papa all riled up. Papa squeezed me closer in a comforting way and my body quieted down. I was sure he would've killed Cholly Dee, or at least tried to, if I hadn't been there. I looked back and was surprised to see Cholly still lying there in the same spot, his arm thrown over his face like he was trying to ward off a bad dream.

Papa spent the rest of the evening in his chair, chewing on his pipe, staring into the fire. I hated those durn fugitives for all the troubles they were causing. Heaven was the best reward for the hardest life, Papa said. Maybe Raymond wasn't all that bad if Papa saw him to be a fit husband for me. Maybe I did owe it to Papa, to Knotwild. My life had been pleasant up till now, and maybe such a meager hardship as marriage would be rewarded in heaven.

I busied myself by sorting and hanging herbs and roots to dry. One thing Granmam taught me that I faired well at was herbs. I figured how to look them up in Rev Jeff's library and found it simple to identify the ones we used in the woods. For Papa's sleeping tea, we used skullcap, chamomile, hawthorn berries, and valerian root, which Granmam used to call all-heal. Granmam used to warn me to only use a bit of the valerian, or else Papa might not wake up for a week! The stuff stank to high heaven, but the cats sure loved it. When I brought it home from the woods, they'd all follow me and even scratch at the door when I ground it up. Papa loved the smell, too, but I had to wear a rag over my nose and mouth when I handled it. Sometimes, if Papa really couldn't sleep, Granmam would have me put in a tiny pinch of rosy periwinkle, but that could be dangerous—too much was poison. The flowers were pretty, though, and I dried them for winter bouquets. Granmam used to say that eating the flowers would open your heart to love, but I never found that written in any of Rev's books.

I prepared Papa's tea and used a bit more valerian than usual and a pinch of the periwinkle. By the wrinkles over his eyes, I could tell he was going to need it. I made myself some tea for my cough: yarrow, horehound, anise, and lots of honey. I'd only drink it if it tasted sweet. My chest was still rattling like a baby's toy.

I handed Papa his steaming cup and sat at his feet with my own, blowing on the top, making ripples in the dark water.

"Thanks, Mite," he said, and patted my head absently.

We were quiet for a long while, just staring into the fire. After I fell into another coughing fit, he said, "I don't like the sound of that. I'd hoped that since you wasn't real sickly these last two winters, this one'd be the same."

"It's just from all the excitement, Papa," I said. We continued to sip at our tea in silence. I could see Papa's wrinkles relax, so I decided the time was right.

"Papa, why'd Cholly Dee call my mother Adlile when her name was Lily?"

He wiped his hand over his face, covering his eyes and massaging his temples.

"Her African name was Adlile. We called her Lily for short."

"I didn't know that! You never even told me she was a real African! Did she remember Africa? What was it like?" That little seed of knowledge sprouted a whole tree of curiosity in my head.

Papa sipped his tea under shaded eyes. "She remembered quite a bit, I reckon. Rev Jeff bought her directly from there the year or so before we married. But we didn't talk much about it. She didn't . . . talk much. . . ."

"Did she speak English like we do?"

"She picked it up right quick. The auctioneer Rev bought her from was using her to talk with the other Africans on the ship—they all spoke different languages, I suppose. She must've talked to the whole lot of them, even picked up some of that Portuguese language from the sailors. Lily was strange like that."

This was the most I'd heard Papa say about my mother ever. Granmam would say a few kind things about her, like she was pretty and a good mother, but never much more.

"Did you love her right away, Papa? I mean, like how they say in stories?"

Papa uncovered his eyes and looked down at me with a sad, weak smile. "I don't know how they say in stories, but I did love her as soon as I laid eyes on her. She had the most delicate beauty I'd ever seen. I remember I thought she was like a queen would look if I ever saw one. Even when they had her up on that auction block, she held her head high. She was dignified in a way I'd never seen. Yes, I loved her right away."

"I knew it! I knew it was like in a story. You were meant to be together!" Chills ran up and down my spine. I imagined my parents, so young and beautiful, destined to fall in love, like in one of Shakespeare's plays.

"Why'd Cholly say you treated her like a prize? 'Cause you were so proud of her?" He covered his eyes again and gave no answer, so I kept talking. "That's probably why he's so jealous all the time—'cause the smartest colored woman in all of Maryland was in love with you!"

Papa swallowed the rest of his tea.

"Maybe," he mumbled, and stood up quickly. "I don't care what goes on inside Cholly Dee's head. Not anymore."

Papa set his cup on the table and went to his bed. I heard him fall upon it and begin snoring. I put my cup down beside my drying herbs and went to pull off Papa's boots. Sometimes when I'd given him his tea like I did tonight, he'd fall sleep with his boots on and ruin the bed-clothes. Herbs was the only way Papa would sleep sound. Granmam said he'd be up most nights, even as a boy, wor-rying over whatever came into his head. He'd be meaner than a caged bobcat after a sleepless night.

As I wrestled with his left boot, he rolled over onto his

back and mumbled, "I won her fair and square, Cholly . . . fair and square."

I held my breath for a moment, but he just went back to snoring. I returned to the fireplace and added more hot water to my cup. I stared at my reflection in the copper kettle, wearing my mother's dress, wondering which parts of me resembled her. I didn't see much that was queen-like, though. As I finished my last sip of tea, I noticed a small pink flower — rosy periwinkle — sitting at the bottom of my cup.

That night I tossed and turned, and I woke up wishing I'd put valerian into my teacup, too. My chest was wheezing throughout the night. I had to stifle my coughs in my pillow so as not to wake Papa. I turned on my side and looked out the window. It was still fairly dark outside; the rough edges of the horizon were releasing into pale blue. I lay there thinking about what Papa had said about my mother.

At some point in the night, I dreamed about Africa. I was walking through a thick forest with strange plants and brilliant flowers I'd never seen before. My mother was with me and I wasn't afraid. When we got to a clearing, there was a small village not far away. We stood at the edge of the forest but didn't go any farther. I looked up at my mother as she touched my face. She pointed to a small house, where a boy emerged, smiling and waving at us.

The dream vexed me so, I couldn't find my way back to sleep. Before the first bird knew it was time to wake, I got up and tiptoed to where I'd hidden my gift from Rev, deep in the chest that held my grandmother's keepsakes and some of my great-grandmother's things. My mother didn't live here long enough to have very many things to keep. I opened the envelope, but I couldn't make out much of Rev's letter in the blue darkness. I dressed in my riding clothes, leaving the pendant by my bedside and tucking the note and newspaper into the folds of my smock. I went as quietly as I could down the stairs from my loft; the main room was chilly. Papa was still snoring away in the same position I'd left him in last night.

I stirred up the embers of the fire and added a few logs to stoke it, then quickly threw together the ingredients to make a cornbread cake for Papa's breakfast and shoved the covered pan into the embers to cook. I didn't want him growling at me like he did yesterday. I prepared his coffee, too, leaving it on the hearth to keep hot. I went out to look after the cows so Papa would have fresh milk. The cows were a bit surprised to see me so early, I think. I did a few other quick chores in the brightening darkness, hoping that Papa wouldn't have much to fuss at me about if I was late returning.

Finally I threw an extra blanket on Mayapple and wrapped another around myself before I lifted myself onto her back. The morning was colder than the day before, with even more fog. I tried to ignore the pain of breathing. The ground was stiff with frost, crunching under her every step. I had her walk till the house was out of sight, when I felt it was safe to trot, and then we let out into a full gallop. Even through the dark mist, Mayapple knew exactly where she was going.

We halted at the riverbank. I dismounted and let Mayapple rest. The sky was opening up with light, but the sun was still just below the mountain range. The fog hanging above the river was thick as cotton; I struggled to see as I climbed down to the riverside and pulled out the letter, settling into my usual place. There was a break of light just where I sat, so I could clearly read.

My Dear Willow,

I said our usual birthday prayer for you. I am sending you this gift as an early wedding present as well as for your birthday. Your father says you are looking forward to starting a family soon, and although you seem so young, I suppose it is time for such thoughts. I still think of you as just a tiny thing clutching at my knee, hungry for life. I know your grandparents and mother, God rest their souls, are proud of the fine woman you are becoming.

Yours Truly in the Spirit of the Lord,
Rev Jeff

I was wearing a frown as I finished the letter. Though I was getting more used to the idea of marriage, 'cause I knew it would please Papa, I hated that he told Rev such things that weren't exactly true. I sighed heavy; the creaking inside my lungs matched the wind creaking through the tree limbs above my head. I pulled the newspaper out and studied it as best I could. It was a page from the *Boston News–Letter.* There were mostly ship logs and notices, but there was one small article that announced that in November the Boston Female Medical College would be opened — the first medical school devoted to educating females to become doctors. The article denounced women practicing medicine, and as I read, the idea struck something hard in my heart. I'd never get to go to such a school if I even wanted to, just 'cause of my color and my station in life. Without thinking, I tore the paper and Rev's letter up as small as I could and threw them both into the river. I pulled my copybook from its hiding place and began to write.

September 11, 1848

Dear Mama:
The difrence betwixt yesterday and today glare hard. Now I kno there be no sofness lef in this world for

me. Please do not judge me for thinking of things in such
a hard, jealous way, but I cant help it. Papa is fixd
to marry me off quick, and I cant keep his pace. What
make it so wrong for a woman to determin her own fate?
Papa say if I was a boy, he send me off to learn. I am no
boy, but I could learn just as well.

Maybe the thought of his own death make Papa
want to be sure to keep me safe. Tho that thougt keep my
angry heart from racing an my hands from trembuls,
the man he want for me is no one I might think to love.
This man has no subtullies. But I am just a lowly girl
and wors a slave with no say. I feel shame, an I kno I
must face my responsibilite here an bare my cross as Papa
say. But to you only I will tell: I want no part of this
marriage.

Mama, what am I to do?

Just then I heard a branch break on the bank above
me, then Mayapple snorted and stomped once, twice.
I suddenly remembered that Boss H might still be out
patrolling for the fugitives in the early light. I tried to hold
my breath, waiting to hear the sound of horses, but my
chest felt like it might bust open. No horses came. Just to
be safe, I stuffed my copybook back into its hiding place
and slowly stood to look around. I heard more branches

breaking and the scuffling of leaves. Mayapple snorted and stomped again. She was standing close to the bank, looking into the distance, with her head and tail held high. Someone was out there. My heart beat as thick as grits in my throat.

"What is it, girl?" I whispered to Mayapple, who walked up to me impatiently. Before I could even stroke her long brown face, she used it to push me back toward her saddle, telling me it was time to go. I took her direction and gathered up the reins. I could feel Mayapple's muscles quivering under my hand as I tried to steady her. I could just barely make out Mr. Mason and Mr. Dixon's marker through the fog past Mama's grave. North.

The light was shifting through the fog in such a peculiar way; it gave me the notion to walk into the fog, past Mama's grave, just to see what it felt like. *If I stepped over my mama's grave, I'd be free.* I shivered, put my foot in the stirrup, and swung up into the saddle. As I struggled to keep Mayapple still, a loud, clear, sweet whistle cut through the fog from the north of me. Mayapple snorted again and danced in a nervous circle.

"Whoa, girl. Settle yourself." I leaned forward to speak into her twitching ear and patted her neck while trying to figure where and who the whistle was from.

Shuffling sounds—someone walking fast from the woods to the west. Then another whistle, this time more timid and dry.

A breeze shifted the fog, sending leaves floating down from the trees, making enough light for me to see a dark-brown figure, handsomely dressed in a long oilskin coat, standing on the other side of the clearing, the Pennsylvania side. Something about him reminded me of how Papa looked when he preached—proud, but not exactly in the same way. He was relaxed, with his fists on his hips. He looked to the west; I didn't reckon he saw me. He cupped his hand over his mouth, and the same strong, sweet tune as the first whistle floated out of him.

Not far off from the woods that tumbled down from the mountains, another colored man scurried forward. This man didn't look near the same as the other. He was clearly afraid, crouching low and looking every which way as he ran forward toward the clearing. His clothes were tattered, and I could see his feet were bare.

The man from the north beckoned to the man from the southwest. Just then, Mayapple whinnied loudly, warning the two unfamiliar men. Both men froze, their faces turned in my direction. The man from the north still stood his ground in the same proud way. The man from the west crouched down farther, trying to hide himself in the tall grass. I tightened my grasp on the reins but didn't make another move.

The man from the north looked young, my age—he was smiling wide as he raised his hand and waved to me.

Stupidly, I raised a hand to wave back, until I realized that he was waving me closer, signaling me to come with them. The notion tangled itself in my head so wildly that my body jerked in response. Mayapple needed no further notice; she took it as her signal to run full speed back home.

When May finally stormed into the barn, both our chests were heaving; sweat pouring from our steaming skin. The rumbling wheeze deep in my lungs was loud; it hurt to breathe through my mouth. I could only sip the air. Fear didn't hit me until we were halfway back home, and then it hit hard. Was I going to tell Papa? Half of me wanted to do the right thing; the other half wasn't sure what the right thing was. I reckoned if I told Papa about the men I saw, he'd go tell Boss H and they'd be caught. But I wasn't sure; they were already over the state line by now. I knew the law allowed slaveholders to cross state lines to look for their slaves, but maybe since Rawlins didn't own them, it'd be unlawful for him to try to catch them.

If Boss H caught up to them . . . worse, what he'd do to the one on the other side of the Line! Colored men wasn't supposed to be that kind of proud.

My eyes clouded as I led Mayapple over to the watering trough and almost fell into it myself. My legs were weak and my head was swimming, worrying over what to tell

Papa. My breath felt like it was clawing its way out of my chest, where there was a slow-burning heat churning up my insides. I knew I needed to get back into the house, out of the cold morning air. I opened the corral gate so May could go in; I hardly had the strength to close it. Stumbling up to the cabin, I fell against the front door. My mouth was bone-dry; I couldn't call out for Papa 'cause I could scarcely catch my breath. I sank slowly to my knees in the doorway, wondering why everything was getting so dark. . . .

September 9, 1848   Haven, Pennsylvania

Son, 'member what I tole you—go slow. Take your time. There ain't nothing more suspicious than a black boy in a hurry."

"I'm a man now, Father. I know how the world works."

"Just 'cause your name mean 'wise' don't mean you know everything. 'Sides, seventeen years don't make a man anyhow," Atlantus scoffed. "In fact, what I done and did by your time was all in chains. I was more man than you and still not a man. You was born free and have soft hands smelling like books. Don't tell me you a man. I'll know it when I see it." He grabbed Cato's hand to chide him, but silently his heart broke with the thought that it might be the last time he ever saw his son's ink-stained fingers again.

Cato didn't see the tenderness in his father's eyes or he might not have pulled his arm back so roughly. Not wanting to fight before his departure, Cato stiffly extended his hand again to his father. He wanted them to shake to show respect, but really he was seething inside. He was more than man enough to take this trip. He had been meticulous when preparing and told no one of his real mission, not even his father. Atlantus didn't even know how to read signs, study maps, or write passes in a white man's delicate scrawl. Cato was confident that his manhood was in his cunning. This trip would prove it.

Besides, Cato thought, *there's been plenty of times I've traveled with father delivering hogs and manure. And once we even went as far as Pittsburgh and into Ohio.*

Atlantus's company regularly traveled from their freed-black community of Haven all the way to New York to deliver goods they sold and traded with other freed blacks there. Atlantus's business as a teamster made him the wealthiest man in town, since he'd eagerly ride long hours with deliveries that the white teamsters shied away from due to danger or stench. Atlantus regularly carried TNT to the railroads through Indian country all by himself. His company employed most of the men in their town with jobs as farmers, carpenters, welders, and drivers. Many of the women were employed as domestic workers at nearby farms and in town; some had organized a drop-off/pickup laundry service with Atlantus, and it made them all a fair profit.

To Cato, the business was essentially all tote and carry. Pick up here, drop off there. Cato had watched it grow since he was a boy. He was proud of his father's shrewd tenacity.

Atlantus had bought his own freedom only after he'd saved first for his wife. When Cato's mother died, he was only about nine years old; he was the oldest and had her to himself for several years before his sisters were born, so her death was devastating to him. Since then, Atlantus had become more miserly and bitter. He owned more than enough horses and rigs and had plenty of men to work for him, but he fretted over the railroads and canals taking his business away. Now he would watch over his workers like an overseer, chastising them and Cato for every small mistake. Every night Atlantus would count out his money and tally his figures until the candles burned out. Then, every morning, he would make Cato recount everything and write the figures in the ledgers. Although Atlantus could figure numbers well enough and could write them, too, he always told Cato that he sent him to learn with a private tutor in the closest white town, Columbia, so he could make sure it was all put down properly.

A *legitimate freeborn man must have an education,* Atlantus always said when Cato struggled with his studies. Although Atlantus wanted Cato to take over the business when he turned eighteen, Cato had ideas of his own. His tutor, Elihu, was a respected member of the Religious Society of Friends and a retired mapmaker who had explored and recorded most of Pennsylvania and western New York up to and beyond Lake Erie. Cato had stared at those maps for years on end.

Part of Cato wanted to tell his father the truth about his journey, but he knew what Atlantus would say: *I didn't pay for your education so you could go chasing after trouble. You worth too much for that.* So Cato let Atlantus believe that this was like any other delivery.

Now Atlantus was checking the rigging on Cato's four-horse team for the fifth time—lifting each horse's leg, examining its shoeing—even though he'd watched Cato hitch up the horses less than an hour ago. Atlantus was not a big man, smaller than his son, but his muscle was made of concrete. Cato tapped his food impatiently, waiting for his father to finish examining the rigging, although he wanted to tell the old man to leave him alone and let him go.

"Got your papers?" Atlantus asked, retightening the rigging.

"Of course." Cato tapped the pocket of his oilskin coat, right over his heart.

"If someone gets a mind, though, them papers is just made a thin wood. You know that, huh? Easy to go right up in smoke if you look like you'd bring a good dollar at market."

Cato couldn't help rolling his eyes. Through his teeth he said, "I'll be fine."

Atlantus roughly grabbed his son's hand again, only this time he pulled him into a full embrace.

"Bring yourself back safe, hear?"

Cato's anger melted as his father choked on his words. "But I'd be lying if I said I wouldn't rather see you dead then slaved."

Less than an hour later, Cato cautiously drove his team through the busy streets of Columbia, Pennsylvania, a vital center for transportation to the West. The town had rapidly grown and changed now that the trains regularly traveled between here and Philadelphia and since the new canals gave easier access farther into the North, East, and West than ever before. Cato picked up some deliveries at the train depot, then made his way across the Susquehanna to Wrightsville on the world's longest covered bridge. Even though the nearly two-mile-long bridge was quite modern and he'd taken it many times, it still made Cato nervous to cross above the rushing river with so much traffic, including trains. Atlantus said that when he'd first settled in the area, there was only a ferry pulled by oxen that would sometimes get confused and drown in the middle of crossing the river.

Cato made his first official stops exactly as his father had planned, mainly delivering farming tools and mercantile. He dropped off tools to the blacksmith and picked up two saddles from the tannery in Wrightsville, just over the bridge. Seed bags, crates of fabric, and two plows went to the general store in York. Cato marveled at William Goodridge's new five-story building—the tallest in York. Atlantus, who knew William, complained that the mulatto would only do business with whites, but Elihu's Friends hinted that Goodridge often helped fugitive slaves. Cato supposed that Atlantus might've been jealous of Goodridge's expansive wealth—the man owned his own rail line and a newspaper, not to mention his retail and real-estate holdings.

Wool linens, a barrel of cheese, twelve cases of bottled wine, six crates of pickled and preserved food made by the women of Haven, and a new silverware set for dining were all dropped at a tavern near Gettysburg. Along the way, Cato delivered the saddles and some small packages and letters to a few remote farmers. After that, he went to the home of an ex-fugitive woman and her three children.

She would tell no one who their father was, but she lived meagerly in the home her brother had built by the river. The brother had died only a year after they had escaped together with the children. The Friends, or Quakers, as people jokingly called them, told Cato about her, and he took it upon himself to leave a basket of preserved goods and smoked meats at her door. No one answered when he knocked, but he saw some brown children with blond hair peeking out the loft window.

He made four short stops in between to refresh himself and the horses. On the road, Cato visited with his father's friends or business partners, even just to water the horses; they would have alerted his father if he didn't.

As the road stretched south and he passed farms and estates, Cato wondered how many of them were also a part of the plot to aid fugitives. A few people sent money to abolitionist groups or subscribed to antislavery newsletters. Black and white women alike successfully organized donations or made clothing and food for those newly freed. Others would educate ex-slaves or even give space in their homes temporarily to hide a fugitive. Living that close to Mason and Dixon's line, folks didn't talk much about what they did, not even to trusted friends. Though many whites on this side of the Line wouldn't think twice about helping a stranger in need, no matter their color, there were still just as many who would have no problem going to church the same day they cashed in on the reward for some black man's ransom. Cato didn't dare to ask or speak of his mission, for fear of exposing not only himself but also others who made up the fragile web working to erode slavery, even if it was only a few souls at a time.

Having no real companions, Cato had no one he trusted to tell his dreams to. He tried not to take his position in his father's company for granted, but it made him distant from the other men in Haven. He had tried to teach some of them how to read and write — they were eager to learn, and many did so successfully — but they still regarded him as the boss's son instead of as a friend. Still, Cato held informal classes after church on Sundays, devoted to educating the men, while his sisters tutored the women and children in Bible study. Atlantus never attended services. "I paid to have the durn church built," he'd say. "Ain't that enough?"

Although Elihu had donated books, there were few to go around for teaching basic skills. Cato knew he was not a very good teacher. He could go on and on about a subject only to find his students looking at him with confusion and boredom.

Increasingly, there were men and sometimes even women and children who, on their way to cross the Susquehanna River, came through Haven from the deep South. Cato found that some were trained to repeat long passages of the Bible or classical poetry by their masters, and many of them were quite eloquent in their delivery.

But most travelers did not stay long in Haven. They lived on the road until they couldn't run anymore. Although Cato usually spent his time studying or in duty of his family, on the nights travelers came to town, he made sure to find out where they were to pay his respects and hear their stories. They always had interesting tales and interpretations of the world they traveled.

Last year, a young man about Cato's age called Jim was found nearly dead in the woods. When he got well, he finally revealed that he had been living free for many years with a community of Scotch-Irish high up in the lonely Appalachian Mountains after escaping from Savannah, Georgia, when he was just a boy. They had taught him how to read, write, and calculate very well. He said that before he left to find his own life off the mountain, they warned him that others would not be as kind. He'd found that out right away — he was grabbed in Charlottesville, Virginia, by two colored men, probably kidnappers for a local auctioneer.

"I asked them for directions, and they pretended to be friendly," he explained. "They offered to drive me somewhere, but I didn't feel right to go with them. They offered to buy me food, and I was so hungry I couldn't refuse. Next thing I knew, they had me tied up."

Jim would say nothing else about it except that they managed to carry him all the way into Delaware before he managed to escape.

They continued to talk deep into the night, Cato sharing the news of the world. Jim had mostly been taught religious texts, so Cato was eager to share his pamphlets and newspapers with someone with a firm foundation in reading.

"What's that giant black smoke monster that screams so loud?" Jim had asked Cato almost right away. "I saw it from the woods once; those metal things nearly kilt me with fright."

It took Cato a long time to figure out that Jim had meant a train. Although the railroads were growing like vines out of most major cities in the Northeast and South, many rural people had still never seen an actual locomotive. Cato could remember seeing the first train that came to Columbia when he was a boy, how he had trembled and grabbed at his father's hand.

Cato found himself explaining the whole concept of a locomotive engine and was embarrassed for going on, but Jim followed right along, even asking Cato to draw pictures.

"You think they might ever let me work on one of those trains up north?" Jim asked. Cato shrugged; he didn't want to disappoint Jim by saying no.

The next day, Cato was sorely disappointed to find that Jim had left before first light. As much as he understood Jim's need to move on, Cato felt as though he'd lost a friend. He envied Jim for having no attachments, free as a train barreling into the future.

Cato knew the world was changing rapidly—he was constantly inspired by so many new inventions, technology, and ideas! A man in Baltimore had just invented a machine that would reduce the amount of people it would take to harvest wheat—perhaps without the need of so many, it would also help carve away at the tumor of slavery. Elihu, an active abolitionist, received newspapers, books, pamphlets, and letters from action-minded people around the world. Revolutions were happening in Europe and even Haiti—common people demanding *égalité*! Taking freedom rather than waiting a moment longer for it to be given. Down with the rich abusing and enslaving the masses! There was even some interesting news recently about a man named Karl Marx who was calling his ideas *socialism*. He thought everyone should get equal shares of everything.

Cato had just finished reading Frederick Douglass's book, was subscriber to the *North Star* newspaper, and even wrote the man a letter of thanks and praise. Douglass himself wrote back to him, encouraging him to help in the efforts of freedom and equality. Cato was also a devoted subscriber of William Lloyd Garrison's liberal abolitionist newspaper, *The Liberator.*

All of that, and perhaps including the fact that Cato was born the same year as Nat Turner's bloody revolution, inspired and perhaps even obligated Cato to seek out an opportunity to aid the enslaved seeking freedom. Since Turner could read and write, many states outlawed slaves learning to read the Bible or going to Sunday school unless supervised by whites. They justified their tyranny by saying that an enlightened mind was too dangerous in a Negro. Cato and Elihu had many heated discussions about slavery that kept them up, locked in disagreement, for many long nights.

Elihu believed in gradual emancipation, while Cato rejected anything but immediate equality. They both agreed that things might get worse before they got better, just to end the reign of slave power.

Cato longed to be a trailblazer, to explore where freedom was fair, not governed by color or money. He wanted to do more than just seek his own prosperity. There was so much of the West that hadn't been recorded yet. Elihu had taught Cato when he was just a boy how to measure longitude and latitude. He was stern and quiet in the Quaker way, but he had taught Cato everything he knew. Thinking of Elihu made Cato sad, but he sat up straight and squared his shoulders, reminding himself that he was already on his way to doing something remarkable.

The Mason-Dixon Line was easy enough to get to from Gettysburg; Cato left the horses and rig at the location he was told—a Quaker safe house a few miles south of Gettysburg. The farmer would tend Cato's horses and rig until he returned later that day; Cato was then scheduled to head northwest toward Pittsburgh, dropping his live cargo off at another safe point along the way. Under Atlantus's schedule, Cato wouldn't be expected home for at least another ten days after he did a pickup in Pittsburgh.

He carried a pack with a supply of dried meat, hard biscuits, and three flasks of water in case the fugitives were in need, but it wasn't much. He'd even put an extra set of clothes in his bag just to be sure. He also carried an almost-new Colt revolver and twelve handmade bullets, six of which he kept loaded in the barrel. Cato had paid a good sum for the handsome gun; a man who had just come back from the Mexican War had won it in a card game from a real Texas Ranger. It was heavy and awkward in Cato's hands, but he kept the extra ammunition—.44-caliber black-powder paper cartridges—tucked neatly in his oil-skin coat pocket, right next to his freedom papers. In his other pocket he carried a box of locofoco matches he'd bought the last time he was in Philadelphia—a modern tool that was hard to find.

Cato walked to the Line, marking his way with the last lingering stars, starting off just as the moon rose. Through the darkness, he kept his mind busy by remembering how he had met the radical abolitionists at Elihu's funeral, six months ago. Men and women came all the way from Rochester, New York, to pay their respects. Even those liberal Quakers from Philadelphia were surprised at how the Northerners practiced equality, even with women. It was found to be nearly scandalous that these folks traveled so far with a mixed-gender group—some women were not even married, and they all spoke their minds freely.

They had all sat around Elihu's old study after the burial. It was the room in which Cato had learned to read and write, where he would fall asleep by the fire, thinking. To Cato, this room was Elihu himself.

In the Quaker way, anyone who felt they had something to say could raise their voice, but as far as Cato was accustomed, only the men spoke and the women were quiet. Several of the men were moved to tears speaking of Elihu's kindness and devotion to freeing mankind.

When a woman from Rochester whose husband was well respected suddenly said, "I pray that there will be equality and freedom for both races *and* genders one day," there was a loud grumble around the room.

The grumble erupted into a roar when another younger woman said, loudly and confidently, "I pray that soon women will have the right to the vote."

Cato was taken aback. Some people in the room simply stared at their hands or fiddled with their hats; others nodded in agreement. One of Elihu's oldest friends was so furious that he stormed from the room and could not be coaxed back in until "those infernal women" left. Most Quaker men refused to vote themselves, due to their religious convictions.

Surprised as he was, Cato had not been offended by the women's desire to have an equal say; it was what he longed for himself. However, he was not sure that women would ever be given completely equal rights, nor did he truly believe that they deserved them. Cato couldn't imagine a woman understanding complicated topics like politics and science. The summer after the funeral, it was all over the newspapers how some of those very same ladies held a convention in Seneca Falls, New York, to discuss the plight of women. It was said that a man had to preside over the women's convention because none of the women there could handle the responsibility. It was Frederick Douglass who persuaded the group to put women's voting rights on the agenda. Still, Douglass wrote an unflattering article about the gathering in his *North Star;* he called the discussion of women's rights as pointless as discussing animal rights.

After the service, while the abolitionists read a narrative of a slave about his brutal life and daring escape, Cato took Nathanial, one of the men from Rochester, aside and asked what he could to help the cause.

Nathanial pulled at his beard, studying Cato. "We have *packages* that are in *storage* in West Virginia, but we are in need of a safe place for picking them up and someone to deliver them," he said. "But would thee not be fearful? Thine own freedom would be at risk."

"Well, no. I'm the son of a teamster; I can easily do the job," Cato said proudly. He even showed the abolitionist a map he had found in Elihu's things—a perfect spot for picking up "packages," right on the Line.

Nathanial agreed. "We shall contact thee. It may take longer than a fortnight to organize the exchange."

Cato waited anxiously for the letter with his mission, and when it came a week ago, he had memorized and burned it within the hour. Elihu had given him a glimpse of what it was like to learn from books, and as grateful as he was for it, the real world was his teacher now.

．　　．　　．

Just as the sun began peeling back the darkness from the mountaintop, he saw the white granite marker.

He raised his arms and whistled as a sharp wind blew down from the mountains. Cato did this all the time—raising his arms to the wind—ever since he was a child and his father had told him that he was not a slave but free. Cato never felt more exhilarated in his life, delivering the enslaved into freedom!

The morning light broke through the fog as his whistle was answered, and in the close distance, he could see the fugitive coming down from the wooded hills.

Through the fog, Cato heard a horse a short distance away, but as the light broke through the field, he was relieved and surprised to see what he *thought* was another fugitive, riding that copper-maned horse, so he smiled wide and waved. But when the rider merely lifted a reluctant hand, then took off suddenly toward the southeast, Cato froze with fear, realizing how much danger they could be in. The runaway and Cato only had to glance at each other before they both took off running north.

It was all so quick and graceless, not the way Cato had envisioned it in his mind. He thought he would greet the fugitives with open arms, to be a beacon in the dark.

But it didn't happen that way at all.

Cato ran as hard as he could, his eyes fixed northward. Suddenly he yelled out as pain ripped through his leg; the wind was knocked out of him as he hit the ground hard. It felt as if the world had fallen out from under him, he was so confused and shocked. He got a hold of himself quickly, realizing that his leg was almost knee-deep and twisted inside a rabbit hole. Try as he might, he could not lift himself out without groaning in pain—his ankle was stuck, maybe broken.

"Lemme help." The runaway reached out his hand. Cato had almost forgotten him.

"No! Keep running! We don't know who was on that horse—"

The man, who was considerably older than Cato, didn't listen, just grabbed Cato under his arms and pulled him up, despite Cato's writhing protests.

"Look like it's broke on the inside," the man said, looking at Cato's ankle seriously. "Hurt too bad to walk, huh?"

Cato moaned, knowing he wouldn't be able to make the day's walk to the rig. He couldn't expect the man to carry him. Barely able to nod his head, Cato felt himself slipping away.

The next thing he knew, the man was pulling him into a dark, cool place. "Where are we? How far did we get?"

"We ain't too far from where I met you." The man peered at Cato, trying to figure him out. "We in free Pennsylvania now. I saw that marker they said to look for."

"Yes, but they can still come for you, and there's no one to stop them. Run!"

"But we might make it together if we stay in here, give it a few days. There was two more behind me, but they . . . the dogs . . . I couldn't help them, but you . . . ."

Shaking his head, Cato begged, "Please forget about me. You have to go!"

The man shook Cato's hand; it took the rest of Cato's strength before his vision was again consumed with darkness.

Part

Two

She's taken sick on and off all her life, but not like this before. . . ."

"Don't worry, Ryder. This girl's a fighter—she'll pull through. The Lord will take care of her—you'll see. Let's pray. . . ."

"But every time I shut my eyes, I can't help thinking on how . . . She must've put too much of that root in my tea the night before. I didn't even hear her get up, much less hear her collapse right in the doorway. . . . It breaks my heart to think she might've called out for me. . . . If Cholly hadn't come up to find out why the bell wasn't rung on time . . ."

"Don't dwell on that now. What's done is done, and all the rest is in the Lord's hands. Look to Him for guidance."

The familiar voices bit at my ears like chilly winds, but I couldn't open my eyes to see or catch my breath enough to speak. Rev and Papa sat by my bedside, talking and praying together. I always liked listening to them talk; it was like they really were brothers, not master and slave. Tiny's voice found its way into my head, too. I reckon she was caring for me quite a bit. I felt like the world was happening all around me but not with me, like I was stuck in a cellar while the house was full of folks. I don't know how long it was like that.

"The doctor says she'll be fine once the fever breaks. She just needs rest right now."

"Jeff, I know this is all my fault. I could tell she was getting sickly, but I didn't make her stay inside. My head was set on other things. . . ."

"You know you couldn't have done anything about it. You said she's been going out in the early-morning air to sit by her mother's grave. She's like her father once her head is set on something. . . . You couldn't stop her from going out there. The frost just came early this year."

"She's like her mother, too, Jeff. Maybe too much. Kept asking me questions about her the other night. I could barely get up the courage to utter Lily's real name."

"You know I understand the pain of the widower, Ryder. You and I have grown up like two trees, side by side, sharing the same light and the same darkness. At least you still have Willow."

Silence.

"At least you still got Knotwild."

More silence.

"I can't help the position in life that God gave me, Ryder. This place feels like more burden than blessing sometimes."

"Then maybe you should think about passing your burden down to us."

"I think all of this worrying has set you off. You know my hands are tied by the law. It doesn't look like things are going to change for our peculiar institution anytime soon."

"Don't give it to me. Give it to her."

"What are you suggesting, Ryder?"

"You and I both know she's the only heir Knotwild has after us."

Wood scraping wood; footsteps around the room.

"I don't know what you're talking about. Knotwild has no direct heir after me."

"Don't do that to me, Jeff. If we've shared the same light and darkness all these years, don't pretend you're in the dark now. We share the same blood, cousin."

The footsteps stop cold.

"You're talking nonsense, Ryder. You must be tired from staying up with your daughter."

"No, I'm as clear as a bell and you know it, Jeff. My great-grandmother and your great-grandfather . . . My grandmother and your grandfather were siblings."

"Stop now before you insult me, Ryder."

"Jeff, I'm not trying to insult you. I want what's best for Knotwild, to keep it in the family so it's not lost to strangers or to the government when we're gone. You don't want to see that any more than I do. Slavery won't last forever. You yourself believe it. You could claim Willow as yours. Emancipate her in your will, and her children are the legal heirs."

"I don't know if the law would allow that. Besides, I might marry again."

Silence.

"You found someone as angelic as your Clarissa?"

"I don't have to tell you that no woman could live up to her."

"I remember when you used to tell me everything, Jeff. You said we was going to make Knotwild our own, our family, together. And when I comforted you in your grief, you said it would be just us for now on — you, me — and Willow would bring us our joy. She's done that. Give her children this land by claiming her as your own."

Sounds of hard footsteps crossing the floor; the door creaking open and slamming shut.

Something was cooking; I could smell the fire and food. Yet I was still dreaming I was a wretched fugitive lost in the North, buried under a mountain of snow. Tiny's high voice came to me from somewhere near. My eyes, which had seemed nailed shut for so long, finally fluttered open. I found myself lying in Papa's bedchamber, in pain. There was something cold, hard, and wet all around me — ice. Must've been for the fever. They'd done that to me once before when I was a child and couldn't shake a bout of pneumonia. Rev had even had the doctor leech my blood.

My throat was sore and dry, but I tried to call out anyway. Nothing more than a squeak peeped from my mouth. I tried again, but I just ended up coughing. My arms were pinned under so much weight. Papa must've emptied out the icehouse for me. I tried to lift my hands again, but I was too weak. I could only turn my head a little to look out the window next to the bed. The tulip trees were yellowing. . . . How long had I been . . . ?

Heavy feet shuffled into the room. I looked up to see Tiny's broad cheeks shining brightly. She almost fell on me, she was so glad to see me awake.

"Aww, girl! I was sure you'd wake yourself today!" She laughed heartily. "Somethin' told me and I was right! I told your Papa to keep in for another hour, 'stead a shoein' the horses, but he say he couldn't stand to see your lips turn blue from all that ice!"

She stood at the end of the bed and clapped her hands, thrilled by her own determination. "But I knew you'd wake today! I knew that ice was gonna pull you out that fever! I'm gonna tell everybody right now!"

"Tiny," I whispered, praying she'd hear me before she rushed out of the room.

"What you want, honey?"

"Too cold . . ." was all I could get out.

"I'm sure, but you must wait for Master Jeffries and your Papa to give the all rights. I'll be back. Just try to think up some hot soup or somethin' like that."

I lay there for what seemed to be forever, racked with chill and teeth chatter, trying to figure out everything that had happened. All I could remember was fog, and a dream about Papa and Rev. . . . None of it made any sense to me, so mostly I just tried to keep still. I traced the words of my thoughts with my finger on the stiffened, frosty linens:

Mama I wish you was here

I heard someone running up to the cabin door.

"Oh, thank God!" Rev's voice trembled as he knelt down beside the bed. "Merciful God, thank you for bringing her back to us!"

Papa came rushing in. His face crumpled into tearful joy. He knelt down next to Rev and fished my hand out of the ice. My fingers were puckered and wrinkled like an old woman's. I could barely feel them except for the piercing pain. Papa kept whispering "Thank you, thank you" while Rev continued to pray.

How long were they going to leave me like this?

"Please," I croaked out. *"Too cold."* Too deeply lost in their own prayer, neither of them heard me. I tried to squeeze Papa's hand but was too weak and numb from the ice.

Tiny came back into the cabin, huffing and puffing. She fell against the door frame for a moment and wheezed. "I sent word down to the fields; everybody been worried so."

I gave Tiny a pleading look, hoping she'd understand.

"Y'all might pull that girl out that ice before she catch a whole 'nother fever!" she said after a moment.

Papa and Rev got up without saying anything to each other and began to haul me up out of the bed. Ice crackled and clunked onto the floor. I had no strength to help myself and only hoped that Tiny was the one who had changed my clothes and wrapped me in muslin.

Rev and Tiny pulled the huge washtub I used for the bed linens into the cabin and set it by the hearth, taking turns filling it with hot water while Papa wrapped me in blankets. He carried me to Granmam's chair, where he rubbed my hands and feet and gently blew on them. I began to feel some sensation in my toes, but it was painful—all pins and needles. My body continued to quiver from the cold. My head swirled with thoughts and questions; I was now unsure of what I'd dreamed and what was real. There was a heavy, noticeable silence between my father and Rev. Tiny did all the talking as she heated water to add to the tub.

"I'm telling you, Willow, honey. We all thoughts you're gonna meet your mama up in heaven the way you took that fever so quick. Your poor little body was convulsing so, and you kept crying out 'bout who knows what, something 'bout somebody walking 'cross your poor mama's grave."

"I don't remember," I whispered. Rev excused himself quietly.

"Papa?" It took a lot of effort to lift my head, to look him in the eye.

"Hush, now, child," he said, rocking me steadily. "Hold your tongue till you get your strength."

They put me in the tub; Papa busied himself collecting and cleaning up the ice while Tiny sat with me while I soaked in the warm water. It felt like I was thawing from the inside out. It was nice to breathe easy again—I was able to guide Tiny on what herbs to steep for my tea. I even had her put some herbs in the bath, chamomile and lavender, which soothed me; the scent made me feel like somehow Granmam was with me. Tiny could barely keep her mouth closed, telling me all the goings-on I'd missed in the past two weeks.

". . . and Rachel had twin boys! They healthy but howls all night, like a pack a wolves all by theyselves. At Merriend they'd fetch a pretty price. . . ."

I winced at the thought of babies being sold. Tiny paused a long moment before she exhaled. I reckon she was thinking on her own children. She didn't talk about them often; I figure it must've been too painful. She told me once that the only thing she could do was kiss them all good-bye. I reckon that's another reason why she's so good at those tiny stitches — before she started sewing, her hands would shake something awful if they weren't busy.

"Ain't nobody sleeping down in the quarters since the twins came on Tuesday. I tried stuffing cotton in my ears, but it don't work. . . ."

Tiny would sometimes sit with Old Samuel and the children while she sewed. She talked to them, told them stories to make them laugh, but she never held them.

"I don't reckon I'd be able to let 'em go if I got my hands on 'em," was all she said once I finally got up the courage to ask her about it.

Tiny shook her head, blinking into the fire a few times, and then slowly continued to ramble on about old Rex chasing a fox out of the henhouse. I was grateful she didn't expect much conversation from me.

I stretched my legs so they hung out over the side of the washtub. There wasn't much room in there, but enough to cover my belly and chest. The fire kept my legs from getting too cold.

". . . and don't you know they caught them fugitives? Two of 'em up in the mountains, trying to cross the border. They rode 'em pass here on the way back south or wherever it is they takes 'em. Wanted us to see 'em as an example. Somebody let the dogs at 'em."

I struggled to sit up in the tub, sloshing water all over the floor. "What'd they look like, Tiny?" I asked. Memories of seeing two men in the woods became clear, and my curiosity leaped at me like a flame.

"They looking a mighty mess, I'd say."

I sank back down into the cooling water. Was it possible that those were the two men I'd seen in the woods? Was I the reason they were caught? The thought twanged a note of sadness in me. . . .

"Ooh! You got goose skin, girl! 'Bout time you getting on outta there." Tiny came and helped me out of the tub. I was still very weak. I had to lean against her as she helped me dry off and put on a clean nightdress. I sat in Granmam's chair wrapped in blankets while Tiny prepared broth for me. After I was settled, she opened the front door and told Papa he could come in. He busied himself by making the bed up for me. Papa didn't say much, but he touched my head every time he passed by me in the chair. I wondered when Rev would be back. For now, I could only sip my tea, stare into the fire, and think.

It was a few days before I could do much else *besides* sitting by the fire or lying in bed and thinking. Papa wanted me to keep sleeping in his bed in case I felt faint climbing up and down from the loft—the small stairs leading up to it made a sharp turn, which he worried could be dangerous.

For a week after I woke up, Papa slept on a pallet by the fire if he slept at all. He wasn't drinking his tea at night 'cause he wanted to make sure to be there if I needed him.

It was hard not to have a book to read. Papa let me have the Bible for no more than an hour when no one else was around, but I'd read it so many times that I could only stare at the pages. Mostly I tried to piece together what I'd seen before I fell sick and the dreams I had after. The conversation I thought I had heard. . . . I surely remembered going out to the river and what I saw there—the young man in the oilskin coat with his arms wide open to the world. Where did pride like that come from?

I couldn't stop seeing him, waving at me to come to him. I couldn't help feeling shame burn at my face when I finally remembered the longing I'd felt to go. I couldn't imagine seeing a man like him in chains, chased and mauled by dogs, and it vexed me worse that the very thought nearly brought me to tears.

Rev came by to see me a few times, but only when Papa was out working.

"So, my dear," Rev said, sitting next to me by the fire. "Are you feeling any better?"

"Much better, thank you, Rev. I hope Tiny is taking care of you well enough. How was your trip to Boston? What interesting things happen there?"

"My trip was quite exhilarating, indeed. Boston is a lovely city, with fascinating sights, like the new telegraph poles with wires that swing to and fro when the birds sit upon them. But it would not suit me to live there. I enjoy our quiet here at Knotwild."

"Me too, but I would love to see a big city like that!"

"You would, wouldn't you? Perhaps when you get better you will."

"Really? Then I'll be better tomorrow, Rev!"

He laughed and we were our old selves again.

"By the way," Rev said, pulling a book out of his jacket pocket, "it took me going all the way up to Boston to find out about a fine poet from Baltimore. He is a rather morose fellow, but the way he turns a phrase endears my heart! A fine young woman introduced me to him—Edgar A. Poe.

I have been lacking in my literary studies for a long while, and it was refreshing to find a woman who enjoyed poetry. It touched me deeply."

I didn't pay attention to what he was saying—I might've been staring at the biggest chunk of gold in the world; I wanted that book so bad. The cover read, THE RAVEN AND OTHER POEMS.

"You always enjoyed reciting poetry, so I thought I might teach you my favorite verse."

"Oh, yes!" I wanted to get closer to see the words myself, but without his invitation, it would have been improper. In our usual way, he would read the poem aloud once, straight through, so I could hear how it should sound. Then he would say a line and have me repeat it until I had it memorized.

Rev cleared his throat as he began to read the poem "Eulalie" aloud.

"I dwelt alone
In a world of moan,
And my soul was a stagnant tide,
Till the fair and gentle Eulalie became my blushing bride—"

As I leaned in closer, my mouth watering as if I were smelling steak, Papa walked in. Neither he nor Rev looked at each other or spoke for a heavy moment until I coughed, breaking the silence. My hopes were that Rev would continue reading.

"I have matters to attend to," Rev said, and stood up suddenly and awkwardly, stumbling over his chair. Papa called out after him, but Rev didn't turn as he left.

"Papa?"

"I just came up to check on you, Mite. I see you're doing just fine, so I'll get back to work." He left almost as quick as he had come in.

I turned back to the fire, remembering again what I thought I'd heard while I was sick. I didn't want to believe it 'cause part of me was confused and somehow ashamed about what my father was trying to do—make Rev feel guilty enough to will Knotwild to me. The other part of me was frightened by Rev's reaction. I understood the law might make it hard for him to just hand everything over to Papa, but if what Papa had said was true, why would Rev hesitate? It all made me uneasy. I wished I'd never gone out to the river that morning, that I'd just stayed at home, done my chores, and been a good daughter.

I was finally allowed to crawl up to my loft and finish recovering in my own bed. Most of my energy was restored and I was able to take care of myself, but still couldn't do much. It was a Sunday night, not too cold. From my window, I could see a fire burning in the middle of the quarters. There was a full, bright moon, so I could clearly see folks sitting around, plates of food steaming with what I imagined was fried fish. Someone—when I squinted I could just make out that it was Cholly Dee—had everyone's attention, surely telling a far-fetched lie, by the way they all watched him waving his arms and making wild gestures as he talked. I could even make out Tiny, her body bobbing up and down with laughter.

I thought about how embarrassing it was that Cholly Dee had found me, passed out at my front door. And then came the terrible thought that Cholly knew things about my mother that I didn't. And, worse yet, the possibility that Papa had hidden the truth all this time about he and Rev perhaps being blood relatives. . . .

I hated feeling this way, all confused with mistrust. By moonlight I tried rereading a volume of Shakespeare's sonnets I'd forgotten that I'd hidden in my mattress long ago, but my mind was spinning with questions. I had found the book in the attic, so I didn't think Rev would miss it. It had taken me months to read just one poem and understand it. I often pondered on how strange Shakespeare wrote. Even though we both knew the same language, it was different. Did he speak the same way he put words on the page? Now that I had most of the poems memorized, their familiarity brought me little comfort.

•   •   •

Thankfully, as the days went on and preparations for the annual trip to the market in Baltimore began to beg for his attention, Papa came up to check on me less and less. The same with Tiny and Rev. When I was young, I used to cherish the days I was left alone to recover from illness. Now I yearned to get out and ride, to take Mayapple back to the spot where I'd seen the men. More than anything, I wanted to get my copybook; writing always helped me figure things out. I wrote little notes with my finger in the dust under my bed:

Roses do not bloom here enouf
for me to know all their sweet names.

On another one of Rev's short visits, I worked up the courage to ask what had happened to the fugitives; I was tired of wondering.

"Tiny said something about fugitives in the woods, Rev. You know what she was talking about?"

"Oh, I don't know all the details," he replied distractedly. "It was just before I returned. I believe one of them recently died from the wounds he suffered getting caught. The other is being held in Taneytown for now. That's all I know."

My heart felt like a lightning storm was ripping through it.

"Rev . . . If you don't mind, I think I need to go lie down now for a bit."

"Are you ill again? Shall I get Tiny or your father?"

"No, I just . . . It's sad to hear, is all." I couldn't at look him, fearing I might cry.

"About the fugitives? It is upsetting. They were found so close to here. I'll let you rest now, Willow. I need you to get well soon."

I smiled and nodded the best I could as he patted my head and left. For the rest of the afternoon, I stayed in up in the loft, with a tight brow, watching yellow and copper leaves drift past my window.

It was almost another long week before Papa let me venture outside. He made sure I was wrapped in several layers, even though the weather was suddenly unseasonably warm, and he made me promise only to walk down to Mayapple's stall, visiting for only a quarter hour before returning. May nearly broke down her stall door when she saw me. I fed her all the apples and carrots I was able to carry and the one lump of sugar Papa didn't see me take. I stepped inside the stall to hug Mayapple's long neck. Someone else entered the stables. I heard Cholly Dee's voice coaxing another horse, Macho, out of his stall. I swallowed hard, then I called, "Cholly Dee, how did you know my mother's African name?"

Cholly stopped dead in his tracks. He turned to face me and stared for what seemed like an eternity.

"We spoke the same language," he said quietly. He licked his lips and tipped his hat to me. "Good to see you up and about, miss."

He turned and mounted the horse.

"Wait!" I called after him. He looked back at me. Just as I was about to ask him more about my mother, Papa walked into the stable.

"Where you think you're going, Cholly?" Papa demanded.

"I'm goin' to town. I tole the Reverend."

"No, you ain't," Papa said, standing in the middle of the stable door. The light and dust sparkled around him, making him look like a wrathful angel. "You got too much to do before we have to go down to Baltimore market. We got bushels that still need tying and wagons that need loading. There ain't nothing in town you got business for today."

"Move aside, Ryder. I'm goin' to Taneytown. They'll be takin' that runaway to the auction block in Baltimore, so I want him to know a friendly face gonna be in the crowd. The Reverend wrote me a pass."

I just about swallowed my tongue hearing that. He would be able to tell me if that fugitive was the young man in the oilskin coat.

"But Rev don't know how much work needs to happen before we leave," Papa said. "I'm in charge of that, so *I* say if you can go."

"I'm goin' no matter what yuh say, Ryder. Go ask *Massa*." He rode out of the stable. Papa could only step aside as he passed.

"You best be back before dark!" Papa shouted after him.

I stroked Mayapple's mane a few more times until Papa bellowed, "Time's up, girl! Let's go!"

Papa marched up toward the big house, where Rev was heading toward us. I walked slowly behind Papa. Papa greeted Rev with his arms across his chest, his foot tapping like he was keeping time with a rabbit's heartbeat.

"I had things for Cholly to do around here. Why'd you let him go?" Papa said through his teeth.

"I think it does no harm for Cholly Dee to exhibit some compassion toward this man," Rev was saying. "Even a fugitive's troubled heart needs that. He'll be sold in Baltimore in the next week. Cholly promised to speak to him about doing what his next master asks of him so that he will not get himself into any more trouble."

"Ha! Don't be foolish, Jeff. Cholly's probably just gonna gamble!" Papa's voice was raised, and he struggled to control it when Rev cut him a sharp look. "We got work to do around here! Ain't got time for . . . for things that don't even concern us. I need Cholly Dee to get the hands fixed to load the wagons in two days' time. Now I have to supervise the hands *and* organize the inventory."

"Is that what you're concerned about, Ryder? A few hours' inconvenience?" Rev sighed loudly. "I trust that Cholly will do the right thing and be back tonight and have the hands ready in time, even if you can't handle his work today."

"You know I ain't shirking no work. It's just . . . you usually let me know before you write passes, is all."

"I was just coming down to tell you that, Ryder." They stood there in silence until Rev finally stepped around my father to greet me. "How are you feeling today, Willow? How's your breathing?"

"I'm feeling almost right, Rev." I tried to smile brightly and bring some peace between them.

"Well, good. Then I think if the doctor says it's safe, you shall accompany us to Baltimore. I'll need you to assist me; I'll be attending some important meetings."

Baltimore! I nodded, trying hard not to show my excitement. I'd surely see the fugitive, see if it was the one that waved at me and know if he was alive!

"I don't think she's ready . . ." Papa began.

"But as I said, I need her. So we'll let the doctor decide. I sent word with Cholly Dee, asking him to come out here tomorrow." He paused, then said, "I will be taking dinner at Merriend this evening. I'll ride by myself." Then he turned curtly and walked back into his house.

We went into our own cabin; the air was getting heavy with late-afternoon light. Papa carelessly threw wood into the hearth when we got inside, making the embers pop and jump. "I guess since you're feeling better, you can make supper," Papa said.

Tiny had left us half a roasted chicken, and there were plenty of root vegetables in the pantry. I prepared a thin soup while Papa paced the floor.

The sun was setting frightfully quick. Papa's shadow grew large in the firelight, taking up the light of the room.

My mind was on the fugitive when I suddenly chopped into my own finger while aiming for a carrot. I gasped and went closer to the fire to clearly see the damage.

"You cut?" Papa asked. He peered over my shoulder as several drops of blood hit the hearthstone. He finally lit a candle. He was always stingy with them this time of year, before the coming winter darkness.

I examined the gash, then went to rinse it in the basin. The cut was clean and not too deep. "It ain't that bad," I said to Papa, "but bad enough to cause trouble. Can you hand me a rag and Granmam's ointment out of the cupboard?"

"Plenty of folks getting sick and dying from such a

small thing," Papa reminded me. After I put on the ointment and wrapped my finger tight with a clean piece of muslin, I sat down in Granmam's chair; all the excitement took the wind out of me.

"You handled that just as your Granmam would've, Mite." Papa looked down at me, sincerely concerned. "You did what needed to be done and didn't think too hard. Understand what I mean?"

I nodded slowly, unsure what he was going to say next.

"I want you to go on this trip to Baltimore. I worry over your health, but maybe it might be good for you after all. There'll be things you never seen before, and I think you're grown enough to handle it." He began to pace in front of the fire. "But only if the doctor says you're healthy enough."

As far as I recalled, Granmam never went to Baltimore; I'd been told it was only a man's trip. I couldn't believe it. I wanted to kick up my heels!

"In Baltimore, you'll have to take care of Rev's needs before he even knows he has them." Papa talked quickly without looking at me. "Usually he travels taking care of his own self, but he seems to have something else in mind for this trip. So you got to keep your ears and eyes open, Mite." Papa stopped and leaned against the hearth to find a bit of light for his pipe. "And tell me everything." He pointed the end of the pipe in my direction. "Promise?"

"'Course, Papa. But what would Rev ever keep from you? You all just like brothers."

"Some things he forget to tell me, like today with Cholly Dee. He just got a lot on his mind lately. It's our job to know what white folks want before they do. That's the only way we can get them to do what *we* need," he said mysteriously.

I had more questions, but the crease in Papa's forehead as he stared into the fire told me to keep my thoughts to myself. The rest of the evening passed with Silence sitting at the head of our table.

The next day, the doctor came and took my pulse as though he were handling worms. He even held a sachet of lavender to his nose as if my very scent offended him. Papa and Rev were both present, standing at opposite ends of the room. After the first time Dr. Bell came to Knotwild to see me, Papa, Rev, and I all made fun of how delicate he was for a doctor.

Dr. Bell opened his bag and pulled out an instrument he used to listen to my chest. Our old doctor would just put his ear right over my heart. The last time I was sick was the first time I saw it.

"What's that thing called again?"

"Quiet," he hissed.

"It's called a stethoscope, Willow," Rev said patiently. "It's a tool to hear your lungs and heart better."

"Steth-o-scope . . ." I repeated under my breath.

"I said *quiet*!" Dr. Bell raised his voice sharply.

"Sorry, sir."

He listened to my back and chest again, pressing the lavender against his nose.

Rev continued talking anyway. "It was invented by a French doctor who didn't want to put his head against the bosom of a very plump lady patient," he said, his eyes twinkling with mischief. I couldn't contain my laughter, and I even heard Papa chuckle a bit.

Dr. Bell put his tools away roughly and stood with his nose in the air.

"Reverend Jeffries," he said with disgust. "I graduated from the University of Pennsylvania School of Medicine with high honors. I refuse to come here and examine your slaves if you refuse to give me the respect I deserve in front of them. Knotwild is the only plantation where I am asked to treat slaves. Frankly, I'd rather examine the horses." With that, he collected his things and walked out the door. Rev went after him, apologizing.

Dr. Bell wasn't the same doctor who treated me as I grew up. Dr. Yoder had been a kindly old man who knew and had treated my family and Rev's, back to my grandparents. He had worked with my grandmother to treat the field hands when they were in need, and Granmam had often shared her herbs with him. There would be none of that with Dr. Bell.

As Papa went to shut the door, I saw Rev nodding to Dr. Bell, who wasn't finished complaining. Rev pulled out his billfold and handed a near fistful of money to Dr. Bell. Papa said nothing, but his vein was popping again.

Rev briefly came in a few moments later to say that Dr. Bell had approved me to travel. I nearly leaped with joy, until I saw the stony look on Papa's face.

The next few days got real busy with preparations. Since I'd fallen ill, I hadn't had the chance to clean the house, and some of the rooms still had canvas over the furniture since Rev was away so long. I spent a few days putting the house halfway right again. Rev had been living very meagerly, and he even let Tiny serve him in the kitchen rather than the dining room.

The rest of my time was spent pressing and packing his finest clothes and organizing some of his papers, which I took the chance to read. He had correspondence with many churches in the state as well as abroad. Particularly he was writing to a deacon in a church in England about a visit and making inquiry about something called a lodge in Baltimore.

I was reading a newspaper article about how they were

going to hold the presidential elections on the same day for all the states for the first time this year when Rev walked in. I was gawking while I was supposed to be folding his shirts.

"Finding anything interesting?" he asked. My cheeks grew hot, and I bowed my head.

"I . . . I'm sorry," I stammered. "I was just glancing at it."

"So how well do you read these days? I suspected you had been practicing." He came farther into the room and sat at his desk. "Come here. Let's see what you've learned."

I was reluctant, but I wanted to show him what I was capable of. I stood behind him and put the newspaper on his desk. He pointed to a section for me to read. When I finished reading the paragraph aloud, I looked at Rev. He was impressed. He turned the page, pointed to another section, and I read it—this time my voice was steadier and I didn't stammer over any words. I read two paragraphs instead of just one.

"Well." Rev Jeff stared at me. "Your father has been helping you?"

"No. No one helps me. I just practice. Papa don't like me to read much besides the Bible. You won't tell him, will you, Rev?"

"I won't tell him, but I'm fairly sure he knows you're hiding some of your abilities." Rev studied my face seriously for a moment. "Willow, do you know how much trouble we would all be in if anyone else found this out?"

"I . . . I'm sorry! I don't want trouble!" I was nearly fit to cry. "I just . . . I just . . . love it so!"

"Now, now." He patted my arm. "Calm yourself. I'm proud of you, although I shouldn't be. I just want to be sure you understand the importance of keeping this secret." He smiled kindly.

If Rev gave his blessing to my reading, then perhaps . . .

"I can write nearly well enough, too," I blurted out. "I practice all the time. My spelling's real bad, but I make do. I love figuring how a proper sentence works—" I stopped. Rev's face was clouded with trouble. He stood up and paced the room.

"Willow, reading a little is one thing, but writing . . . This puts you in a strange dilemma in the world. You are getting older, and it no longer serves as a . . . novelty. . . . Your station in life forbids it." Reverend looked solemn as he paced the room.

"None of this is your fault, Willow." Rev looked out the window; from here we could see clear down to the barns. All the hands were packing up the wagons for market. "I should have never taught you . . . or your father when we were boys. These are simply the laws we live by. Rawlins was saying something last night that I'm beginning to think is true—it is more of a burden to be a slaveholder than to be a slave. I am beholden to my family's land and traditions, and yet I feel a calling to do other things than being a farmer. You can't ever truly comprehend. . . ."

His words were a dagger in my heart.

"Besides, Willow," he said, "too much reading and writing will just decrease your ability to find contentment in your life as a . . . servant . . . and a wife."

I curtsied low, keeping my eyes on the floor. "Yes, of course, sir. I best get back to your packing now."

"True enough." He sighed deeply. "Promise me you will put no more effort into writing, and if you must read, from now on let it be *only* the Bible. Understand?"

"Yes, sir. I understand."

Packing my own things for Baltimore wasn't hard. I wore my only suitable dress—Mama's. I still felt small and clumsy in it. I also wore a thick wool cape that used to belong to Rev's wife, Clarissa. It had some moth holes, but Tiny sewed them up right quick. Rev gave me Clarissa's soft old kid gloves and boots, and her wool bonnet, too.

Tiny had me carry a large basket of her embroideries, some that had to be delivered to ladies in the city, but mostly to sell at Lexington Market. Traveling to Baltimore was the same as going to the ends of the earth. Taneytown had its share of hustle and bustle, but that was only on market days. I'd been once with Papa on a regular old

Thursday, and you could yell down Main Street and everybody would turn their head clear to the other end. Even though I'd only been there barely enough times to count on both hands, it always made me as skittish as Mayapple on a moonless night. My heart would race, and I made sure to cling on to Papa real tight. He wouldn't ever say it aloud, but I often got a notion that Papa was uncomfortable there, too, though he'd been to Taneytown as well as Baltimore more than once every year of his life.

Hidden at the bottom of Tiny's basket was Mr. Shakespeare's play *Romeo and Juliet.* I couldn't help myself from bringing it along at the last moment, despite Rev's words. I had begun it many times, but it always took me hours of staring at the same few lines before I understood. I often whispered the words aloud in my head while doing chores, making memory of them. It sent chills up and down my spine to read about "star-cross'd lovers." I was bewitched to puzzle out the rest of the second act. Reading Mr. Shakespeare made me reckon on how some writings were straight, like a Choctaw's arrow, while others wrapped around themselves like snakes in the sun. Although I longed to bring my copybook to write in so I'd always remember my journey and could record new words, I didn't dare. Instead, I made a promise to myself to remember everything so I could write it all out when I got home.

•   •   •

The morning we left was quiet. Not just 'cause it was before dawn but 'cause of the mood among the men; the trees talked to the wind more than anyone spoke to another. Papa and Rev weren't saying more than they had to, Papa was certainly not talking to Cholly, and Cholly seemed like he was mad at everyone, 'specially me. The other hands who were traveling with us were Rachel's husband, Lou; Mattie's husband, Sirus; and Julia Caroline's man, David. They sensed the mood and only spoke in grunts and whispers. I knew all of the men but had never held a conversation that I could remember. The wives had all come up to the wagons to see the men off. They greeted me as cordial as usual and complimented my new fineries again. But when Rev told me to sit in the coach with him, as there was still quite a sharp chill in the air, I know I heard one of them choke back a gasp. . . . Or was it laughter? It sank my heart down to the bottom of a bitter sea.

I figured they were jealous of Rev's showing favor to me. Granmam always said it was natural for folks to taste vinegar when what they couldn't have smelled sweet. I would be seeing and doing things they only dreamed of. But all the same, I suddenly felt jealous of them, too; they had love. Raymond wasn't such a bad fellow. I just didn't love him. It would make everything so much easier if I did. It wasn't that I didn't want to have a family; I just wanted to do it in my own time. I wondered if that was even possible for a woman like me. Maybe if I talked to Papa again, he'd understand.

"What makes you sigh so heavily, Willow?" Rev asked from the darkness where he reclined on his side of the coach. We kept the shades down to help keep the cold air out, and there was only one small lantern that gave off a meek, wavering glow. I hadn't realized I'd made any sound.

"I'm sorry, Rev—it's nothing. . . ."

"Were you thinking of your beau?" His voice was teasing. "Your father told me you would be ready to marry this spring. Don't worry—we will work out the details soon enough."

All I could manage to say was "Pardon, sir?"

"Mr. Rawlins and I just have to work out a deal. Your Raymond will drive a hard bargain if he's as clever as your father says." Rev chuckled. "You'll be big with child this time next year, I bet!"

I gasped for air.

"Willow? What is it? I hope the cold air hasn't affected you."

"I—I don't want to marry Raymond! I don't love him!" Every muscle in my body turned to wood; my head thumped a horrid beat. At once I regretted my words.

"Stop being foolish." Rev's voice sounded less amused. "You two have a little lovers' quarrel? It happens in every engagement. I, too, am in a little quarrel with my . . ." He trailed off. "Willow, I'm going to tell you why I wanted you to come on this trip with me. I am going to Baltimore to ask for the hand of a lady, a fine lady. Finer than perhaps I should pursue . . ." He trailed off again, then started up. "She's quite beautiful and like a fragile bird in some ways. I don't want to rush things, but . . ." I could hear Rev rubbing his hands together, as if to loose them from a tight hold. "Her name is Evelyn Downdry. I want to be sure of her—if she truly loves only me. I've brought you to find out from her maid, a girl about your age named Silvey. I want to know if Mistress Evelyn has any other serious suitors. You can do that, can't you? And you need not let your father hear of this. I will tell him when I decide."

I could have crawled out of my skin. I knew my father would want to know everything, and this news particularly would drive him mad. But I reckoned that if I did this for Rev, he might be in a mood to hear me out about not marrying Raymond.

"Rev, you know I would help you in any way that I can." I was silent for a while. "But please . . . I truly don't want to marry Raymond," I finally said. "I barely know him, and Papa told me to just think on it!"

"You don't need to think to get married! Why, your

mother and father barely said ten words before their nuptials. You coloreds don't need all of the pleasantries that whites require."

"But, Rev! I don't love him!"

Just then the carriage lurched, and my basket toppled over, spilling out its contents. As dark as it was, I scrambled to find the hidden book. Rev bent to pick up some of the handkerchiefs, and just as I saw it, his hand was upon it. My blood ran cold.

"Willow . . ." Rev said quietly, holding the book by the light to see what it was. "This is from my library. You stole from me?"

"No, Rev! I only . . . I only meant to borrow it."

"*This* must be why you talk of not wanting to marry this suitable buck that your father has chosen for you. How dare you be so ungrateful! Reading books like these will only lead you to dreaming beyond your station. A girl like you can't afford to think of *love.*"

We rode in silence after that.

By the time the sun rose, Rev still hadn't spat a word— just closed his eyes and put his head back. I wasn't sure what hurt me worse—Papa's betrayal or Rev Jeff's. The silence was deep among all of us now. I tried to busy my shaking hands by folding the handkerchiefs again.

When the window shades were glowing with sunlight, Rev finally opened his eyes. He carefully drew the shades back and looked out at the day.

"Reverend, please . . ." I started. I was suddenly afraid he was thinking of selling me away.

"Willow, be silent. When we stop you will go sit with your father. You will tell him that I have been asleep and that we said nothing. That is all I have to say to you now." He leaned back again and closed his eyes.

It was true that Shakespeare wasn't helping the idea of love from growing out of my head like the very braid of my own hair. There was nothing bad about Raymond. He would probably be a good provider. He was clever, after all. I remembered what Rev said about Papa and my mother not knowing each other before they wed. Perhaps I would grow to love Raymond.

I tried to soothe myself by trying to recall the last bits I'd memorized in *Romeo and Juliet*:

> *True, I talk of dreams,*
> *Which are the children of an idle brain,*
> *Begot of nothing but vain fantasy,*
> *Which is as thin of substance as the air*
> *And more inconstant than the wind, who woos*
> *Even now the frozen bosom of the north,*

And, being anger'd, puffs away from thence,
Turning his face to the dew-dropping south.

The only part of Romeo's reply I could recall went something like *some consequence yet hanging in the stars.* I didn't figure it out fully, and now, with the book in Rev's hands, I never would.

Baltimore is frightful strange and strange wonderful. We arrived weary on Monday afternoon after two tense, quiet days on the road. I was riding up high with Papa, and long before we even got there, I could see the city ahead of us, on a hill by the bay. Tall ships were entering and leaving the harbor. People had taken out lunches and stopped to eat or rest along the banks of the river. There were more buildings and churches than I could count. It looked like the city was alive, breathing smoke.

"What's that tall white spike sticking up from the middle of the city?" I asked.

"It's a monument," Papa said. "A memorial for President Washington, I think. They love monuments in this city. They've got a few, I hear. Never been to see them myself. I'm mostly busy, so I don't get to wander."

We went past the train station and were stopped in a line of wagons, so we got to watch a train departing.

Rev had told me about trains before our trip; he had ridden one between New York and Boston. The trains were loud and their smoke dirty; I was more frightened than amused and ended up sneezing black soot for the rest of the afternoon.

Rev and I stayed in a place called Fountain Inn, which is a large beautiful building where the very President Washington himself is said to have stopped for a few nights. Rev's room was nice and comfortable, but I stayed in the maids' dormitory. It was at the rear and bottom floor of the building, next to the stables. It must have been some kind of curing shed at one time, because the walls smelled of smoked meat.

Papa and the rest of the men stayed at Three Tuns, a tavern near the office of a well-known slave auctioneer named Woolfolk, I heard someone say. I wondered if it was the same auction block my mama knew when she was bought by Rev. The men's lodgings were the closest to Lexington Market and had enough space for all our horses and rigs chocked with goods. Papa and the rest of the men rented only two beds where slaves stay, since they'd be taking turns guarding what we planned to sell.

Where I was staying, many of the maids seemed friendly enough but I was afraid to speak. When we left each other, Papa said, "Keep your head down, ears open, and mouth shut, 'cause so many of these women are of the bad kind. One can't tell who's friend or foe here in the city."

The first night we were there, Rev got himself gussied up to have dinner with Mistress Evelyn. He called me into his rooms; he was staring into the mirror seriously, struggling to adjust his white evening cravat. There was a book laid out on the bed called *Neckclothitania,* I think; with a glance I was able to read that it showed different types of fashionable knots appropriate for gentlemen's neckwear. I have never known Rev to fuss about his looks, but he was particular tonight.

"Mistress Evelyn has arrived in Baltimore," Rev said, clearly frustrated about his tie. "She is also staying at this inn. Remember, while we are dining, you are to find out from Silvey if Evelyn has other beaus besides me. But be discrete about it! This is a delicate matter, and I trust . . . Oh, damn!"

I nearly jumped out of my skin hearing Rev curse. I heard Cholly Dee say much worse, but this was the first time I could recall Rev saying anything ungodly. He ripped the scarf off his neck and threw it on the floor. His hands were shaking as he crossed the room and poured himself some port wine from a carafe. Rev sat in the desk chair, looking exhausted.

"Rev . . ." I went and picked up the assaulted neck scarf. I had spent hours stiffening it to crispness with starch, but it was now limp in my hands. I stole a glance at the book, but many of the words were in a language I couldn't understand.

"Which knot were you trying?" I asked.

Rev looked at me and then the book. He sighed heavily. "The *Trone d'Amour.* There's not enough starch in the scarf anymore, and I don't have time to wait for you to do it again."

"I know what you said about me reading and all, Rev,"—I picked up the book and pointed at a picture— "but I think that the Mail Coach style does not require as much starch, and I can probably tie it for you. The style you were after is real complicated and fancy, but this one will save you time and still look *fashionable.*" That was a new word I read on a sign when we passed a ladies' shop on the way into town.

Rev stared at me for another moment before taking another drink and nodding. He sat still while I worked the knot around his neck, reading the instructions silently to myself. Rev was never a drinker, but he finished his glass of wine quickly.

"The proper tie should be formal, and this style isn't . . ." he began, looking in the mirror like he'd lost his puppy. "I should cancel the dinner. I'm too old for this anyway. Who am I to think Evelyn would want a simple reverend's farm life?"

He was about to take the tie off when I stopped him again. "You're a fine catch for any lady, Rev," I assured him. "Perhaps if we put a lovely pin on it . . ."

I knew I had packed his diamond stud pin, so I went to his things to fetch it. When I brought it to him, he twirled it between his fingers so the diamond caught the light.

"My dear Clarissa gave this to me when we were betrothed," he told me. "It was the first gift . . ." He studied me. "I haven't felt this way about a woman since her. . . ."

"I'm sure she would've wanted you to be happy, Rev." I smiled, took the pin from his hand, and positioned it on his cravat. In spite of everything, I still had deep love for Rev. As Papa would say, Rev provided for us, so it was our duty to provide for him. I truly wanted him to be happy. After all, wasn't it the law, not Rev, who made things the way they were for slaves?

"There! You look right handsome. Don't worry about nothing—I'll find out all you need to know, Rev."

Silvey, Mistress Evelyn's maid, was 'bout my age, but something made her seem much older. I felt as though I were a teething child around her, rather than a young woman of fifteen years. Silvey talked as though she knew everything about life, and she told me some as we walked through the streets of Baltimore that night while Rev was with Mistress Evelyn.

"I been in that saloon over there," Silvey pointed out, as though she were telling me she had found a shiny penny.

"Why?" I had trouble keeping up with her as we walked. I was surprised there were so many people out and about at the dinner hour on a Monday.

"I had to deliver a message to Mr. Downdry. He let me stand next to him for luck when he threw the dice. He won, but I nearly fell faint from all the beer he let me drink!"

"*Mr.* Downdry?"

"Mistress Evelyn's first husband. He's . . . dead."

"Oh. I'm so sorry to hear that. I suppose that's what she and Rev have in common."

"Have what in common?" Silvey said, looking around distractedly. We had walked down toward the docks. I could smell the harbor but couldn't see it.

"The Reverend is also widowed."

"So?" Silvey still looked confused. Finally she shrugged and said, "Oh, sure, you're right."

We stopped on a corner by a gas lamppost — I nearly cheered with delight when the man came around to light it — I'd never seen such a wonderful thing before. Silvey looked embarrassed to be with me; she kept searching the crowd.

"Are we waiting for someone?" I asked. It was getting cold and dark. I looked at my pendant watch — it was almost nine; time for me to get back to attend to Rev Jeff.

Across the street was a house where women were leaning out of the windows, calling to the men below. Drunken men and women were falling around and singing outside of the saloon.

Finally I spoke up. "I don't feel safe here."

Silvey looked at me and laughed. "We're waiting on my brother. He should be here soon."

I thought it might be as good a time as any to ask my question.

"Does your mistress have any other suitors besides the Reverend?"

Silvey laughed at me again. "Mistress already be fixed on marrying your Rev."

"She's that sure of her love for him?"

"Love? She can't find nobody else to take her and her son."

"But why?" I felt silly every time I opened my mouth.

Silvey rolled her eyes. "You'll see. Mistress ain't no real harm. Long as she's got her medicines, she props up real nice. The Reverend seems like a gentle and patient man, but he'll have to be a saint to put up with Mistress and Philippe. They both need a lot of, uh . . . attention. . . . Oh, good—here comes Little Luck."

Silvey's brother was about seven or eight years old; without saying a word, he just took my hand and tugged. As I turned back to Silvey, she was already walking away with a young brown-skinned man wearing the clothes of a sailor. He handed Silvey a bottle, and she took a long swig.

"Where're you going?" I called out to her over my shoulder.

"I'll see you later at the inn," she said, the sailor's arm looped around her neck. "Little Luck's gonna take you back."

Little Luck pulled at my arm. I looked back at Silvey again; she and the sailor were kissing passionately right there in the street. My cheeks burned as I let Little Luck lead me away.

Although quite small, Little Luck was quick and smart. I didn't know that he couldn't hear or speak until I needed to ask him to slow down. I called his name till my throat was sore. Finally I stopped still and didn't move. He turned, smiled, and seemed to apologize, making movements with his hands to make me understand.

We continued at a slower pace, but just as we turned down the next street, there was a brawl between some men. They knocked over a lantern in the confusion, and it set a pile of trash ablaze right next to a wooden shed. While I was agape at the scene, Little Luck tugged me with all his might. We ran down a complicated maze of alleys and even through the back shed of a house. A scruffy-looking family—I counted seven in all—was sitting at the table with only a few slices of bread among them. They looked up without surprise; the children all waved and smiled. They already knew Little Luck.

Luck pulled two small apples from his pockets and set them in front of the children, who squealed with delight. We didn't stop for more than a moment, and he never let go of my hand.

Luck looked back at me several times and flashed a big grin as he led me safely through the streets. But as soon as I saw the inn, he dropped my hand, waved, and ran back in the direction we had just left.

Rev asked me what I had found out about Mistress Evelyn as soon as I entered to prepare his rooms for the night.

"Silvey said there was no one else and her mistress is eager to marry you," I said quietly. Rev's face lit up.

"Really? I'm so relieved. She acts . . . differently . . . sometimes and I just wondered if perhaps there was someone else," he said, sitting at the edge of his chair. He smiled in a giddy way and even gave me a shiny Lady Liberty dime for my trouble. I almost didn't take it, knowing that I hadn't told him the whole story.

"Tomorrow afternoon I will be meeting with Evelyn's father's acquaintances at their fraternal lodge. I'll need to look sharp—I'm hoping they'll ask me to join. Evelyn thinks these things are quite important."

He looked so excited that I reckoned he might not have

been all that mad to find out he was the only suitor she could find.

When I went down to the maids' lodging, there were six of us jammed up in a room with only four beds. Two girls slept on the floor by the small woodstove because their masters would not or could not pay for beds, which cost more. They were worthless flea-ridden cots, anyway; I itched all night.

The next morning was the first market day; I barely slept. I was up early to make sure that Rev's blue vest collar had stayed pressed and that his formal striped trousers were pleated correctly. I was finished brushing the black long-tailed morning coat and top hat before Rev even woke up. By the time I brought up his breakfast tray, he was wearing his pants, braces, and shirt. I helped him attach his collar with his tie again and made sure he was looking his best, just before the sun rose. I wanted to get to the market as early as I could.

"Willow, would you like to see what Evelyn looks like?" Rev asked while eating his eggs.

"Of course, sir," I responded. I was distracted, shining his boots.

"Look, you can see her right here!" he said, holding up a tiny picture of a solemn woman in layers of lace, holding a fan. It looked too real to be a painting, though the coloring was unnatural.

"Evelyn had it made for me; it's called a daguerreotype—it's as though they freeze time onto paper! She's beautiful, isn't she?"

I wanted to know more of how this extraordinary thing was made, but from the window I saw the sun rising over the harbor. "She is lovely, Rev," I replied. I finished his shoes and wished him good luck as I left.

Although the mistress was lovely, I soon found out what Silvey had hinted at. The night before, Mistress Evelyn had told Silvey that she was in the mood for a fresh peach even though they are so far out of season. One of Mistress Evelyn's friends had heard that new locomotive trains with cars stocked with ice were bringing all kinds of luxuries from the South and the islands for market day. Mistress Evelyn told Silvey that Little Luck would get locked in the cellar for a week if he didn't bring one back for her.

I wasn't supposed to know about it, and I wouldn't have if I hadn't forgotten my gloves and returned to hear the other girls talking about it. They were betting on Little Luck's quest.

I walked in as Claudia, one of the other maids, was saying, "He's gonna get eaten alive by the cellar rats! There ain't no peaches to be found in all a Baltymore." Silvey winked at Little Luck and put down quite a bit of pocket change.

"Oh, just wait—he'll bring back one for you, too." Silvey laughed.

"How can he even know you *want* a peach, not an apple?" I whispered to Silvey. "How do you tell him anything? He always seems to know everything."

She smiled proudly and patted her brother's head. "We got our ways."

Little Luck escorted me to Knotwild's stall at the market, where I sold Tiny's kerchiefs for the handsome price of one nickel each. Cholly Dee told the men who dawdled over the kerchiefs that their women were fighting over which of their sweethearts would buy one for them first. All those kerchiefs went quick! Tiny had wanted to split her portion of her sales with me since it was my idea and I did all the selling. 'Course, Rev Jeff still made the largest sum, but I was glad to have every bit of spending change.

Afterward, I sat atop our wagon for a while and watched all the people go by. It was six in the morning when the open market bell had sounded, but with the gas lamps on, it didn't matter if it was dark. The men started setting up at four thirty in the morning, but Papa said he got there at three to stake out their spot.

Little Luck had dropped me at the market at quarter to eight, according to my pendant clock. He came back at ten thirty with a black eye and a near bucketful of bruised but honest-to-goodness peaches. I bought a small slice of cold meat for him to hold against the bruise. I never knew the full story of how he got either, but he proudly drew me pictures in the dirt of a dog, a fat man, several squares (ice?), something that might have been a train, and maybe a hammer, but I did not know what to make of it. He and Silvey celebrated that night by eating a full crab meal at a café. On the back stoop, of course, but it was special just the same.

Little Luck continued to keep me from getting lost over the next few days, and he was thoughtful enough to point out some sights, like the fancy monument to President Washington I had seen on my way into town. It was taller than some of the trees at Knotwild and was shining white with mythic griffins. I remembered what they were from some of Rev's books about the Greeks and Romans.

It was a good thing I had Luck; I was easily distracted, reading newspaper scraps and all the signs everywhere. Once I saw a man walking around wearing two boards tied together over his shoulders, his body sandwiched in the middle. On one side, the sign read, FINE APPAREL FOR FINE PEOPLE and it had a crude drawing of a well-dressed couple. The other side, when the man turned around, read,

BARGAIN PRICES AT OUR STORE! with the name and location to find such bargains. I marveled over it for some time.

When I came to my senses, I found myself turned around on a street that wasn't familiar, and I began to take fright. A moment later, I turned another corner to find Little Luck running errands and doing whatever else would earn him a penny or two. He led me back to Papa as if I was a child.

I was surprised how many people of different shades I saw on the streets. Some of the colored people wore fine clothes; some wore rags. Since the next market day wasn't until Friday, Silvey and I had a few occasions to walk together in the afternoons or evenings while her mistress and the Reverend were occupied.

One time, Silvey had to deliver a message to Mistress Evelyn's aunt in Mount Vernon and allowed me to tag along. She pointed out which businesses were owned by free blacks. There were several black churches she pointed out as well; the African Methodists had the most beautiful church, with colored windows.

"Sometimes if you go after church on Sundays, they help people learn to read," she said. "And I heard the nuns have regular school for black Catholic girls."

I was joyous and jealous at the same time. We would be

leaving on Saturday after market to return to Knotwild, so I couldn't go to any service or the after school.

"Do you attend?" I asked, breathless. Silvey didn't respond. City people walked very fast. I quickly found that it was crucial in order not to get pick-pocketed, trampled by both animal and human feet, or pushed into muddy piles of trash.

We were walking through a large square that held another massive marble monument. It was inscribed with words I couldn't read, but I did see the word *battle.* I marveled at its size and grace for only a moment before having to catch up with Silvey.

"You can't be standing around too long in places like this or you'll be asked to show your papers," she said, her eyes straight ahead.

"But I have a pass to travel as I please around the city."

Silvey finally looked down at me. She was taller than I by a head.

"Huh. Your *Rev* write you that?"

"Of course."

She slowed her pace and lowered her voice. "Why he ain't got you staying up in his room with him?"

"He didn't want me to sleep on the floor since I get sick easy. Though I'm not sure the maids' quarters at the hotel are much better."

Silvey shook her head and picked up her pace again.

She continued. "We only went to the A.M.E. church once when we were here with Mistress at Christmastime. She mostly stayed with friends, so me and Luck got to have holiday. It was a nice service, but we couldn't stay after. Luck runs errands for them when we're visiting."

I asked Silvey about the mistress's family.

"Her papa dotes on her, and her mama's real pretty like Mistress Evelyn, but she don't ever dress in a fuss. Her aunty's likable enough, and we visit her here often. We'd be staying at her grand house now, but she has other visitors," she said. "Over there, least me and Luck get a bed to share."

"And Mistress Evelyn's son? What's he like?" I asked, but she suddenly changed her mood again and went as stiff as a board.

She only said, "Like most *Southern Gentleman,* I suppose."

"How do you mean?"

"He always gets what he wants."

"I don't understand." I felt like a whimpering puppy.

"Guess you'll have to wait and see."

We had arrived. The four-story, nearly new house was on a corner close to the park. There was new construction going up all around the neighborhood, more big fancy houses. We went around the back, and Silvey knocked on the kitchen door. A white girl, perhaps twelve years old, with red curls exploding from her bonnet, answered.

"Hello, Sally! How you?" Silvey greeted her with genuine affection.

"Silvey! I thought I'd be seeing you soon. How they treating you at the Fountain Inn?" Sally's Irish accent was thick, and I had to listen hard to understand.

We were let in; the fancy modern kitchen was large and had an impressive gas oven. I had seen one like it in a newspaper for nearly one hundred dollars. The whole room was cozy with the smell of baking bread. A fire in a big hearth was outfitted with all kinds of swings and levers for holding pots over the flames.

"You know I'd rather be here!"

"I do miss you and Luck for company. Where's he now?"

"Running errands down at the harbor. We miss you and Cook!"

"Aye, and she'll be after me soon with the rolling pin!" They both laughed.

"I won't keep you. I have a request for Madam Lydia from Mistress Evelyn." Silvey handed over an envelope. "I'm to wait for a response."

"I'll get it to Mrs. Rose. You know where the tea and biscuits are. . . ." She winked and left.

"Sally works here? She gets paid?" I asked. I had never seen a white scullery maid before. Silvey quickly gathered a small snack for us to share.

"You ask too many questions!" She scolded me as she

cut a thin pat of butter to smear on a biscuit. "Cook has a temper like a teakettle! Can't take too much, or Sally really will get the rolling pin. . . ."

"I'm sorry," I said. "It's all so new to me."

Silvey rolled her eyes and handed me half of the biscuit, which was delicious, like nothing I had ever tasted before — not like the plain cornbread that was Granmam's recipe. Silvey and I shared our tea.

"Sally's bonded — indentured. Came over on one of them coffin ships with her family just last year. They all died of that ship fever, so Sally's been left to work off their contracts, too. She may never get her freedom dues till she's an old woman."

There had been an article about the horrible typhus outbreak on board several ships from Ireland. I felt sorry for the girl, but couldn't help thinking, *At least she has the promise of getting free.*

As soon as we were finished, Silvey cleared our place.

I was dying to ask who Mrs. Rose was, when a woman entered the kitchen. She was a wrinkled and stern-looking mulatto who moved noiselessly even though she had on layers of black skirts. "Mrs. Rose," Silvey said, and curtsied, so I did, too.

"Please tell your mistress that Madam cannot continue to be disturbed this week while she is entertaining members of the Democratic Party. Mistress Evelyn is invited to dine tomorrow evening, but if she has any other financial needs, Madam suggests that she ask her father," Mrs. Rose said without emotion.

The big Democratic Convention had been held in Baltimore back in May, so there was still political news and leaflets all over the city. One said that the Democrats supported slavery — they thought freeing slaves would cause "alarming and dangerous consequences."

"Yes, thank you, Mrs. Rose," Silvey said, not taking her eyes from the floor until Mrs. Rose handed her a pouch that jangled with coins. Silvey took it and tucked it into her corset.

Mrs. Rose added, "The sum is exact. Be sure that she gets *all* of it. This is for you." She then gave Silvey two pennies.

Silvey nodded. "Thank you, ma'am."

"How is your brother?" Mrs. Rose inquired politely. Silvey replied that he was well. "Send my regards to your aunt Beth in Annapolis Junction. I trust she is also well?"

Silvey nodded, seeming shy.

At this point the matron turned her head in my direction. "And this?"

I curtsied again awkwardly as Silvey introduced me. "That's Willow. She belongs to Reverend Jeffries."

Mrs. Rose raised an eyebrow and stepped forward to examine me. "The minister farmer? He keeps you well dressed, I see."

"Thank you, ma'am." I didn't know if it was a compliment.

"That's a good sign, for you, Silvey," she said soberly. "Good day, ladies."

With that, she turned and went back up the stairs.

As we left, Sally pressed two more biscuits into Silvey's hands. "Save one for Little Luck!"

Silvey tore a biscuit and gave half to me as we walked away. "I can't stand that stuck-up Mrs. Rose!" she said with a mouthful of biscuit. "She's the housekeeper, but she's been with the family her whole life. Cook says she's Madam Lydia's older half sister, and that's why she puts on so many airs!"

I nearly choked on my half of the treat, but I held my tongue.

Silvey would always wait with me at the same corner after our walks; we'd wait until Little Luck came to escort me back to the inn. Little Luck seemed unhappy to leave his sister, and I realized that Silvey probably arranged this not out of concern for my safety but to have time alone with her beau. I'm also sure that was why Luck always left me in such a hurry.

Her beau would usually wait at the opposite corner, near the saloon, so I never spoke with him. But I could always tell when he was around, 'cause Silvey's face would light up and she would ask how she looked. She was a pretty girl. She always kept herself neat, although her clothes were worn thin and patched, and I once saw her line the bottom of her shoes with newspaper because of holes. Her deep-brown skin wasn't marked from pox, and she had lovely high cheekbones, a dimple, and good teeth when she smiled. Her eyes, framed by thick lashes, had a fresh, giddy spark—she was in love.

Two nights in a row, Silvey came back after dressing her mistress for bed and then left again, not coming back to the maids' dorm until very late. It made me worry; despite her moodiness, I cared about Silvey. Each time, she was up and out the next morning before I woke. I did my best not to let these things distract me from all of Baltimore's sights.

Baltimore is said to be known for its food, and I can say that Papa and I ate quite a bit of it. Thursday afternoon, after I got back from Aunt Lydia's, he and I walked around, and he showed me all the places where rich people ate crabs, clams, apples with fine cheeses, and sweet, pretty cakes. Papa had been busy all week, and I'd hardly seen him.

"So what's Rev got you doing in that fancy inn, Mite?"

Papa nudged me as we sat at the wharf, eating ears of roasted and salted corn. We shared a newspaper heaped with a new type of fried potatoes made in a special French way. The vendor told us that Thomas Jefferson himself loved them, but to me it was just fried potatoes. I wished I could have read the newspaper up close, but the oil ruined the ink.

"Mainly I've been starching and tying fancy neck-scarf knots," I said, trying to make it sound unimportant. I wasn't sure how Papa would react to anything these days.

"What's all that about?"

"It's just fashionable in the city, I reckon."

Papa was quiet for a moment as a big clipper ship pulled into the dock right in front of us. Black and white men alike jumped around everywhere, securing sails and unloading crates, working together good-naturedly, even though Papa said there was often tension between black and white workers. I'd heard someone in the market talking about how there were almost more free blacks than slaves in Baltimore, and everyone wanted paying jobs. The thought brought the man in the oilskin coat to my mind. Just as I was fastening up my courage to ask Papa if he'd heard anything about the fugitives, he spoke again.

"Is Rev going out a lot? To meetings and such? Just churches, or has he met with any lawyers?"

"I don't think he's met with any lawyers. Just some lodge meetings and a lady friend."

Papa stood up and walked in circles, rubbing his head. "What lodge? Who's this friend? A church member?"

"I don't know, Papa. Just someone he fancies, I guess."

"He's courting a woman? How old is she?"

"I wouldn't know. Old enough to have a son older than me," I added reluctantly. He was going to find out sooner or later.

Now Papa was vexed for sure. He asked me all sorts of questions I couldn't answer, like does Mistress Evelyn own land or a house of her own. He was so distressed that I suggested we walk for a while.

"You'd think he'd let me know something like this," Papa mumbled. "I should've never . . ."

We turned a corner to find a mixed-race crowd gathered around a man standing on a box. He wore a long white beard and the simple dress of a Quaker. His voice rose above the clamor of the docks. The man waved a stack of pamphlets as he talked.

"How can a man go to church one day and whip another human the next? How do *you* sit next to that same man in church?" He pointed to the crowd, who were also whispering commentary to themselves.

A man with a German accent said, "I'd sit next to that

slaver because he owns *my* home, too! He probably even owns the church!" A few people, mostly whites, laughed.

Papa and I kept walking around the edges of the crowd, which was growing thicker as the man spoke.

"God did not give us this land so that we should grow rich on another man's back. Slavery is an evil that needs to be destroyed!"

A black woman was saying to her friend, "He's right! Being a slave in this city is miserable when so many others are free! My sister's mistress says she'll let her buy her freedom, but she won't allow her to find more work. Then my own mistress says she'd be happy to emancipate me, but she couldn't bear to allow my daughter to part from hers. What can I do? She *owns* my daughter. I could be free but my daughter can't? *I* can't bear that."

Papa grabbed my hand and pushed harder through the crowd. I caught a glimpse of the pamphlets being passed around; the cover had a sketch of a man on his knees wearing chains. Someone else was selling other books. One was titled *Narrative of the Life of Frederick Douglass, an American Slave, Written by Himself.* The other one I couldn't see.

"A female slave wrote this book of poetry. . . ."

I had nearly wrenched that book from the man's hands when Papa yanked me out of reach.

·   ·   ·

"Willow!" Papa was shaking my arm. "We're here."

We had walked the whole way back to the Fountain Inn. I just kept seeing those books in my head. . . . Written by slaves themselves.

"Those abolitionist radicals always rousing trouble. You upset?"

"No, Papa. I'm fine. . . . Just lemme catch my breath." But I wasn't fine. My hands were trembling to get ahold of those writings I saw.

"Yes, it's always surprising to see white men trying to cause violence over this sort of thing. Can't wait to get back home, safe from all this."

"Papa," I whispered, "you think slavery is a *good* thing?"

"I don't think it's the best way but it's the only way we got right now, and at least we have our kin." He squeezed my shoulder gently.

"'Sides, the British got rid of it, and I think one day soon this government will, too. I pray for our leaders to have wisdom, but for right now I'm trying to keep what *we've* got that's good. You understand me? I'm just trying to keep us *and our generations* together, Mite."

I was walking back from the market the next day when I saw Cholly Dee not too far ahead. Papa had said he often went down to the waterfront houses where I'd seen the women calling to the men on the street. I was with Little

Luck, so I grabbed his hand and followed. To my surprise, Cholly went to the slave market instead. Little Luck pulled at my hand so hard; he didn't want to go near. I reckoned I knew my way, so I let him go, covered my head with my shawl, and followed on my own.

Cholly went to the gate where the slaves were allowed to roam around a small dirty yard when auctions wasn't going, though some were kept in small, cramped brick pens. It was guarded heavy, but Cholly slipped something into the biggest guard's hand and the guard turned as if he suddenly didn't see Cholly. It began to rain as I watched from around the corner. Cholly called to one of the men, and though I was not so close, I felt for sure it was not either of the men I had seen that morning by Mama's grave. I found myself trembling, thinking again of the man from the North in the oilskin coat. Was he now dead?

Cholly and this man in the auction yard shook hands long and hard and said words that seemed to straighten the fugitive's back. After a bit, the guard pushed Cholly away with his gun. Before I could even hide myself, Cholly saw me directly. I turned to run, but he caught up with me, grabbed my arm, and shook me so hard I cried out.

"You following me? You wanna see this?" He was right up in my face. "You wanna know what this all about? You've never been to an auction house, right?" Then he dragged me to see the people 'bout to get sold.

I could see small groups, perhaps families, huddled together, more than one of their faces streaked with tears. The single men had little or no life in them. They all wore hard faces. Fearful, angry faces. Some women paced the yard, not noticing the cold rain, trying to outwalk fate. Some held each other with hopeless arms. My heart sank deep seeing them. Just then a distinguished white man wearing a thick beaver-fur coat yelled up to everybody to look lively, 'cause they were starting the sale.

I twisted and wrenched myself to get out of Cholly Dee's hands; I wanted to run so fast back to my papa or even to Rev, but Cholly would not have it so.

He caught up with me again and clamped his big hand down on the back of my neck so I could not run but only be steered like an ox.

"You're gonna see the whole thing through; you grown enough now to see this. It's about time you see the world how it really be."

Another man—called himself the auctioneer—came to the front and started rattling off numbers like a snake. None of those for sale was fresh off the boat—Papa told me real Africans is hard to come by these days. I thought of my mama so lonely on the auction block, and it tore my heart.

One family was broken up, and to see that tragedy unfold was more potent than any Shakespeare.

"*Sold!*" boomed the auctioneer. It rang in my ears like a gunshot. "To the gentleman from Virginia!"

The father went first, and his stone face did break for just a moment. He gathered himself enough to tell his three children to be good and to press a final kiss on his wife's lips. Romeo and Juliet could not have kissed more tender.

"*SOLD!* Two for the price of one!"

The mother wept quiet as the auctioneer pulled away her children. They got to stay together at least.

"*SOLD!*"

The mother fetched only a meager price and a long journey south.

"I've seen enough! Let me go!" I begged Cholly, but I was scared to struggle or scream, lest someone take attention and sell me, too.

"I just wanted to know if it was the same men who got caught out by that Mason-Dixon Line," I said, crying.

He looked me hard in the eyes, then dragged me out the auction house to roar at me some more.

"How you know where they was caught?" he demanded.

I thought real quick. "Rev told me."

"Girl, you sure think you something. Think you know all kinds of things, but you know nothing. The men who got caught weren't by Knotwild. They were up in the mountains crossing from West Virginnie," Cholly said, loosening his grip on me and spitting tobacco in the street.

My chin set to quivering and my nerves were all shattered. The men caught weren't the men I'd seen.

"You better be careful, skulking around the city like a mountain cat. Shouldn't you be sitting at Rev's knee?" Cholly looked me up and down. "They fixing to marry you off real soon, eh?"

I looked away and nodded. He was still holding my arm.

"I wonder how a *smart* girl like you gonna take to married life. You so used to easy living, you don't even know how to do real work. Bet you don't even know what a husband would want from you."

I yanked my arm away from him. I had had enough of him. "Cholly Dee, you're the one who knows nothing! You're ignorant and jealous of my parents, just 'cause they was in love and you never had nothing like it. And you never will!"

"Is that what he tole you?" He fell out in a wicked laughter. "He tole you some *love* story? Your papa thinks love can be won in a rooster match."

"What are you talking about?" I demanded.

"Ask your papa."

As shocked as I was, I ran straight back to the Fountain Inn.

•   •   •

Rev was out visiting the lodge again, so I let myself into his room to lay out his evening clothes for his dinner with Mistress Evelyn and the Democrats at Aunt Lydia's house. I wanted some peace and quiet after all that horribleness. We were leaving tomorrow afternoon, and I was relieved. I wanted to pack up all of Rev's things and return to my home. Papa was right: city life was not for me.

Rev wasn't supposed to return until six. It was only ten minutes to five, so I figured I would take my time getting that fancy necktie all starched out.

I lit the fire and the lamps before I took off my damp cloak and laid it by the hearth to dry. I went over to Rev's desk to get the newspaper I saw sitting on top. It was my usual habit to find something to read while I waited for the iron to get hot. Yesterday's newspaper was on the desk, and I picked it up without thinking.

There was a telegram underneath it, the first I'd ever seen. I marveled at how different it was from the writing in newspapers and in books. Every sentence was butchered to the quick. Telegrams were paid for by the letter, it seemed.

JOIN LODGE MARRY EVELYN SPRING STOP
TALK KNOTWILD BUSINESS SOON STOP
M. WICKOFF

Next to it was a letter from the lodge. I couldn't help but pick it up — it said that being a member of the lodge meant that Rev would be responsible to "support the values and holdings of his fellow lodge members as well as the interests of southern slaveholders."

Just then I heard footsteps in the hall. I put the newspaper where I found it as the key turned in the lock and picked up the necktie just as Rev entered. He was startled but pleased to see me.

"How was your day, sir?" I asked, stepping away from the desk to help him out of his cloak and boots.

"It was certainly busy. I came back early because the weather is so dreadful."

Just then a terrible cough came out of me as if to testify, and I began to wheeze.

"You just got in as well?" Rev said, seeing my cloak steaming before the fire. "Why don't you sit and get warm. You can starch the tie after."

"The kettle still has enough water in it from the morning to make tea enough for both of us," I offered. He nodded and sat down in the armchair while I prepared the tea.

"Not your granmam's herbs, but this India stuff is quite good," Rev commented cheerfully. Mistress Evelyn had given Rev a box of the latest delicacy — black Assam tea. "I do miss her, your granmam. She raised me and your father as her own."

The stress of the day, the confusion, lies, and questions unanswered suddenly struck lightning in my heart, and I began to cry. Rev sat in silence while I cleaned up my face with one of Tiny's kerchiefs.

"I guess I miss her, too, Rev. Her and my mama."

Rev continued his silence for a while.

"Willow," Rev spoke sharply, "you mention your mother and it makes me sad to remember her, her inability to . . . conform. I am going to ask Evelyn for her hand in marriage tonight, and I am certain she will accept. I know the time is now or never. I am giving you an opportunity, Willow, a choice. I don't envy you for it, but I think . . ." He paused.

He stood up and began to pace the room. I stayed quiet and still.

"I am quite clear about the kind of woman my future wife is. She is delicate and demanding of high standards, something I value more as I age. But that is something that will require a great deal of change at Knotwild. Much more will be demanded of you, in addition to your poor health and . . . wifely duties." He stopped here and glanced in my direction.

"I understand that you are not like most women of your station in life. It's my fault for indulging you and your father all these years. It's led us all down a treacherous path to this very crossroads. Willow, you seem to have deeper feelings and thoughts . . . and it pains my Christian sensibilities . . . so I will offer you this . . . *gift* . . . as my penance." He sat down again and took a sip of his tea with unsteady hands.

I stayed still until I could barely stand it any longer. "I don't understand, Rev."

"This is hard for me, Willow. What I'm about to say you are never to repeat, no matter what. Your father will be inconsolable for a while, but . . . Willow, if you can read Shakespeare . . . I know of a school in the North that will take certain Negro girls who show promise. . . ."

I nearly clapped my hands with glee. "School? Me? I can go to school?"

"If you go, I will no longer be financially responsible for you. You would have to work for your keep, Willow."

"Of course! That's fine!"

"And you would have to leave immediately. . . ."

"Well, Papa will drive me there, right? I'll make him understand on the way. . . ."

"No, Willow. If you go to this school you must cut all ties to Knotwild. Word of this cannot get into the wrong ears. My reputation as a southern gentleman is at stake. If you go I shall tell everyone that you ran off. I will provide you with a small amount of money for coach fare and to help you get started, but you will have to get to the school yourself, and from now on, fend for yourself. It's the cost of your education and freedom, if that is what you desire above all else."

"I can't even say good-bye? Can't I write a letter to Papa, at least?"

"No . . . I'm sorry. Not even your father. It's too risky. No one can find out I supported this. My generosity is in letting you go. The choice is yours."

"What if I don't go?" I asked.

"You will return to Knotwild with us, and you will marry the man your father has chosen for you. You will go about your duties without complaint or incident. You will not pick up another book again . . . or else you shall risk being sold."

"Sir, I . . ."

"Do you understand what I am saying?"

I nodded.

"Then I will not speak of it further. I will expect your answer by tomorrow before we leave. If I hear that you have mentioned this to anyone, I will have to sell you far south before we leave Baltimore. Do you understand?"

I bit my lip, nodded again, and went back to my duties. Rev sat before the fire unmoved until I told him that his things were ready.

"Willow," he said, "I know this might seem harsh, but you don't understand how the world works; neither does your father, really. There are certain ideas and responsibilities only a white man can truly grasp."

"Yes, sir." I curtsied quickly and left the room.

I fled straight down to the maids' dormitory, though it was the last place I wanted to be.

"Well, don't you look like a right princess rather than a slave!" Silvey was the only one in the room; there was a sharp odor of alcohol. "Where you think you going in all them fine clothes? I could take them from you like that." She tried to snap her fingers. "You know nothing 'bout how cruel dis world is out here, girl. Take me: Mistress find out the truth about her son, *I'd* be the one in trouble. . . ."

She took a long swig from a flask.

"What do you mean?"

"I ain't spelling out a thing to you!" Silvey slurred. "Ain't nobody told me how it would be, so you got to find out on your own, too."

Papa often said that men drink to excess 'cause they're running away from something. He'd never said why a woman would do such a thing.

I wasn't in the mood for this, so I began to ready myself for bed, though I knew I wasn't going to be able to sleep much. That I couldn't go out into the dark night of Baltimore alone depressed my spirits even more. Even from my bed, I knew I'd hear the sounds of a city that never stopped moaning — from tolling bells to the folks begging and sick in the streets to the sounds of the slaves being marched in from the boats to the auction house.

As I unbuttoned the little carved shells on my dress, I wished for my mama. I had no one to guide me. All I wanted was to ride off into the woods to think. If I went to school, I couldn't do that again, at least not with Mayapple. And to never again visit my mama's grave? And Papa . . . Oh, how I wished I could talk to him. To tell him everything, then beg him for answers, for the truth.

"What you standing there for?" Silvey demanded.

"Got lost in my thoughts," I said, turning away.

"You thinking all the damn time." She opened the flask and drank again. I could smell the spirits from across the room, but there was another scent, something almost sweet.

"What is that?" I asked.

"It's medicine."

I had seen all kinds of medicines advertised in the city — promising all kinds of miracles — but I wondered what was really in those bottles. Granmam taught me to use a small amount of brandy or whiskey to make herbal tinctures or to quiet pains.

"Never mind. It's none of my business." I didn't want to argue. I just lay down on the bed, pulled my cloak close around me, and shut my eyes. What would the school be like? The other students and teachers? What would I study? Was I smart enough to be a doctor? Could I write a book? Just as I started liking the ideas I was having about being a real educated woman, I heard Silvey sob.

I tried to ignore her, but it made me feel like even more of a wretch.

"You worried about your mistress moving?" I finally asked. "I'm sure you'll love Knotwild — it's the most beautiful place God ever made. Maybe I can even show you how to ride. . . ." I stopped. I wasn't even sure I would be there.

"Ain't everybody want to live way out there in the country!" she snapped. "I'm just fine with where we live now! Mistress house less than a half day's ride from Baltimore, so we come to the city all the time. We stay with Mistress's mother's family in Annapolis Junction, too, and I like going there 'cause my mama's sister there. And that's the only other family I got 'sides Luck. Sometimes we get to ride the B&O railroad there and back. Now Mistress talking like she want to leave Little Luck in Annapolis Junction, and if she got you, why she need me?" Silvey began to sob heavily. "My fella, George, worked himself free and now he's working on a boat. He said he'd work for me and Little Luck to get free, too. . . . Now I'll never see him again!"

It hit me. If I went to school, Silvey and Little Luck would have a better chance of staying together at Knotwild.

"C'mon, let's go outside," I said. I wished I could tell her something to console her.

Silvey finally let me help her up and out to the out-houses, where she vomited a few times. The cold air sobered us both. I got a bucket of fresh water and helped her wash her face and neck. Something caught my eye in the darkness near the stables. I tried to get Silvey to hurry up, but she was stumbling. Suddenly Little Luck stepped out of the shadows. I had wondered where he slept, and now I shivered to think that he was spending his nights with the horses. He helped me get Silvey inside without anyone noticing.

"You might as well just get in." Silvey pointed to Little Luck and then the bed. "He hide out by the stables till he can come in when the lights go out," she explained to me. "We cover him up real good, and he don't move too much. Then he up real early in the morning, so nobody mind him."

"Why didn't Mistress Evelyn get him a room?"

"She don't care! Her father gave her money for both of us to sleep, but Mistress wanted to use that money for herself. And she get money from her aunty, too! Besides, there's too many rough boys sleeping on the kitchen floor. I don't let him sleep without me in a strange place, any-how." Silvey began to cry again. Little Luck hugged his sis-ter with all the might he had. He was so clever, it was easy to forget how vulnerable and young he was.

"Go to bed," I told Silvey without conviction. "Try not to think so much." I nearly choked on my own words.

The next morning, both Silvey and Luck were gone before the sun rose. I didn't sleep, tossing from my thoughts and itching from the fleas. I'd made no conclusions about what to do, for myself or for them.

After I attended to Rev's packing, I went down to the market. I wanted to see my papa. On the way, I saw the same man who was speaking at the docks. He had another crowd around him, not as big as the one before. I tried my best to stay as far away as I could while still hearing what he said. I wondered if I could get ahold of those books without anyone knowing.

If I went to school, I wouldn't ever have to worry about anybody seeing me with books.

"Revolutions are happening all around the world!" the man shouted. "France and Russia both fight for equality of the classes. Why not here? Why not now? Why not to save your fellow man?"

A well-dressed white couple walked past. "What is 'equality of the classes,' Alexander?" the wife asked.

"Radical rubbish" was the husband's only reply. "Not fit for a delicate lady's ears."

I found myself creeping closer and closer to the books

being sold by white man my age, but I became startled when he smiled at me quite boldly and held up a book. I was close enough to read that it was by the slave Phillis Wheatley. He opened the book to show the drawing inside, a girl who looked like me, sitting at a desk, thinking, writing. Real poetry published in a book by a black slave girl like me? My heart ached in my chest, and I thought I might faint. Just as I reached out to touch the book, two colored women came and stood beside me. I could tell that they were not slaves by their clothes and the way they spoke so freely.

"Tsk, tsk. So sad how she ended up," one woman said.

"The poet? How so?" her friend asked.

"You remember my cousin, the business owner in Boston? He said that she died heartbroken, penniless, and alone."

"Well, I suppose that's what happens when a black girl thinks herself a poet."

They both shook their heads with pity, and it brought me horror. I did not want to be pitied like that. I did not want to die alone!

———————

Cato opened his eyes again. His body was in an awkward and painful position, lying on his pack inside of a large hollowed oak. The tree stood against some large boulders, creating just enough space for Cato to be somewhat protected and undetectable. The runaway had helped him before he set off on his own—he'd put some large pine branches against the opening so Cato would have something of a door. Cato could see out but not be seen himself.

After hours of throbbing pain and violent chills, Cato was now awake enough to take off his pack and drink some water from his canteen. He wrapped his ankle with a handkerchief of his mother's that he carried in remembrance. As a boy, when Cato had wept for his mother, his dry-eyed father had shoved her handkerchief in his face and told him that a free black man should never cry for anything except the loss of his freedom. Despite that, Cato sometimes heard his father weeping alone in his room late at night.

Cato's ankle was swollen to the size of his two hands clasped in desperate prayer. The handkerchief made Cato catch up enough courage to set his crooked ankle himself; he took his belt and two sturdy pieces of bark and bit down on the strap of his pack to keep from howling in agony. After he popped the bone back into place and supported it with the wood and belt, Cato passed out again, salt drying on his own cheeks.

After the fifth day of lying in humiliation and pain in the hollow of the massive tree, Cato was desperate with boredom. He thought on Nat Turner and wondered what he had really done when he ran away from the plantation and spent thirty days in the woods before the Spirit told him to return to the plantation to gather men and plan for his bloody revolution. After the revolution, before he was caught, Turner had made himself a hideout from some discarded wood. Cato had studied the case closely. He felt that Turner's so-called confession wasn't to be believed, since he was not the one who wrote it.

"The man was delusional, possessed by nothing but the devil," Elihu would say, agitatedly tapping the tobacco in his pipe.

"We do not know his true perspective," Cato reasoned, steadfast in his belief.

"We *do* know Turner's true perspective—*pure violence.*"

"But, Elihu—isn't that why we fight against slavery? Because *it* is pure, violent evil. Let us not pretend that Africans were brought here and kept here for their labor skills. They were brought here to be treated as the white man's mule—worse, in many cases. And how does a master subdue a slave? More often than not, it's through that same evil violence. I don't try to justify Turner's actions, but I don't see how anyone could justify his hanging without calling for the hangings of all the white men responsible for his enslavement."

Elihu had scratched his beard but remained silent for

the rest of the evening. As a Quaker, Elihu abhorred all violence, but he was still conservative by Cato's standards.

When Cato had questioned his father about Turner, Atlantus only grunted. The one time Atlantus answered, it stayed with Cato as much as any of Elihu's words. "A man forced to live without dignity is as wild as any beast."

As he aged, Atlantus became more and more wary of runaways. A handful of times there'd been kidnappers, ransom hogs, who'd tried to catch a few folks from Haven by waiting in the woods. Once, one even boldly walked into the settlement, but they all found that Haven was quite prepared to defend itself. Atlantus feared more of the same, and perhaps worse. His disdain showed when Cato wished aloud that he'd had more time to talk with the runaway Jim, whom he'd gotten along with so well.

"What'd you expect?" Atlantus scoffed. "I'm surprised he stayed so long! He had blood on his hands when they found him! Runaways bring danger with them everywhere, just as thick as the dirt under their nails. I bought my freedom, fair and square. Can't nobody make me to run nowhere."

In that cramped tree that windy, hungry, rainy night, Cato choked back tears remembering.

Cato had studied the maps so well that they seemed to be imprinted behind his eyes, for they were there even now,

mocking him in his fitful dreams. He had planned and cal-
culated his route with a telescope, vernier, and compass. At
night in the tree when he heard the baying of distant dogs,
Cato tried not to let himself wish that he'd listened to his
father and stayed home with his books. Elihu would have
thought Cato's unfortunate predicament served him right.
He had told no one where he was going, not even the farmer
tending his horses, so no one knew where to look for him.
The Quaker would have made Cato keep two weeks of silence
for such a simpleminded error. Cato assumed that the maps
and tools would be his shield and his sword. But they are
nothing but thin wood, as his father would say. And a map
was only as good as its maker, Elihu would have told him.

Cato still prided himself on being a rough-and-ready
man's son. He'd been taught to protect himself and his
sisters since he was a boy. Atlantus would have at least
approved of his son's ability to procure and carry a fine
revolver for times of need. There was always a shotgun
hidden under the driver's seat of every one of his father's
rigs. Cato cursed himself for not bringing one of those, too.
There were no laws against free blacks carrying hunting
weapons in Pennsylvania, but a revolver was an easy way to
multiply your trouble. Maryland was a devoted slave state,
and any blacks carrying guns were outlaws. He knew that.
And he had no plans of letting himself get sold.

The oak was big enough for Cato to stretch out his

hurt leg if he propped it up inside the tree. This lessened the pain, but as soon as he put his leg down, it throbbed terribly. He could only fit completely inside if he was half sitting up, so the position, even leaning up against his pack, was causing him to cramp all over. Each night he would try to drag himself farther and farther out of the tree, just to lie flat for a while and stretch before he crawled back inside. It was more than a week before Cato felt like he could try standing a little. The swelling on his ankle had gone down a good bit, and he was desperate to walk farther north, deeper into Pennsylvania, to find a better place to hide. He was very aware of the short distance between himself and the Line. The first night he tried to stand up against the tree, he thought he saw the Mason-Dixon marker glowing white in the darkness, but then the pain thrashed through him and he struggled to get back into his hideaway.

Somewhere in the second week, he ran out of rations and was wearing the second set of clothes he brought on top of the first for added warmth. He was getting hungry and was ready to do almost anything to eat. He considered using the revolver to hunt, but he needed to conserve his ammunition for an emergency. Besides, the amount of noise and smoke from one shot would surely draw attention. He made himself a very crude slingshot, but it broke after he killed a tiny chipmunk. He barely thought it worthy of making a suspicious fire. Two days later, he cursed himself for not having eaten it.

Cato knew the cardinal directions, but couldn't grasp if he was in a populated area or not. The map had shown two farms in the close vicinity, and a small river near the Mason-Dixon Line to the southwest, not far from where he met the fugitive. The river curved north into Pennsylvania, but that was too far for him to walk.

One dusky evening, when Cato was finally able to stand and take a few steps with the help of a tree branch as a crutch, he went in search of food. In his coat pocket, his free hand gripped the revolver. Limping around was noisy business, so he didn't dare go far, but he did find a clutch of quail eggs in the grass nearby. He could hear the mother quail complaining in the distance, but he ate all of her eggs anyway. Farther ahead he could hear the river. He started in the direction of the sound, but his ankle began throbbing, and so he turned back, afraid he would not have the strength to find his way in the gathering dark.

It was another two days before Cato could get to the river. He went little by little, a few yards at a time, marking his way by folding and tying bundles of high grass into knots, or crossing sticks to show the way back. Reluctant as he was to set foot into the land of slave power, his hunger and thirst propelled him, so he did not much care which state he drank from. He saluted the Mason-Dixon marker as he hobbled past it.

Cato rested with his back against the trees, wary of daylight. The river embankment was deep, rocky, and slick. Since the waters were receding, he was able to find a spot where he could wrestle his way down by the roots of a huge old willow tree that was rooted deep into the riverbed. He lay flat on his belly to drink the cold rushing water from his cupped hand. It ran down his throat and chest, he drank so greedily. Filling his canteens, Cato spotted a fish and, without thought, grabbed at it. To his own surprise, he caught it, but it slipped out of his hands before he could get his bowie knife from his belt. After some scavenging among the rocks, he found some crawfish and even pried a bit of meat out of some freshwater clams before it got dark. It was not enough to satisfy him, but he consoled himself by thinking he would come back the next day with a steadier hand.

Climbing gingerly back up the tree's hulking roots, Cato stuck his hand into a crevice to pull himself up. He nearly fell backward when his hands touched not dirt but something else. He pulled out a leather-wrapped parcel. Unable to tell what it was without a lantern, he tucked it into his coat and continued climbing up the roots of the massive tree. Cato waited until he was securely in his hiding place to open what he'd found. In the spare light, he could see it was a book, a diary of some sort, but couldn't make out the handwriting.

It was the first time he anticipated what the morning light would bring.

Finding the copybook was like finding a treasure. He watched the stars all night, begging them to quicken their paces. By the first ray of sunlight, he was absorbed in the page, deciphering what began as rough chicken scratch and eventually blossomed into sentiments, ideas . . . prayers, all written as letters to a mother. Cato wished he had thought to write to his own mother to help make sense of grief and loneliness. Although the copybook author's writing was imperfect, she crafted her words with utmost care. He was reminded how Elihu had often accused him of having fine penmanship but little art with the written word.

His favorite entry was this:

May 5, 1848

Dearest Mama,
I sit here so quiet sometimes it feel like I am this

tree, the very bark and branches. I watch birds and spell
out the names—C-A-R-D-I-N-A-L, W-0-0-D-P-E-
C-K-E-R, 0-R-I-0-L-E.

When I was little I would ask Granmam about
the birds, their names. She could only say, thats the red
bird, theres that noisy bird, that orange one makes a
strange nest. But Rev Jeff would say something different
when wed take our walks in the woods. He would
sometimes visit here with me back then. He was the one
who tole me to pray by your grave.

It wasnt til Granmam gave me my first chore that
I found out about the birds. I got in her way, no matter
what I did. She put two rags in my hands and tells me
dust and tidy the library.

Your mama used to dust the books real good, she tole
me. See if you can, too.

I didnt dust one thing, Mama. I dont know how
you was so good at it. I seemd to get swallowd into the
books like they was the whale and I was Jonah. The
first book I open was big and sat on top of a pile tall as
me. There, colord drawings of birds, still and yet live
at the same time, startle me at first. Some was of bird
skeletons and innards, and then it fascinated me, true
to the word. I stayd glued at the pictures and tried to
cipher the letters next to them. Papa and Rev often read

the Bible to me while I sat at their lap, so I already
knew the letters made the words and the words made
the stories.

If Granmam hadnt called my name so many times
I would have stayed staring at the pictures and words til
night shadowed the pages.

Is it such a crime for me to know the names of simple
creatures?

Time does get away from me now and I must get
home to my chores. Ive learned another new word:
D-R-U-D-G-E-R-Y.

Your loving daughter
Willow

Cato couldn't help but be moved by the purity of the
writer's spirit. Cato was almost in tears by the time he finished the last entry.

Besides the abolitionists from Rochester, Cato knew no
women who would dare question any man or speak against
social customs in public. Like most men he knew, Cato
believed that it was a man's responsibility to care for the
women in his family. His sisters would become the property of their husbands. Cato had never seen a problem with
this outlook until he found the copybook. It had never
occurred to him how a woman was enslaved by the bonds

of marriage and of kinship. Free to study, to seek her own truth without a man? To have children only if and when she chose? How radical an idea!

Cato had once stolen a peek at his oldest sister's diary, but it was a boring account of her daily habits, speculation on those she thought admired her at a party in the city, and a constant lament about becoming a spinster. His sisters were praying to get married. And because their father was too wrapped up in his business to think of anyone's social life, Cato had to chaperone visits and escort his sisters to parties. It bored him. He had no interest in the lace-and-ruffle women who fluttered and puffed around him. Cato had no shortage of prospects, unlike his sisters. Free and profitable black men were rare. But how could he involve himself with one of these women? Who would understand his need to explore, to matter in the world?

Now, however, his mind was fixed upon what this girl, the writer of these letters, would look and sound like. Above all, Cato pondered how someone so clever could bear staying confined.

He read the journal again and again and began to shake off his guilt for prying into her life, he began to think that perhaps his mission wasn't to deliver the fugitives after all, but that fate had put him at this moment in time to help this one girl.

He sat up straight, compelled to do something . . . anything. . . . When the graphite pencil fell out of the leather pouch, he believed it to be a sign. He wrote only one word — three little letters — the most urgent thing, the only thing, he could convey. . . .

Part

Three

Dear Mama,

This is the las letter I ever will write you. Why, Mama, is this world so full of burden? I never knew such agonys and my tears run low, but they say this is life an responsibilities the only way to salvation.

Mama, I never knew your life so well, and now I think I know it even less. Cholly Dees face mocks me in my dreams. Always hes there laughing. Something he knows I dont know. Not one of my prayers for truth been answered, an now I reckon they never will.

Granmam used to say I pay too much attention to what lies in front of my face and not enough on what around me. I suppose its true. I try to see the world with wide eyes, but it is so pale and bleak these days. Responsibilite feel like chains. I remember how Romeo was so lost after his Rosalyn, and I, too, feel the same woes.

Rev offered me a generous gift to free my mind. But I boarded the coach for the long ride back to Knotwild. I refused freedom for fear, Mama. For comfort. What does that make me? Coward or fool? Perhaps both.

My thought is clear that I must be here at Knotwild. It is my fate, and I cannot leave Papa. Baltimore frighten and enchant me, but I see how if you have no friend in the world, you can get so lost. My weak lungs and heart remind me. Silvey and Little Luck remind me. Phillis Wheatley, God bless her, remind me.

Oh but, Mama, I will tell you. Even in the loud rumble of the city, I could hear the wild geese call as they flew north.

Rev is so pleasd I chose to come back. He tole Papa he planning to marry Mistress Evelyn in the spring, but Papa barely smile. He feel betraed and even cheated, maybe. I think Papa feel we supposed to be next in line for Knotwild. How this can be I dont know, but I mus learn not to fret so over mens affairs. As a woman and

slave, I must remember I have no right! It makes my
mouth bitter, and, Mama, I think you know that well.
Granmam prolly did, too.

I came back to Knotwild so I dont have to say good-
bye to my loved ones who are living, even tho I must say
good-bye to you, the one who is dead. I will not write
here at this nook of tree again, for I promised Rev. It
pains me to think it, but I can only keep promises to the
living.

Forgive me, Mama, and know you are always
always always in my heart.

Your loving daughter
Willow

After I wrote my name for the last time, I sat sobbing
all over the page. The journey home from Baltimore was
still festering like a sore, as Papa had wanted to discuss the
details of my nuptials.

"I bet you excited for Tiny to start planning out your
dress, huh?" he'd said.

I had nodded and tried to smile.

"Get whatever lace and ruffles you want. I got some
money saved up."

"Thanks, Papa."

"Rev says Raymond's exact value is going to have to be

decided. 'Course, Rawlins wanted to take as much of Rev's money as he could," Papa said.

"You're a real investment to Rev, Willow. That means your children will also be worth a lot more. The Rev'll have to make sure the doctor is paid well when it comes time for you to give birth. . . ."

"Papa!" I had said, horrified.

"No, Willow." He'd lowered his voice and leaned closer. "This is serious. You need to have a real doctor when you with child. I want someone with real medical learning taking care of you."

"But that doctor hates me! I can't even think about having him—"

Papa had given me a sharp look, stopping the conversation cold.

Suddenly, through my mess of tears, I noticed one of my journal pages was folded over. I never do that.

Who might have found my writings? Was it Rev? Papa? My hands trembled as I opened to the entry. It was one I dated September 12:

> *But to you only, I will say: I want no part of this marriage. Mama, what am I to do?*

RUN

I feared my heart might stop right then. For a brief moment, my mind caught on to the idea that somehow my mama had come back to tell me she wanted me to flee. . . .

I looked back down at the scrawl, neat and delicate despite the wide, flat edge of the pencil. The writer had pressed down hard; I could trace the impression of the word with my fingertips on the next three pages.

I climbed up the embankment and looked cautiously over at the Pennsylvania side. It was as calm and peaceful as the Maryland side. If it weren't for the granite marker set by Mason and Dixon, no one could tell the difference between the two. I recalled the young man in the oilskin coat. I felt that same warm tingling from somewhere deep inside, the same as when I first saw him, arms outstretched.

That's when it occurred to me that I had to burn my writings, and something strong told me I should do it as soon as I could. If after all the sacrifices I had already made, someone found my secrets and could expose them . . . I couldn't bear the thought. I had no way to make a fire, so I would have to come back.

I glanced at my pendant clock. It was time to go any-way. As soon as he started talking about me preparing for my "wifely duties," I told Papa that I needed to visit mama's grave. The mention of Mama always softened him. I said I also needed to set some rabbit and turkey traps, which takes a long time, but not all day. Now I set the traps, gathered up Mayapple's reins, and slowly started home.

Suddenly Mayapple reared up, giving me a fright and nearly throwing me off.

"Woman, you too pretty to be alone out here!"

I looked around desperately, Mayapple was turning in circles, but no one appeared.

"You look almost too pretty for me to be looking at, in fact!"

"Show yourself!" I called out, and hoped my voice didn't tremble.

Finally Raymond stepped out from behind a tree, grinning.

"Hello" was all I could manage to say from behind my false smile. I tried to ignore that he had scared me on purpose. I had been trying to soften myself to the thought of him.

"Now, that ain't no way to greet your betrothed, woman! Get down here and say it proper." He grabbed Mayapple's rein and held her so I had to get down. May didn't like it at all. She pulled and yanked and nearly broke her bit until I took the reins from Raymond's hands.

"How are you?" I asked, trying to sound politely interested. I had not expected to see him so soon, not until Rev was going to Merriend next week.

"Wait—how'd you get away from Boss H?" I asked, and he laughed.

"I tole Boss H I could catch him a plump turkey for his dinner. Then I jumped a wagon on over here to see if I could get a glimpse of you." He looked me up and down again.

"I saw you take off on this-here horse. I never knew you could ride. Almost as good as a white man, too! Me, I never took up horses, always being in the fields. Prolly have to learn now, since I'll be coach driver like your pa soon. Can't wait to get dressed up all fancy and drive past that old Merriend and just wave real polite-like to those fools in the fields. Guess I'll have to start somewhere. Lemme try this one here. Shoot, if you can ride her, it can't be too hard!"

"Raymond, She's particular. I don't think you should . . ." I tried to warn him.

"Someone's gonna have to ride her, since you won't be riding no more once we married! Can't have no wife of mine riding a horse!" He climbed up in the saddle awkwardly; I held the reins and talked to May in low tones to try to soothe her. Her eyes were rolling as though she were likely to throw a fit.

"I'll just walk you on her . . . to teach you," I told him.

"Let 'er go! I don't need a woman to teach me nothing!"

He pushed me off of the reins with his foot and kicked

into Mayapple hard, and with that she reared, then bucked him clear over her head. Then she ran like the devil himself was chasing her. I wanted to laugh, scream, and cry, all at once.

Instead, I went to see if he was hurt. "Are you all right? I tried to tell you . . ."

"Get off me!" He pushed me away roughly. Luckily he had landed in a bed of leaves dropped down from a sycamore tree. He got up, rubbing his behind. "That horse oughta be shot!"

"She's really sweet once she gets to know you," I offered.

"You mocking me, girl?"

I tried to take a step back, but he grabbed my arm tight.

"No," I said. He was breathing heavy, and his breath smelled sour.

He pulled me closer and tighter so that I had to look into his glaring eyes. "I can't stand a woman who don't know her place. Woman got no right to laugh at a man! If we was married right now I'd box your ears!"

I tried to turn my face away again. "Please. . . . You're hurting me!"

He slid his hand down my arm and grasped my hand. "Seems like I should get a kiss for all my troubles."

"We should wait until we jump the broom," I said quickly.

"We just about married. Unless . . . You ain't partial to no one else, is you?" Raymond tightened his grip again.

"No! I just promised my father . . . and Rev . . . that I would save myself completely for my wedding night." I had never actually made that promise, but I hoped he believed it.

His body stiffened as he pressed himself against me to whisper in my ear.

"I like hearing you saving up just for me, but you and me both know all that just talk. When I want a kiss, you damn well better give me one."

We struggled for barely a moment when a bright song broke out of the woods.

"Down by the riverside, I'm gonna lay my burdens down . . . Ain't gonna study war no more . . ."

Just then, no other than Cholly Dee walked up with Mayapple trailing behind him. Raymond let go of me. I nearly cried out with joy. Never in my life was I so glad to see Cholly.

"Well, well, well," he said, amused. "I saw this horse without her usual rider and I set out here thinkin' I'd find you thrown and half broken. 'Specially when this horse, who never been no friend of mine, walked right up to me and stared in my face till I walked with her in this direction. But now I see you weren't really needing me, now, was you?"

I ran over to Mayapple and threw my arms around her neck. I couldn't bear to look at either of the men.

Cholly kept a hold on May's reins so I couldn't lead her away.

"Naw, I can't say we was needing you," Raymond answered gruffly. "Who you, anyway?"

"How you do?" Cholly said. I could see a flicker of annoyance at Raymond's bad manners. Cholly took off his hat and dipped into a flourished bow. "Forgive me for not introducing myself. *Miss* Willow knows me."

"Raymond, this Cholly Dee," I said roughly. I just wanted to get on my horse and go. "He from Knotwild."

"Well, Mr. Cholly Dee," Raymond said, "you can leave me *and my wife* alone now."

"Oh!" Cholly bellowed his low laugh. "I had no idea you done got married already! Excuse me! I guess I best give my congratulations, then." Cholly bowed clownishly again.

"I should be getting back to the house now." I pulled the reins, hoping Cholly would let them go, but he grasped them tighter.

"I'll make sure you get back safe, then," Cholly said firmly. "I wouldn't want your father or your *husband* to worry."

I just shut my mouth and let him lead me home.

"I'd've thought your papa would've made some big announcement 'bout you gettin hitched," Cholly said as we walked away from Raymond.

"There's no announcement to make," I replied stonily. "We didn't jump the broom yet."

"Ah. And when that's gone be, pray tell?"

"Spring . . . after Rev's wedding."

We walked in silence for a moment. I wasn't sure if he knew about Rev, but I just wanted to prove to him that I did know more than he thought.

"You really trying hard to be what they want you to be, huh?" Cholly said after a while. "That's not something Adlile would've done, given the chance."

I stopped in my tracks and gathered every inch of gumption in my soul. "Respectfully, Cholly, I'm tired of all your talk. If you have something to say to me about my mother, come on and tell me. Otherwise, I don't think you should say nothing else to me."

He looked me deep in the eyes, searching for something; then he handed the reins over to me, tipped his hat, and walked away.

The rest of my day was the dull drudgery of endless chores. Rev was so pressed to have everything perfect for Mistress Evelyn's first visit that he told Tiny that she was not to take on any sewing until after the wedding. That way, she and a few other women could help prepare the house, since my weak health hindered me from doing all of the heavy cleaning that needed to be done.

"We want the mistress to feel as though our home is her castle," Rev said more than once.

So it fell to me to supervise and organize tasks, something I'd only seen Granmam do. We had to not only polish the surfaces of everything but also clean out the cellar, the indoor kitchen, and outdoor cookhouse, whitewash the porch floor, and pull up all the rugs to beat and air them. We had to turn and restuff mattresses from rooms that hadn't been opened since before Granmam died, which meant that we also had to chase out a lot of mice, and even a bat that had gotten stuck in one room. I had to get Papa to climb the roof and drop two hens down a chimney that was thick with soot; their flapping wings would sweep out the dirt. Granmam used that trick every few years. Every floor had to be scrubbed with apple vinegar (and then there was more apple vinegar to make), and every piece of linen had to be boiled and bleached — those were my main jobs.

Mistress Evelyn would be bringing her aunt as chaperone, and I prayed that Silvey would be brought along as well — I was a bit afraid to tend to Mistress Evelyn and her aunt in addition to running the house. I wanted to help Silvey talk to Rev about bringing Little Luck to Knotwild, too.

As busy as I was, and no matter how many prayers I said to forget it, at night I could not sleep, thinking of the fine penmanship in my copybook and how I needed to burn it.

I came up with a plan. I suggested to Rev and Papa that the ladies might enjoy some scented linens. I'd soak the sheets in lavender-scented water, and after the final rinse in the river I'd let them dry out in the fragrant breeze of the field by my tree. Meanwhile, I'd collect herbs for sachets to freshen the drawers and closets in the rooms where our guests would lay their heads. Rev thought the idea was a very good one and complimented me on my sensibility about the mysterious needs of fine ladies, of which he knew little.

Washing was a six-step, three- or four-day process in all, not counting the days making the lye soap made of wood ashes and animal fat—a chore saved for winter. I had to prewash the linens and soak them overnight in the lye. Then came scrubbing, boiling, rinsing, and drying. These bed linens didn't have to be scrubbed too hard since they'd been in storage, but there was also toting water and the strength it took to stir the great mess of fabric in the boiling washtub. After that, I had to crank it through the wringer.

Granmam used to handle most of this herself. Rev had bought her one of those fancy new zinc metal washing boards, complete with a little box for her to line with straw to cushion her knees and protect her skirts from getting soaked. Gran had little use for it. She learned as a child that the only way to truly get laundry clean was to beat it over the big smooth river rocks. Although she taught me the same, I didn't mind a few modern conveniences, and I used the new boards and wringer.

All of this just to have an excuse to burn my own words.

As I rode down to the field, I sorely recalled my last encounter with Raymond. I daydreamed that I told Rev and Papa how he treated me and they called the wedding off. Then I remembered everything the both of them had been telling me the past few weeks—responsibility, duty, station. Besides, who else would I marry? I didn't want Rev to take someone from their own family just to be owned by mine.

I toted the washtub and a small batch of linens off the cart; then I got to starting the fire. Once it was going good, I fed it a few more sticks of dry tinder. I'd circled some rocks around it so the tub could sit on top, and I took two buckets to the river to fill the tub. I threw in an armful of lavender with the sheets to boil and soak, and then I walked upstream to my tree.

I found my copybook in my hiding spot, but it had been moved from how I'd left it. My hands refused to steady as I opened the book.

I examined each one of the pages to see if they had any marks, pausing at that first command . . .

RUN

Then in the blank pages at the back of the book I saw another page folded down. There was the same elegant scrawl:

How do you stay enslaved when you live so close to freedom?

I touched the words printed there, and anger boiled up inside of me. Despite my promise to Rev, I grabbed my graphite pencil and wrote:

I am not so much enslaved as beholden. *There is difference—I owe everything to Papa and Rev. They the only family I got and I aim to serve them. Isnt that what we do for those we love? What is freedom without*

our loved ones? Who are you that love does not affect you
so? As Mr. Shakespeare says: "Love is not love which
alters when it alteration finds."

I set the graphite pencil back in the crease of the copybook and put it all back. Nothing could make me burn
it now.

Two days passed in agony before I could find a lie to get
me away again without notice. The housework was tire-
some and supervising the other women worse. As I was
younger than them all and had no desire to boss anyone,
I found myself doing the tasks myself rather than give
direction.

"There you are, Willow." Rev wandered into the dining room, where I was polishing the good silver. Rachel
had been helping me, but she talked so much about her
loving husband and handsome children that I told her we
were finished, even though there were two more trays of
serving spoons and the entire tea set to be done.

"I would like to have a treat for Evelyn and her
aunt when they are here. She wrote and said that chocolate is quite fashionable in Baltimore, and I want her to
know that she can have the finer things so far from the
city. You'll have to make it, of course. I'm going to have

your father order the cacao nuts from the mercantile in Taneytown."

"I'm afraid I don't know how to make chocolate, Rev. I only saw Granmam do it once when I was a child."

All I remembered was watching the long process of roasting, crushing, and unshelling the hard nuts, then mashing them into a paste thick with sugar. I never was able to taste the concoction because it was too precious and thought to be unhealthy for children. Granmam made it into a hot drink at Rev's request one Christmas. He usually wasn't very fond of indulging in sweets.

Rev sighed heavily, but he suddenly brightened and left the room only to come back later with an old cookbook, one I didn't recognize.

"It was my first wife's. When I got out her cloak and gloves for you, I found it; I had forgotten it. I remembered Clarissa used to read recipes aloud to your grandmother and mother to direct them in the kitchen. Perhaps it will help. Let me look."

I couldn't believe that Granmam ever let anyone direct her in the kitchen. She ran the house at Knotwild like she was General Washington himself. I never even heard Rev give her a direction—he gave his opinions and wishes and then she told him how things would be done. Granmam was clear that tradition and her knowledge of it was prized over all. I suddenly realized how Granmam's life must have changed when Rev brought his first wife to Knotwild.

"Yes, here it is . . . the recipe for chocolate. Oh. I see the directions are long and complicated," Rev said with dismay. "I really don't have the time to prattle all of this off. . . ." He looked at me and I knew what was behind his eyes.

"For the sake of convenience, Willow." He pushed the book across the table and then he left the room. I wasn't sure if it was for his convenience or mine.

That very afternoon I told Rev I needed to collect grasses for a new winnowing basket to separate the cacao shells. Of course the old one would have done fine, but Rev didn't question it, only nodded and kept his face in his book.

Mayapple was happy to run free to our sacred place. I was grateful to feel the wind in my face. My heart kept pace with May's gallop when I thought about what might be waiting for me in my copybook.

The cold had broken again and the weather had turned mild for a spell. Papa said it meant a big storm would probably be heading our way. Instead of reading my copybook there by the river, I grabbed it and led Mayapple into the woods to find a quiet place. I reckoned that moving away from my usual perch would be smart.

I opened the book to the last folded page and found a curious response.

To also quote Shakespeare, "These times of woe afford no time to woo." So I will speak plainly— True Love can only be given freely. Perhaps you cannot know what True Love is if you are not truly free. Love from obligation alone is not True Love. Are those you are beholden to also beholden to your oppression? If they keep you enslaved, they are indeed. Unfortunately, being "almost free" is not free. I am not unsympathetic, but I know freedom is worth more than any love wrapped in chains. Self-preservation is the truest love of all. . . .

Yours truly,
A friend

I bristled with the heat of embarrassment that turned into a blazing anger. Who was this . . . brute . . . to say I did not understand true love?

I weighed the options between burning the book or burning my words into the page. The sun was beginning to set—I had to get back. . . .

How cruel of you to judge a stranger. And how rude to invade my deepest thoughts. I have indeed chosen love of

kin over a lonely freedom. Reveal yourself if you know
who I am, what I suffer. If not, let me alone.

I struggled to recall another fancy quote that would make me seem smart, but nothing came to me, so I walked back to the tree and tucked the copybook away. Halfheartedly gathering a few handfuls of grass along the way, I started for home with Mayapple, neither of us in much of a hurry.

I was on my knees — which were swollen and blistered from all the scrubbing and polishing — praying hard that Mistress Evelyn's arrival the next day would bring peace and prosperity to our home. Most of all I asked to be clearly guided on how to best serve the highest purpose meant for me.

My arms ached as I stretched out on the bed; my last chore of the night was churning fresh butter. At dawn I would begin preparing the long list of foods that Mistress Evelyn requested. Rev announced to me only yesterday that her son, Philippe, would be traveling with them, and also that he had invited Rawlins to dine the evening Mistress arrived.

Tiny would be with me in the kitchen the whole day, but she worked best when sitting in one position with busy hands. That would actually serve me some, since Mistress was quite fond of a potato-and-cheese dish that required a lot of peeling, grating, and chopping. There was also a turkey and a goose to be roasted, three different desserts, and four breads to be made. Mistress and her family were apparently ravenous eaters. Rev only required a hearty stew and some cornbread for his supper and a thick porridge for his breakfast. Granmam mostly just made recipes up as she went along, and they always came out perfect. The cookbook Rev gave me from Clarissa, as well as what I'd learned from Granmam, would be my only guides.

Despite all that awaited me, my thoughts were with my journal. It had been almost a week since I'd been to the tree and penned my last entry, and I couldn't stop wondering if . . . whoever it was . . . had written back.

Rex, our hen-chaser, was very old. Since the days were getting shorter, he had somehow gotten the idea in his pea brain to roost on the roof of our cabin instead of the roof of the barn to perform his cock-a-doodle long before the sun had even made up her mind to rise.

"Willow, girl, you might as well get up here and now, 'cause you got work to do," Papa called from below. I didn't answer. "Willow?" he called again.

"Papa," I whined, "I did a lot of it last night! I even churned the butter already. Can't I just sleep for one more hour? Please?"

"Girl, didn't you remember anything your granmam taught you? Even I know you supposed to churn the butter in the morning so it don't sour overnight. You better get up right now!"

I got to the kitchen only after Papa came up, nearly dragged me out the bed, and poured some strong coffee down my throat. Tiny was there already, peeling potatoes.

"I couldn't hardly sleep, I been so excited to finally see our new mistress!" she said before I could mutter good morning. "When I was growin' up in Mississippi, we had lots of fine ladies who would visit. Our own mistress was fine and kind. She would sit with us on the big porch and have us sing and dance for her and tell her stories. I just hope our new mistress be a nice one."

I nodded and peeked at the butter churn. I was so tired last night, I forgot to scrape it clean, and now it was a horrible stinking mess. I set to work cleaning out the churn—the hogs even ran from it when I emptied it into their slop.

I went down to the icehouse to get more cream and check the butter. Papa was right: the two pounds I'd made had gone sour, and two of the cakes I baked yesterday had fallen in the middle. I couldn't read all that carefully since Tiny was in the kitchen, and I had to keep sneaking the cookbook to the outhouse to memorize the directions.

Cholly Dee walked into the icehouse as I was trying to fight the urge to throw the cakes across the room. I nearly screamed at him for surprising me.

"What's got you so bristled?" he asked, chopping off a few chunks of ice into a rag.

"Nothing! Don't use all that ice! I need it."

"I only got a few bits here 'cause Old Samuel's knee is swollen again and this here helps, just like you told him it would. I seen you been busy, so I took it up myself to look in on him. But if you got a problem with that, *Mistress,* I'll go tell Sam to suffer in silence. If you wants, I'll whip him real good, too, for complaining at all."

I could only suck my teeth in response. Before he could leave, I shoved one of the fallen cakes into his hands. It was still good cake, even if it wasn't pretty.

"For Sam," I said without looking him directly in the face. "I'll send down some liniment later to ease his aches."

"That's right kind of you. I'm sure he'll appreciate it." Cholly paused. "Hey, you still go visiting to your mama's grave a lot?"

"Why you want to know?"

"I saw some black bears. Two big mama bears and cubs. So I'm just thinking you need to keep clear for a while. Could be dangerous."

"What're you doing going there, anyway?" I demanded.

"Ain't you just like your papa." He laughed. "Rev asked me to see about plowing some of those meadows out there to plant next spring. Wants to try farming some hemp for ropes. I got to thinking it's a good cash crop these days; you saw all them ships in Baltimore and how much rope gets used for rigging. Rev agreed."

Just then my eye caught the turkey and the goose I'd hung from the rafters to bleed out. They still needed plucking. The smell of the blood made my stomach turn.

"Fine," I said, my mind on the birds. "I'll be careful."

A mere three hours after dawn, I was knee-deep in feathers, sneezing and coughing. I had the cookbook concealed in my lap, and I tried to memorize the gravy recipe while I plucked. *Three cups of chicken stock . . . one tablespoon of flour* (or was that two?) *. . . two tablespoons of lard . . .* I reckoned if I just got all the ingredients right, I could mix it together in the skillet like I'd seen Granmam do. I hoped everything would turn out right.

A shadow appeared over my shoulder as I was about to check the cookbook again. I jumped as Papa squeezed my shoulder gently; I barely had enough time to cover the book in my skirts.

"Relax, Mite! You nervous about all this newness about to come our way?"

"Yes, sir. How 'bout you?"

"I won't lie to you." He sat down in the grass next to me. We had our old familiar feeling suddenly. "With Mistress Evelyn's arrival, we're about to get a glimpse into our future. And that is a frightful prospect. But our fate, far as I can see it, lies with Rev Jeff, and he ain't let me down yet."

I nodded. I yanked a handful of feathers off the goose carcass before I asked, "Papa, you think Rev'll get some more hands around here to help out around the house and caring for Mistress Evelyn and her son? I worry I won't be able to handle it all myself."

"Honey, Rev ain't never been keen on buying fresh bodies just to serve — not since your mama, in fact. He always say we manage just fine. . . . I tole him in Baltimore he should buy a family all together so they fit right in with our ways — and how it could be a real blessing for a family that way."

"You think instead Rev might take on Mistress Evelyn's maid, Silvey, and maybe her brother, Little Luck? They would be so happy to stay together."

Papa got up and kissed my forehead. "We ain't got a say what's going to happen to them. You gotta stop worrying so about other people and more for yourself. You gonna have all this done? Where's Tiny?"

"She's peeling and cutting potatoes. She'll be in the kitchen while I serve. I'm gonna put the fowl over the fire pit soon, and I'm almost finished making the chocolate, then I'll set the table."

"Sounds like you got ahold of things! If you want, I can serve tonight since there's so many people. I think I still have my old butler suit in the trunk."

I laughed, fairly certain that suit wouldn't fit him now. "Thanks, but don't go through all that. It'll just be good to have you around. Hopefully my cooking will satisfy them all."

"I'm sure you'll do our mothers proud, Mite."

It did catch me in my heart the way he said "our mothers." I dropped the goose in the basket and leaped up to hug him, forgetting the cookbook in my lap. I nearly stopped breathing, but with luck it tumbled into the basket of feathers, and in haste and fear, I quickly kicked the whole basket over. I didn't think Papa saw, but he looked at me strangely when I let go of my embrace.

"Your breathing is hard," he said, eyebrows raised. "I can hear your lungs whine for air. You probably do need some more help around here. I'll have Rachel or one of the other girls come up. Here, let me help you with this. . . ."

"No—I'll be fine, Papa!" I jumped in front of the basket protectively. "Just need a strong cup of tea."

He took off his hat and scratched his head. "Fine, but don't get yourself in a bind from pride, girl. Don't hesitate to get some help—"

"Yes, sir," I interrupted. I had a hard enough time keeping the cookbook a secret with just Tiny around.

I was about to go back to the goose when a question popped into my head and out of my mouth at the same time.

"Papa, why hasn't there been no one new since my mama?"

He looked like he hadn't remembered mentioning her before. "Uh . . . the circumstances . . ."

I didn't want to push it, but I couldn't help myself. " 'Cause of Cholly Dee? You and he fought over her, didn't you?"

"You got a lot to do here, Willow. This ain't the time . . ."

"Papa—he said something about a bet?"

"What did he tell you?"

Just then Tiny called out to me, "Willow, that chocolate you makin' smell like it burnt!"

"Take it off the heat!" I yelled.

Papa said, "Take care of that." He turned on his heel and left.

I tucked the cookbook back into the hidden pocket I had crudely sewn into the back of my apron and ran into the kitchen.

●   ●   ●

The evening began in chaos. The chocolate was ruined, and while I was trying to salvage it, I forgot to turn the birds. Luckily the turkey only seared on the outside; I prayed it would be cooked enough on the inside.

In the kitchen, Tiny was still slicing up the cheese for Mistress Evelyn's potato dish. It should've been in the oven an hour earlier. In Clarissa's cookbook, there was a version of the dish that called for a special cheese called *parmesan,* but there were no instructions on how to make it and Papa couldn't get it from town. I used the only type of cheese Granmam ever taught me to make, and I wasn't sure it even had a name, unless you wanted to call it Clover after the cow whose milk it was from. I hoped it would be good enough.

Just as I went into the dining room to set the table, Papa announced that Rawlins had arrived. As I got the dishes in order, I looked out the window at the coach in front of the house—with Raymond sitting next to the driver. I panicked and broke a glass in my hand. I ran into the kitchen, bleeding. My heart was racing as I grabbed a rag and covered the wound. It was just a scratch, but I didn't let on.

"Tiny! I cut myself—" Before she could fuss, I was halfway out the door. "I'm going to take care of it at my cabin. Can you just put those potatoes in the Dutch oven with a layer of cheese and bacon and hang it over the fire, please? I'll be back."

I had to get out of there, and I knew this was my only chance. Raymond would come straight to the kitchen.

"Sure, but—?"

"Then I'm going to see if I can dig up some more parsnips and carrots to roast," I babbled, backing out the door. "Maybe there's a rabbit in a trap I set. . . . I'm afraid there's not going to be enough meat with that goose all burnt up. . . . I'll be back quick!"

I ran into the woods as fast as I could, praying no one saw me escaping. By the time I got to my tree, I was dripping with sweat and my chest felt like it was about to cave in. Seeing Raymond made my whole life flash before my eyes—and I didn't like how it looked.

Self-preservation is the truest love of all. . . .

I reached for my journal, to read the mystery writer's words again, but the hiding spot was empty. My journal was gone.

Dear Willow,

I do know that love is free. Do not look to characters of the past to teach you love. You know that your heart yearns to be free. It is

companionship you need, a guide. See how the
heavens have answered you by sending me?
Please let me explain myself . . .

Cato paused, trying to find the right words. He wanted
to tell Willow everything: how he had arrived at this very
moment. The first time Cato had heard of Knotwild wasn't
from Willow's journal. It was from his tutor, Elihu. Elihu
had traveled to Boston to see some friends. He associated
not only with Quakers but prided himself on his close rela-
tionships with a variety of people. It was in Boston that
he met Reverend Jefferson Jeffries. They heatedly debated
the pros and cons of slavery over a dinner at the home of
a mutual friend. Although they held different viewpoints,
each man held the other in high esteem. Elihu respected
the fact that the Reverend seemed to guide his slaves rather
than rule them and that he trusted a few with the care of
his beloved home while he traveled.

It was not until several months later that Elihu found
himself sitting across from Jefferson again, this time at the
old Darby Library on the outskirts of Philadelphia. They
were doing research—Cato and Elihu. Cato could see it
made the Reverend uneasy to be introduced to a Negro boy
holding books in a library.

Cato had not taken it personally; several of the other

white men in the library behaved the same way. He would have given anything to have a few hours to be left alone to browse the stacks, but the rules didn't allow him to linger in the library, so he made it his habit to make his own list and collect his books along with Elihu's. Officially, he was only Elihu's attendant; it had burned his heart terribly in the beginning, but as the years went by, he focused more on *getting* the books rather than *how* he got them. The Darby Library was the only lending library in all of Pennsylvania, and it was almost a half day's ride from Haven, so they traveled there only once a month.

After he'd met the Reverend, Cato went outside with the crate of books to load up Elihu's carriage. Eventually Elihu left the building and they rode away.

"Interesting fellow," Elihu said. "Slaveholder, unfortunately."

"No wonder he looked so frightened of me." Cato laughed. "He must've thought I was Nat Turner reborn!"

"Don't joke about a massacre, Cato." Elihu spoke in a sharp tone.

"I wasn't joking. Was he afraid I was going to kill him with the book in my hand? Or with my knowledge? That's more likely, isn't it? Elihu, you and I agree that Turner was driven to insanity by the circumstances of slavery."

Elihu sat in contemplation as they rode through the

hilly woods of the Delaware Valley. Cato knew he was wrong for exaggerating the Reverend's reaction, but as soon as the word *slaveholder* was uttered, Cato lost all compassion — especially because the man professed to be a man of God.

"So what did the slave master have to say?" Cato finally asked.

Elihu responded absently, "His land is directly south of the Mason-Dixon. He has an unconventionally gentle way with his slaves, but clearly thinks Negroes are inferior."

"Well, how else could he justify holding them in bondage?"

"He is so proud of this land he prospers from through the toil of others! He invited me to visit! He even drew me a crude map to his place. Said he would guarantee that none of his slaves would say they'd want to leave his . . . What'd he call it? Knotwild. What a name for a plantation!"

They both laughed about it, but neither of them continued the conversation. When Cato found the map in the library books he had to return after Elihu's death, he'd shown it to the abolitionists as the ideal place to meet fugitives. Cato had completely forgotten the Reverend's face until he read about him in Willow's diary. After thinking about it, he resolved to not mention any of this to Willow just yet. He didn't know what her reaction would be.

Finally, Cato wrote:

Meet with me tonight.

It would be getting dark soon. Cato saw a hawk swoop down into the bushes and then climb back up into the sky with a large rodent in its claws. Cato needed to find food himself. He made his way back to the tree to replace the copybook, pausing with pain along the way.

That was when he saw Willow running toward the river.

He longed to call her name out loud but was suddenly shy. During those long nights alone in the woods, he had imagined her smiling at him as she ran into his arms, but now he wished only to hide.

He stood as still as he could, pressed against a tree. He lost sight of her completely when she climbed down into the riverbed.

He got on his hands and knees and tried to crawl forward without making too much noise, keeping an eye on the spot where she'd disappeared. Suddenly, she popped her head up to look around. He planted his face on the ground and froze. He was right by a mound of rocks wearing a very faded coat of whitewash — Mama's grave.

It was a few minutes before Cato got the nerve to sit up. He heard his father's voice in his head, telling him to take control of the situation.

Using the large stick he'd found earlier as a crutch,

he got on his feet. Just then, she climbed up out of the riverbed.

From somewhere deep inside him, a fire roared to life, something he'd never felt before the moment their eyes met.

No matter how long that moment lasted, what followed was the feeling of total exposure, after they both realized that he held her diary in his hand. He started to walk toward her, but she leaped from the riverbed and ran at him with a wild look in her eyes.

Part
Four

The rage was like nothing I had ever felt before — a rush of blood shot straight to my head when I saw the young man in the oilskin coat holding my copybook. It was *he* who had written to me — he who had read my thoughts and dreams . . . and belittled them!

I ran at him and slapped him hard across the face. He fell backward, to my surprise. I had never hit anyone before, and it hurt me more than I ever could've reckoned. My hand and wrist throbbed; my chest heaved, trying to get air.

"What're you tryin' to do to me?" I hissed.

I bent down and snatched my copybook out of his hands but saw how his hand trembled and that he was using a tree branch to sit up. His ankle was bandaged.

"I did nothing to you!" He fought to stand. I didn't bother to help him.

"You insulted me! You stole my secrets! You *tricked* me!" Something fierce was unleashed inside me as we stood there next to my mother's grave.

Finally he was upright, and we looked each other in the face. His clothes were wrinkled and dirty. He smelled like he'd been out in the woods for a long while.

"Willow, I . . ."

I made a sound of utter disgust. He knew my name, knew all my secrets, and I knew nothing about him.

"I realize . . . this is . . ." he began again. "I . . . sincerely apologize. . . . You have every right to be angry . . . but I . . ."

A noisy flock of wild geese suddenly flew up into the trees and made us both jump. Instinctively, I pushed him back down on the ground. He nearly yelled out in pain, so I covered his mouth with my hand and looked around. I could hear a horse galloping in the distance. Someone was getting close. I withdrew my hand, still burning from the touch of his lips.

"What happened to you?" I whispered. "What's your name?"

"*Cato,*" he said through clenched teeth. "I broke my damn ankle."

"I saw you before, but you didn't seem hurt then."

"That was *you*? On the horse?"

I nodded. "You a fugitive, huh?"

He managed to puff up his chest a bit. "I'm freeborn!"

"All right, then, Cato. At least now I know something about you, but right now somebody's coming. I'm supposed to be cooking dinner. . . ."

I could almost see his mouth water.

"You hungry?" I asked. "I'll bring you something. Wait here by the river—I'll be back after midnight." I threw my shawl over him and woefully handed the copybook back. "You'll have to hold this—I can't carry it back." The cookbook was still tucked in my crude pocket. "If you was a gentleman, you'd put it back where you found it," I added.

I got up in time to see the horse and rider in the distance but couldn't make out who it was. Just then Cato grabbed my hand. It sent a shock straight through me.

"Please be safe, Willow."

He was scared for me. My heart melted a bit.

"I'll be back, Cato," I promised, and said a silent prayer that I wouldn't have to break it.

Quick as I could without seeming to be in a hurry, I walked toward the rider. I figured it would be Papa, raving mad. For a moment I feared it would be Raymond. So when I realized it was Cholly Dee on Macho, our biggest and strongest field horse, I had no idea what to say, but I felt relieved.

"C'mon," he said, not looking at me but in the direction I came from. There were too many shadows for him to see anything. I grabbed his hand and climbed up behind him.

"What you doing out here?" he asked.

"Praying."

"What? Why couldn't you just . . . ?"

I offered no explanations, and he grunted loudly with doubt.

"They 'bout to start looking for you," he said over his shoulder, and then clicked his tongue to get Macho moving. The horse moved slowly, since Cholly had clearly been running him hard. Even though Macho was strong enough to carry us both, he wouldn't be able to move as fast getting back.

"Tiny told them you cut your hand or was getting some field greens or somethin, but your papa 'bout to figure something's not right. I saw you run from the kitchen like you was on fire when Rawlins and them pulled up." He turned his head toward me, waiting for me to say something. When I didn't, he shook his head and we rode the rest of the way in silence.

When we got close to the house, he stopped Macho, helped me to climb down, and handed me a rucksack I hadn't noticed he was carrying.

Cholly said, "Maybe you got more nerve than I thought, girl. But now you owe me a talk real soon."

I walked the rest of the way in the ever-quickening darkness. As soon as the lights of the house allowed me to see, I looked inside the bag. Two fish, already gutted. There was also a mess of greens and root vegetables. What a kind thing for Cholly Dee to do! I looked up and saw a figure waiting in the doorway of the kitchen. It was Raymond. My head throbbed, and my chest tightened. Had he seen me and Cholly?

"Well, where you bin, girl? Your daddy was 'bout to send the hounds after you, and Massa Rawlins talking 'bout how much you'd sell for if you were his an' you'd run off."

I held up my wrapped hand. "I had to take care of this, and I had some fish on the line down at the stream I had to get for dinner. When I saw you all roll up, I figured we'd need some more food. I . . . didn't want *my husband* to go hungry."

His eyes lit up. I rolled my eyes as he bowed ridiculously and let me pass through the door. Poor Tiny was very nervous and sweating into the pots. I took the spoon out of her hand and told her to sit and chop herbs, which she did gratefully. Papa came in from the dining room, with that wrinkle burrowed deep in his brow. He was wearing his old butler gear—black pants and a black jacket, but he wore his shirt untucked because his belly was too big.

I said nothing, just slid the fish out of the bag, stuffed

them with onion and herbs, slathered them with grease, and let them sizzle on the pan.

"I had to finish setting that table for you." Papa came up and spoke low and sharp into my ear. "I cleaned up the rest of that broke glass *and* served drinks to the men. You lucky Mistress Evelyn is running late. I'm glad you got some more food, but you can't just be running out like that! You know Tiny's scairt of Rawlins; I thought she might pass out when I asked her to serve. You better take care."

I nodded and kept my eyes on the fish. Papa went back to see to the men.

Raymond stayed in the doorway of the kitchen, watching me hard. Tiny kept him in conversation, asking about every single person she knew over at Merriend plantation. I ignored them both. Eventually, Papa came back and took Raymond down to the stables.

Mistress Evelyn arrived quite late. It was hard to keep the food hot and the men had gotten hungry, so I wanted to serve dinner without her. Rev wanted to wait for Evelyn, but Rawlins complained, having brought two bottles of wine with him, and he had drained most of both already.

Apparently the journey didn't agree with Mistress Evelyn, and she had to take a lot of "medicine." One of the coach's horses had a bad shoe, and they had had to stop at a tavern to have it fixed. She stank of rum. I wondered what Rev thought of this, being that he rarely drank. He seemed to ignore it, but he laughed nervously a few too many times. Mistress Evelyn was jovial, but she hung on Rev's arm like she was unable to stand and fanned herself ferociously.

She *was* quite lovely, even more than her picture had shown, and I could see why Rev fancied her. She had dark rings of curls pinned up by her face in a way I had seen many women in Baltimore do, and her dress was quite fashionable, too. It was made of deep-blue satin with frilly white ruffles and a very tight waist. She had to have been wearing a tight-laced corset; she could barely bend and stood very straight. Her skirt was shaped like a bell and had at least three or four petticoats underneath, maybe even a hoopskirt. I had seen all of these types of fancy lady underclothing advertised in newspapers and in shop windows in Baltimore, but Silvey had also told me how it took hours to dress her mistress.

Mistress Evelyn wore an elegant velvet-lined fox-fur cape with matching velvet fur-trimmed gloves that went halfway up her arm, as well as a fur hat. Her cheeks were bright, perhaps because of the drink, or maybe it was her nature. Evelyn's eyes were bright blue, Rev's favorite color.

They came in to dine right away, since they had all waited so long. I barely got to say hello to Silvey. She was brought along to tend to Mistress Evelyn and her aunt but they had made her ride on the back of the carriage, so she was half froze.

We rushed her into the house; I had Tiny give her tea and set her up in front of the fire to soak her feet. She kept sneezing and splashed the water out of the bucket.

Mistress Evelyn went on and on about the terrible roads as I went in and out of the dining room, filling glasses and serving plates. It was such a strange assortment of food that I served each dish separately. Gran had taught me that that way was for fancy guests, but it made a stack of dishes to clean.

"Even the new wooden plank ones are *atrocious,*" Evelyn said with a nervous giggle while I was serving, and I liked how horrible it made the roads sound. I didn't remember them being "atrocious" when we rode to Baltimore, but I appreciated the new word. I kept saying it over and over again under my breath to keep me from getting too nervous. I think Mistress Evelyn's son heard me, for he kept looking at me strangely for the rest of the night. He was very sullen, and even though Rev kept asking him questions, he would only answer with an "Um-hmm, sir" or "Nuh, sir." Madam Lydia, Mistress Evelyn's aunt, was a nice enough old woman, though she only referred to me as "girl." She was dressed in black and reminded me of Mrs. Rose. It was hard not to see the similarities in their faces.

As I was in and out of the kitchen, Silvey and Tiny talked while Tiny did dishes.

"You got people?" Tiny asked.

Silvey nodded as she warmed her face in the steam of the tea. "My brother and I got a aunt out by Annapolis Junction with Mistress Evelyn's relations. Her and my mama was together since birth, but my mama died when she had my brother."

"I'm so sorry to hear," Tiny said, patting her knee. "But 'least she's got the comforts of heaven now. And you got your aunt and brother. I ain't got nobody, never did."

That touched a sore spot on Silvey. "I ain't gonna have *them* if we move way out here!"

I went to the dining room to take away the dishes from the table and prepare for dessert. The chocolate paste had burned a bit, so I added more sugar and milk. As much as I tried, it ended up being more of a black porridge than a drink. I just gave everybody spoons and hoped they'd think it was a sweet pudding.

Mistress Evelyn was not fooled or impressed. "What is this lumpy mess?" She pushed the dish so violently it spilled onto the table linens. I rushed to clean it up but couldn't get it quick enough because Mistress Evelyn's outfit meant she couldn't lean back far enough to let me wipe around her. Aunt Lydia was trying to help Mistress Evelyn get up, but it was proving difficult with all of her skirts. I tried to help, but my hands were sticky with chocolate. Mistress Evelyn's son, Philippe, sat eating his chocolate, ignoring his mother and aunt. I watched him slyly take his aunt's dessert as she struggled with Mistress Evelyn. Master Rawlins was talking to Rev about the famine happening in Ireland, and they didn't seem to notice the commotion.

"Now all these damn typhus-ridden Irish are coming over by the boatloads. I say we should send them back!" He pounded the table, making the mess even worse.

Rev was trying to be a good host by listening to Rawlins, but he finally interrupted by saying, "I think the ladies are finished."

He stood up and assisted Mistress Evelyn. "We'll escort you ladies to the sitting parlor while we adjourn to the porch for a word. Mr. Rawlins?"

I had never heard him use that word — *adjourn* — before. I repeated it and *atrocious* over and over as I cleaned up the table. No one had finished their meal except Philippe. The turkey was so dry it was brittle, but the gravy was good. At least I could get a soup out of it. There was still one whole fish uneaten, too, so there would be plenty of leftovers to spare for Cato.

While I was cleaning up, I could hear Miss Evelyn in the sitting room complaining to her aunt about the food. Philippe must have fallen asleep, because I could hear him snoring like a saw.

"I will never be able to live in this house if *that girl* is cooking. . . . The potatoes were mush instead of *au gratin.* And what kind of cheese was that? I swear I tasted the cow's cud in it! We'll have to order imported cheeses. . . . I have the refined tastes of the city!" she whined to her aunt. "I'll need a proper cook; Lord knows Silvey can barely boil water to save her life. . . . And don't get me started on the renovations that I'll need on this house! Jeffy will just have to understand that."

Mistress Evelyn's pet name for Rev made me cringe worse than her insults.

Her aunt answered her quietly so I couldn't hear all of it. ". . . your best prospect . . . respectable . . . he's kind and decent . . . more than you could ask . . . until your inheritance . . . for Philippe's sake . . ."

Rev and Rawlins had gone out on the porch to smoke. I had never seen Rev smoke, but Rawlins had brought cigars for them both. As I cleared off the buffet by the window, I could hear them talking. I pulled the curtain closed a bit so they wouldn't see me.

"So why can't you just do like the rest of us and let my boy Raymond have her for a night or two till she gets big?" Rawlins said. "You can't expect me to sell my best darkie!"

Rev was quiet for a moment. "Her father wants to have a proper marriage for Willow. . . ."

"Ha! How you do entertain their fancies! Believe me, they don't need the same things our women do. They do just fine without their men around—popping out a baby is the same as plowing a row to them anyway."

"But you'd be willing to let him visit overnight a few times a month?"

"Sure, on one condition."

Rev chuckled. "I should have known."

I could see Rawlins's teeth shining in the lamplight.

"I figure since their child would be half my property, I should get it when it turns fifteen. . . ."

"Willow!" Papa called to me from the kitchen, and I nearly dropped the trays. He came into the dining room.

When I looked back at the window, Rev was walking Rawlins down to his carriage, shaking his hand. I saw that Boss H was out there, too.

"Come say good-bye to Raymond! What's the matter with you, girl?"

"Papa, I—"

"Go! He's waiting!"

I bit my lip and followed him outside. Boss H was talking to Rev Jeff. ". . . it was just a small one in the kitchen. We put the fire out, but there were some damages. I came 'cause I thought Uncle should know right away. . . ."

"Girl, I thought I'd have to miss you," Raymond said, grabbing me into a rough embrace. "I'll see you soon."

He leaned in to kiss me, but I pulled away. "Not in front of my father."

Raymond tried to hide his anger since Papa was right there, but I could see it in his eyes. "Of course! Not till the *wedding*! You just so pretty, it made me forget." He backed up respectfully and reached out to shake my father's hand.

"Good night, son." Papa shook his hand warmly and patted him on the back. "We're always happy to see you."

My stomach turned. I went back into the kitchen; Tiny and Silvey were there, snickering. I couldn't bear to even hear their comments, so I went straight back into the dining room; there was still a mess to clean up.

Papa found me later while I was scraping the last of the half-eaten food from the plates into the slop bucket for the pigs. I had made up a pallet for Silvey in our cabin, and after she helped Mistress Evelyn and Madam Lydia into their bedclothes, she went right to bed. Tiny had already washed the serving plates and the pots; she'd even swept up the floor and the hearth.

"I see you're upset, honey," she'd said to me before she left. "This a big change of life for you right now. But you gotta smile. You gotta laugh. Else, it's all just misery. 'Sides, you never know what kind of surprise 'round the bend. Like that"—she snapped her fingers—"everything be changed."

How many times had I wanted to pour my heart out to her? I *was* changing, minute by minute. . . . But I couldn't tell her that. Cato was waiting for me.

Papa pulled a stool up to the fire. "You could've kissed Raymond in front of me, Mite. He's just about your husband by now. Rev said he and Rawlins are done negotiating. Didn't give me the details, just said we'd all talk about it after the guests leave." He continued with a smile, "It'll be real nice to see my grandchild around here. Maybe by this time next year—"

"Papa!" Some kind of gumption had boiled up in me. "You don't understand. I can't marry Raymond!"

"Willow!" Papa stood up, knocking over the stool. "Girl, you ain't got to do nothing but what you're told, so be grateful and keep your mouth closed!" He stormed out before I could say anything else.

After I finished in the kitchen, I went down to our cabin. I know Papa was trying to do what he thought best for me— for all of us. He wanted Knotwild to prosper; he wanted the generations of our family to go on, together. But at what cost?

When I opened the door to our cabin, Papa was sitting in his chair by the fire, deep in thought. I began to prepare for his nightly tea. I got down the herbs and put them into the mortar so I could crush them, and I added as much periwinkle and valerian as I thought wouldn't kill him, set it down on the table, and went up to my loft.

Silvey was sleeping soundly, although she moaned a bit. I hid the cookbook in the chest of remnants from the women in my family. Then I quietly changed into my riding clothes, lay down on top of my covers, and waited.

After what seemed like forever, I heard Papa clank his teacup down and get in his own bed. As soon as he was snoring, I was out the door.

Cato watched the moon travel to the highest point in the sky. He watched the Milky Way and the constellations dance their way through the blackness. Sitting still left him not only cold but stiff and aching as well. The shawl Willow had dropped in his lap was now wrapped tight around his face and neck; he could still feel the warmth of her body and smell the scent of her skin.

Never could he remember thinking so much about a girl. His father always said he'd take Cato to Philadelphia to find a suitable wife in the free colored community when the time was right.

"A man got all the time in the world to start a family," Atlantus always said. "You don't need to let none of those little girls trap you yet. Get the business settled first."

Cato wondered when the business would be settled enough for his father to free him to start his own life. . . .

What a risk it was to trust Willow at all. What if she told someone about him to spite him for taking her diary? What if someone followed her? Or what if she decided not to come back? Or what if she *couldn't* come back?

Shaking the thoughts out of his head, he remembered how she had squeezed his hand, the way she had looked into his eyes. That was what had made him trust her. She was coming back because she wanted to, and something made him believe that no one would be able to stop her.

His face and neck were itchy from not shaving. Plus, he smelled horrible—and probably looked even worse. Cato finally decided to get up and walk to the riverbed.

Focusing all of his senses on not breaking any other part of himself in the darkness, Cato eased his way down to the river. His two boxes of locofoco friction matches clanked together in his pocket; the airtight metal tins contained pine sticks dipped in white phosphorus and coated with beeswax. He carried a piece of sandpaper to strike them on. The chemicals were highly flammable and could explode in unexpected ways. A group of radical Democrats up in New York was named after the matches. Their plans had backfired miserably.

Cato hadn't dared to use the matches yet; he had

witnessed a man's whole shirt catch fire while he was trying to demonstrate how to light one.

Cato tried to find a sturdy root to ease the rest of himself down the embankment when the noise of the boxes startled something lurking by the river. Cato froze. The moon wasn't so bright now, but he could make out the figure of an animal downstream—a big animal.

Cato considered taking out his gun, but he was still wary of the attention a shot would bring. The animal didn't move, so neither did he.

I had packed a bundle of food and left it just inside the kitchen door. The lights were out in the house, but I knew the place by heart. I even dared to go into the trunk in the parlor to take one of Granmam's long-forgotten knitted blankets. I wondered if this was what Papa meant when he talked of the devil's temptations seducing the soul.

I didn't care! I had to get to Cato.

I didn't even bother to saddle Mayapple. I opened the stable, and she let me lead her out with a click of my tongue. When we were a safe distance from Knotwild, I made the same noise again, and she stopped and let me climb up on her back by gripping her mane. I wrapped my arms around her neck and whispered, "Run."

Cato held his breath as long as he could, but he was sure the animal could sense him. As soon as he exhaled, he could hear a low growl. Was it a cougar? Cougars generally kept to the mountains, he reasoned. Would bears be hibernating by now? As chilled as Cato was, the weather was unseasonably mild. He realized, too, that the only easy way in or out of the riverbed was exactly where he was clinging to the roots of the willow tree. Cato reached his hand into his pocket and gripped one box of matches, pressing on the opening seam carefully with his thumb. Hearing another growl but not seeing any movement, Cato didn't want to use any of his supplies in haste. The sound of the rushing water mingled with the other sounds of the forest, and he couldn't be sure what he was hearing or where it was coming from. There were so many shadows that for a moment, he thought he was mistaken.

Squinting to see better, he realized there was more than one animal — a large creature and two smaller ones. A mama bear and her cubs.

His father always told a story of how he awoke one night, three days into a seven-day haul, to the sound of glass breaking. A box of jars filled with honey had been discovered by a big black bear. Atlantus hadn't thought to hang the goods up in a tree like the rest of his vittles — the honey was sealed in glass and packed in crates under layers of straw. But somehow that creature had sniffed it out and was quick to break open the crates, smash the jars, and lick up the sweet goo wherever it was found. Knowing it was a matter of time before the bear cut its tongue or paw and went raving mad, Cato's father quickly grabbed the last two sticks still burning from the dying fire. He crept up to the bear and burned its behind. While it leaped into the air with fright, Atlantus shouted as loud as he could, waving the glowing sticks in front of him. "That bear was so surprised," Atlantus would say, laughing, with tears in his eyes, "he nearly left his skin behind for me to have as a remembrance!"

Cato tried to climb back up to get out of the way, but he slipped and slid farther down. The mama bear was making louder, heavier grunts and growls. She would kill to keep her little ones safe. Cato gathered his courage and pushed himself away from the safety of the tree. He half fell, half rolled onto the river's shore, hoping to get as far from the bears as he could. He tumbled on his knees and finally landed on his left side. His left hand was chafed and cut by the sharp rocks, but he held on to the box of matches with his right hand.

The mama bear roared and stood up on her hind legs. The cubs cowered together. The bear charged forward a bit, then went back to her cubs. Cato scrambled backward as far as he could without falling into the swift waters. He pulled the matchbox open, and somehow, in one graceful movement, fire and sparks exploded all around. The bear charged forward again, but afraid of the fire and now able to see that Cato was at a safe distance, she allowed her cubs to climb safely up the embankment, and then she climbed up herself, backward to watch Cato, who burned the tips of his fingers, holding the light as far away from himself as he could.

As we were coming up on the river, Mayapple stopped dead in her tracks, nearly throwing me off her back. I tried to kick her forward, but she wouldn't budge. I had no reins to lead her if I hopped off. I reckoned if something was scaring her that badly, it was something that should be making me nervous, too. I almost thought about turning back. If Cato was caught, there was absolutely nothing I could do for him. In fact, I might end up making things worse.

Then I heard what Mayapple sensed. A bear's roar came distinctly from the riverbank, then the flicker of a small but powerful light sputtered in the darkness. I could make out the figures of two little bear cubs scrambling up out of the riverbed, followed by the grunting mama herself. Mayapple backed up slowly, instinctually. The bears ran off west, toward the mountains. Papa had always told me to respect the bears, especially the mamas. Most times they would run off when they saw folks, but he said bears don't see all too well and could stalk you like you was prey. Mama bears, though, were a different matter.

Once the bears were a safe distance away, I left Mayapple and told her I'd never feed her again if she ran off without me.

"Cato? Cato! You down there?" I whispered as loud as I could.

I heard groaning by the bank of the river, so I got down there quickly. "Cato?" I whispered.

"Here," he moaned. I ran to him.

"Willow." His voice sounded weak. "There was a bear. . . . I'm so glad you're here, Willow. . . . I was so . . . worried. . . ." His voice trailed away, but I was able to find him without falling in the dark. He had passed out. I couldn't feel any blood leaking out of him, and his face and head weren't dented from a bear paw, like I'd feared. But he was lying on his bandaged leg, so I'm sure the pain was making him feverish.

I pulled the canteen filled with warm herbal tea out of the sack I had brought and pressed it to his lips. Gran had a good remedy for chills and pain — comfrey, horsetail, willow bark, and skunk cabbage. I had made some for Silvey with valerian, since she was still shivering and sore from the ride.

I propped Cato's shoulders up on my legs, tilted his head back over my thigh, and tipped the concoction down his throat, praying he wouldn't choke. He didn't but seemed to revive slightly. I gave him another sip, and he opened his eyes and moaned a bit more. After a moment, he was able to drink on his own.

"So . . . how'd we . . . ?" he asked. It wasn't proper for him to be lying in my lap. I nearly injured him again, pushing him off of me. He managed to sit himself upright. As he leaned back on a large rock, I rummaged around in the bag, pulling out the food I'd brought. Truly I wanted to fill the heavy silence between us. He saw the turkey leg and tore into it, as well as the fish I had wrapped in parchment, thanking me with a full mouth. After he ate, he sighed and belched contentedly.

"Excuse me. I'm so sorry. All this time in the woods and I've lost my manners in front of a lady," he quickly explained. "I was trying to put this back where it belonged. . . ."

He handed me my copybook. It was a wonder he had held on to it.

"Thank you," I said, taking it back. "Just get better so

you can go back to wherever you from, where black children are born free."

He laughed, but I hadn't meant to be funny. After hearing what Rev and Rawlins said, I couldn't help but feel sore.

"I didn't mean to laugh," he said after a moment. "It's just . . . my father always says all children are free until somebody tells them they're enslaved."

"Your papa free, too?"

"Yup," Cato said, taking more sips of tea. "He bought his freedom and my mother's, too."

"Oh" was all I could say.

"And my sisters are free, too. . . . I'll give you three guesses of what our last name is."

"I don't feel like playing games with you."

"Aww, now, don't be that way. Even in the dark I can see you frown. C'mon, just take one guess."

"I don't know. . . . Freeman." Silvey told me that almost every free person in Baltimore took on that name.

"You're right! It's kind of obvious, don't you think? My father changed his name as soon as he got his papers and married my mother. Said he never wanted to carry his master's name again."

I thought of how Papa always said we should be proud to carry the Jeffries name as our own. He said it was an honor.

"Ain't your mama missing you now?" I asked.

He was quiet for a moment. "She passed away, like yours, but I was nearly ten."

My heart squeezed for him.

"You still want to know how I got into this predicament?" Cato asked, clearly changing the subject.

I repeated the word *predicament* again in my head. "Yes," I said, "tell me about your *predicament.*" I was trying to sound as though I already knew the word. I guessed it meant his unfortunate situation. Or maybe it meant "broke ankle." I wasn't sure.

He told me his story, how he came down here from his town he called Haven.

"You mean they *all* free where you come from? Living in a town together?" This was a very different North from the one my papa had told about. "How they get along without whites to pay for things?"

He laughed again. I must've sounded like a simpleton, but I wasn't enjoying being mocked.

"We work! Still for the white man, most times. But my father owns his own hauling company, and most of our customers are white. We need the whites just as much as they need us. My teacher was a Quaker. . . ."

"Quakers let *us* be teachers? How? I know Quakers are different from regular whites . . . but I didn't know they let folks like us into the religion, too."

"My teacher was a white man. But there are plenty of *Negro* Quakers, and my sisters are tutored by a Quaker woman who was educated in Philadelphia at the Institute for Colored Youth."

"What's that?"

"A school for colored children. There's talk of one day making it into a teachers' college."

"A teachers' college just for blacks? And girls can go, too?"

"Yes."

"Just over in Philadelphia?"

"Yes. My teacher said that the best way for us all to get along is to live and work side by side, so we can see how we're all the same in God's eyes."

He continued talking, telling me how he came down here to help some fugitives and broke his ankle. I barely heard the whole thing; I was still stuck on colored teachers. When he said that he walked here from near Gettysburg and then fell, I cut into his story.

"You broke your ankle the same day you saw me?"

"I can't believe that was you on the horse that fateful morning. I thought you were a man! Why'd you run away?"

"I always wear men's clothes to ride. It's just more . . . comfortable. I ran off 'cause I didn't know who you was! We'd heard of some fugitives in the mountains. I paused. "They caught some fugitives up in the mountains the day before, you know."

Now it was his turn to be silent. "So I didn't help anyone after all," he muttered. "I just caused more harm. . . ." His head hung low.

"But that one . . . the one you got over the border . . . he's safe, I'm sure."

"I hope so. My father says I'm no good at anything but keeping books. Maybe he's right." He pounded his fist on the ground. "I should've listened to him and stayed at home," he muttered.

I felt bad for his *predicament*. He seemed to really care.

"If I were you, I'd've been happy to just be allowed to read and study and go about as I pleased," I said without thinking. "I wouldn't be worried about nobody else."

"You sound like my father."

"I sound like *my own* father!"

We both laughed at that. Then came the uncomfortable silence again.

"Do you ever think of the future?"

His question was so strange and sudden that I laughed nervously again.

"You mean, like, when I'm old?"

"Well, yes, but also beyond that. Do you think slavery will end?"

"Oh, that. I don't think it'll happen anytime soon.

Papa says too much needs to be done to build this country before they let go of free work."

"But what do *you* think, Willow? I know you have lots of thoughts; I read a whole lot of them. The 'eggs in your nest.'"

Sadly, I remembered my own words. "I'm just a girl. I'm not supposed to think like that."

"I *admire* how much you think . . ." he said kindly. "My sisters don't think half as much as you, and they're educated. I want to know your opinions."

"Well," I began slowly. "I think my papa's right in some ways. Nobody wants to give up when they've got it good. But when you tell me things about black towns and colored schools and whites worshipping with blacks . . . I can't help but have some hope that things will change."

"Me too," he agreed. "Maybe one day we'll all actually *want* to live and work together."

I bent over laughing into my shawl to muffle the sound. "Oh, yes, and colored children will be given the same opportunities as white children? It'll take five hundred years! We might live on the moon by then!"

Cato laughed, too, but not as heartily as I. "Maybe it might not take that long. That's why I came out here. I'm hoping that I can do something to quicken the pace to freedom and equality for us all. . . ."

I liked the grand way he said that.

"Can I ask you something else, Willow?"

"Why you asking like I'd take offense?"

"Because you might!"

"Well, I guess we won't know till you ask!" We laughed again. I reckoned I'd never had such an interesting conversation before.

"How can you be content to stay here?" he asked. "I mean, with the Mason-Dixon Line right over your shoulder, it's hard to believe you don't drive yourself crazy with the notion to escape. You wrote that you had the chance in Baltimore; why didn't you take it?"

"To do what? Leave my father and the only home I've ever known? And go where?" I demanded. "Sure, Rev offered me something that I'll never have the chance for again, but it would be nothing if I didn't have my family. I couldn't break Papa's heart like that; I couldn't abandon him. I got responsibilities here."

"But, Willow, don't you have a responsibility to yourself? You deserve to be free. Don't you think your mother would have wanted that for you?"

"How *dare* you! You know nothing about her!" I stood up as he protested. I should've known he'd start talking some mischief about me leaving Knotwild. "It's almost first light," I said. "There's hard-boiled eggs and a roasted yam in the bag here. Should keep you for a day. You should start back to your town soon. You don't belong here."

Cato was struggling to get up. "Willow, I didn't mean any harm! I just . . . I just think it's *you* who doesn't belong *here.*" He fell back down; his leg was pretty bad off. I could tell he wouldn't be able to make it back out of the riverbed, much less all the way back over the Line.

The moon was getting herself ready to set. The sky was still dark, just getting pale around the edges. It was enough for me to see the pain in Cato's face. He wiped at his eyes quickly when he realized I was watching.

"Can't seem to do anything right, no matter how hard I try. No matter how good my intent." His voice was low and unsteady.

Angry as I was, I understood how he felt. I knelt back down, but he wouldn't look me in the face. I wasn't sure what to say. I knew he wanted to help me like I wanted to help Silvey and Little Luck. It struck me that moment that he was the only man who was actually trying to get me to help myself.

"You better stay down here. 'Least till you get some rest." I pulled the blanket out of the bag and tried to make him comfortable.

I could tell he was exhausted; I knew I was. He leaned back and let me prop his hurt leg up on some rocks.

"You should go," he said. "I don't want you to get into any trouble on my account. Thank you for all your help, Willow. Please don't risk anything else for me; it's too dangerous for both of us."

"You really want to know what I think?"

He smiled. It was the first time I'd seen it properly, and my cheeks burned as I found myself admiring his looks. "I think you should wait here till I come back to bring you some stronger herbs for the pain. When you wake up, you should stick that ankle in the river for a bit. The cold will help. And you need to keep off that foot for a while so it can really heal."

"Thanks, *Doctor*. But I think I need to head back over the Line. I've got a little hideout."

"Where?"

He was silent for so long I thought he had fallen asleep. "It's a secret."

"What? You have all my secrets and I can't know that?" My fists rested on my hips.

"Willow — if it comes down to it — I don't want you to have to have the burden of knowing. You're already endangering yourself coming out here. Please understand."

My palms opened and rested at my sides. As much as I hated it, I knew he was probably right. "Fine, but you can't go anywhere right now. Promise you'll stay here? Get some sleep. You'll be safer here than in the woods."

He reluctantly agreed by yawning loudly.

"Write in my book in the morning to let me know you left all right. Don't do anything . . . *radical.*" I pulled that word out of my memory from Baltimore. "'Least let me know . . . *if* you'll return. I'll come back as soon as it's safe."

"Yes, Willow, please be safe." He reached out his hand in the darkness.

I let my fingers brush against his as I hurried away.

Cato dreamed of maps. He dreamed of miles of pathways and roads and tracks that led west to the shining blue sea. He didn't realize it at first, but Willow was with him, right beside him, holding his hand. It was if their hands were the same hand. Their steps were the same. They followed the maps together and then they drew their own. They created and planned their own world where they were both free.

He woke with a start, surprised to be waking in the open, next to the river. But he relaxed, remembering the night before; thanks to Willow, he was warm and rested, with the sun shining full on him. How long had it been since he slept so soundly? What had she put in that tea? She had cared for him, so attentively. She knew exactly what to do. Remembering that she instructed him to put his ankle in the river, he sat up, stretched, and looked around; a bloodred cardinal sat boldly on a nearby branch, calling, *"Purdy, purdy, purdy!"* complimenting his mate.

He looked into the bag Willow had left. The eggs were perfect, and they revived him. At the bottom of the sack was a cake of homemade lavender soap. He laughed to himself; she knew how to give a hint. Figuring he was all alone, he peeled off his layers of clothes to try to get himself clean.

Afterward, he felt much better, although chilled to the bone. Wrapping his waist in the blanket Willow had left, he put his coat back on and washed a few of his undergarments, laying them out on a sunny, flat rock. His ankle looked much better, but it throbbed when he stood. Still, he felt strong and optimistic. Perhaps he should try to get back to his rig tonight. . . .

It was almost seven weeks since he spent his first night in the woods. Surely he must begin walking north tonight. As much as he cherished the image in his dream, he did not want to cause Willow any more distress or inconvenience. He thought of Jim and realized how painful it must have been for him to leave the comfort of Haven. Finally Cato understood that sometimes moving on means you really cared most about the ones you left behind.

If Willow did not agree to leave with him tonight, he would only stay long enough to say good-bye.

By the time I got back to Knotwild, I had to begin to prepare breakfast for our guests. Tiny would be doing a lot of the outdoor chores, like milking the cows and gathering the eggs. Papa would come up to the house kitchen for his breakfast. As the sun rose, I had the dining table set and the porridge bubbling, so I let myself take a quick nap on the floor in front of the fire. It wasn't long before I thought I heard the bell ringing, but I told myself it was a dream. Soon after, Papa was shaking me.

"'Least you got your chores under control. What time did you get up here?" he said.

"I . . . I couldn't sleep, worrying everything wouldn't get done. I've been here all night," I said as I served him his breakfast.

"Then why you got your riding clothes on?" Papa caught my wrist when I put his bowl in front of him.

"Oh, I took Mayapple out for a while at first light. Not far," I lied cautiously. "I know you don't like me out in the dark. I just thought it would help me sleep to get some fresh air. I came back so tired, I fell asleep right here."

Papa grunted and released my hand. "Sorry you didn't sleep, Mite. If you want to go change now, I'll stay till you get back — in case they need anything."

"Thanks, I will."

Back in my loft, Silvey was sleeping. I woke her, but

she was still groggy and feverish. I dressed quickly and made a healing tea with extra birch bark to help sweat out the cold. She hadn't drunk much of what I made her last night. This time I put in extra honey and mint to sweeten the taste, and she drank it down quick. I gave her a little porridge, but she threw up in my washbasin.

"Willow," Papa called, "Mistress wants Silvey. Tell her to hurry."

I came down the stairs. "Silvey's sick, Papa."

"You'd better get going, then," he said.

I could hear Mistress Evelyn calling from outside the house. When I arrived at her room, she was still in bed. Aunt Lydia was sharing the bed with her but was still snoring; she seemed not to hear her niece bellowing. By now it was nearly seven thirty, and Rev would be ready to begin the day. I knew he had planned to take Mistress Evelyn to Taneytown to meet some of his friends, but when I realized that she couldn't even dress herself without Silvey, I knew it was going to be a long day.

"I expect my tea first thing in the morning," she said, her lips pursed tightly. I couldn't help but notice that her face seemed to have much less of a rosy glow, and there were wrinkles now where there had not been any last night. She looked downright green around the edges of her face, and her head was tied up as though she had a tooth-ache. I also noticed that she had a lot less hair—and then I saw the rest of it sitting at the dressing table.

"I require my medication with my tea in the mornings for my headaches. Hurry and look in my bags; get the bottle of tincture. My head feels like it's in a vise!"

I went into her bags and found where she kept a host of "medicines"—two bottles that had fancy labels reading DR. NICKELBEE'S HEAL-ALL TONIC WILL HEAL ALL, but the corks stank of rum. There were also pills, liniments, packets of teas, and a small bottle labeled, LAUDANUM. I'd only seen our old doctor give it to someone who had broken bones or to women with breech babies.

"Yes—that's it. . . . Give it to me." Her hands shook as she reached out for the bottle. I was surprised that she hadn't just gotten out of the bed to get it herself.

"Silvey usually does it," she complained. "I don't remember how much. . . ." She didn't seem to worry for long, simply squirted half the dropper down her throat.

"Ma'am, don't you think that's enough? It's mighty strong," I said as she went to fill the dropper again.

"What do you know?" she demanded. "Go get my tea. And bring me toast with a soft egg. Auntie will want one, too."

"Of course, ma'am. I'll go ask Silvey how much she usually gives you so you don't take too much."

She didn't seem to hear me. Instead she closed her eyes, lay back on her pillows, and half smiled while waving me away. I took the bottle and dropper out of her other hand so that it didn't spill. She fought me for a moment but finally let me take it.

I went downstairs to make her tea and breakfast. Rev was out on the porch talking to Papa and Cholly Dee. Philippe was at the dining table, waiting to be served.

"Good morning, sir," I said. "I'll have your porridge out shortly."

"Ham and potatoes," he said without looking at me. "And two eggs."

I stopped in my tracks. "That will require much more time for preparation, sir," I said through clenched teeth.

"*Preparation?* You talk different from Silvey," he said, finally looking at me sideways.

"I learned that from Scripture—Rev often speaks of how we should live in preparation of the Lord."

He snorted. "Just make my breakfast."

"Of course, sir."

I went to the kitchen, poured water for tea, and sliced and set the ham to frying. I'd never seen people eat so much on a regular day. I cracked four eggs into the pan. In Baltimore at Rev's hotel, I had seen folks dining in luxury, but I reckoned it was just 'cause they were away from home and enjoying themselves. Perhaps these folks here considered themselves on holiday. I couldn't begrudge them that; they were guests, after all. I reminded myself to ask Silvey for more detailed instructions.

I used the back stairs to deliver Mistress's tea. I heard snoring, but it was nigh eight thirty. I'd never known anyone to sleep so long. I knocked softly and let myself in.

"Your tea, miss?" I said as I entered. Mistress Evelyn had fallen back to sleep, and her aunt didn't seem to have woken up, so I set the cup down beside the bed.

"Ma'am?" I cleared my throat just to be sure. I shook Madam Lydia's shoulder.

"What is it?" Aunt Lydia woke and propped herself up on her elbow. She rubbed her eyes and looked at me. "What time is it?"

"Eight fifteen. Miss Evelyn took her medicine and I brought her tea. Your breakfast will be up soon."

We both looked at Evelyn, who was sleeping quite soundly and drooling down her cheek. Lydia shook her, but Evelyn did not rouse a bit.

"Ma'am? Do you know how much medicine Mistress usually takes? Silvey isn't well, and I don't know the correct"—I was about to say *dosage* but I thought better of it—"amount."

"Let me see." Aunt Lydia thought about it, wiping the

sleep from her eyes. "I don't normally see her take her medicine, but I believe the doctor told her to take three drops a day in her tea."

Laudanum was a potent medicine made from opium. I had gotten to half read an article in a bit of the Baltimore newspaper I found; it happened that people wasted away taking the stuff.

"Ma'am, she took half the dropper!"

"My word!" Aunt Lydia frowned. She began shaking Evelyn again and calling her name while patting her cheeks. "Haven't you any smelling salts, girl?"

I shook my head. Granmam didn't believe in such things. She'd say if a body was meant to sleep, let it, but I don't think she'd ever seen anything like this.

"I'll go make some coffee," I said. "That should help."

I ran back downstairs. I turned the ham, which was almost burned, and luckily there were still potatoes from last night that I just reheated in the pan with four eggs. While it cooked, I hurried upstairs with the coffee.

Lydia was patting Evelyn's hand, still calling her name. Mistress was murmuring to be left alone. I handed Aunt Lydia the coffee, then moved to go back downstairs.

"Wait! You have to help me get her to drink it. Hold her head." She poured some of the coffee into Evelyn's mouth, but it was hot and she spat most of it out onto the bedclothes. I was worried about Evelyn, but I couldn't help but tally my chores for the day, including rewashing these linens.

"Leave me 'lone," Mistress Evelyn slurred.

"Ma'am, perhaps we should do as she says and let her sleep a bit. I have to go serve Master Philippe breakfast, but I'll be back after I find out from Silvey what she knows about the medicine."

Aunt Lydia sighed. "I suppose. . . ." She shook her head at her niece and drank the coffee herself.

I went down and finally served Philippe his breakfast. It hadn't burned, since I had forgotten to stoke the fire before I set everything in the pan. Rev had come back in to the dining room and was trying to get a conversation out of Philippe. He wasn't having much luck.

"So . . . son . . . what are your prospects for a position?" Rev inquired.

Philippe shrugged and continued looking at his newspaper.

"Are you interested in farming?" Rev Jeff tried again.

"Maybe" was all Philippe replied, and he dug into his food immediately.

"Business?"

Philippe nodded and continued to chew.

I went down to my house, carrying toast. I hoped Silvey

could keep it down; I poured more of that tea I brewed last night and took it up to her. She was sleeping but sat up when I called her name. I told her what had happened.

Silvey laughed. "She been taking almost a half dropper of that for weeks now. She's got friends who take it, and they all take about that much. Why you think they all be fainting all the time? If it's not the tight corsets — it's that."

"But that's a dangerous medicine," I said, clicking my tongue in dismay. "You have to be careful with it."

"Well, when you deal with this family, you find out how much a body can take."

"What do you mean by that?"

"Just make sure she keeps her medicines close."

"Why does she need so many medications?"

"Pain." Silvey sipped her tea like she was not sure if she should like it.

My patience was growing thin. "From what? Just tell me. I have too many things to do."

"Promise you won't tell your pa *or* the Rev."

I laughed and thought, *Just add it to the list.* "I promise."

"Evelyn's first husband, Philippe's father, died, but he was old and she didn't care much 'cause her father had made her marry him. Her second husband didn't die in a carriage accident, like she be telling everyone. He didn't die at all. She was pregnant with his baby, but then she lost it. He left her when the doctors said she couldn't have no more children. He said he heard people were finding gold in California and he was going there to try to pay off their debts."

I was stunned into silence. Once I gathered my wits, I asked, "But what if he comes back?"

"Well, he wrote some months ago and asked to have all his things sent down to Texas. Her friend in South Carolina is married to one of his brothers. She said Mr. Richard had found a señorita and she was already big with his baby. Evelyn's father paid some judge to say they never was married."

"That's terrible! Poor Evelyn. No wonder she's so . . ."

"Oh, don't feel too sorry for her! She's been like this since for as long as I can remember, just without the medicines to keep her smiling. I think Mr. Richard would've left sooner but didn't have a good enough excuse. They both liked to spend money too much. Now Evelyn's father's putting his foot down. He wants to see her married so Philippe can have decent prospects. I should've begged Mr. Richard to take me with him."

"But don't you think she'll tell Rev?"

"Not as long as she can help it. And you better not, either." Silvey lay back down. Her teacup was still half full, but the toast was gone. "So now you got to deal with her today. Like I said, just keep her medicine close and make sure she eats something soon. She's a good one for getting food made and not eating nothing. Then she'll spew the medicine, so it's better she eats. That tea she has is from the doctor, too, for between the times she takes the tincture in the morning and the rum she drinks at night. Oh, and I packed smelling salts in her bag."

"You're looking much better, Silvey," I tried. "Don't you think you can come and help me? I could really use you."

"Huh! You ain't *using* me," she said, and pulled the blankets around her chin. "I still feel ill, but I'll get up in the afternoon if you do a few things for me."

I thought of how I just brought her breakfast in bed and cleaned up her vomit, but I wanted her to cover for me so I could go see Cato. "What?"

"Get Mistress and her aunt dressed . . . and bring me some rum or whiskey for this tea. . . ."

Dressing Aunt Lydia meant laying out her undergarments, helping her into them, and hooking up the back of the dress. She kept her hair braided and twisted in a bun. It wasn't so bad. Mistress Evelyn, on the other hand, was a trial indeed. Luckily, Lydia stayed to help. We had to use the smelling salts to wake her, then struggled to get her to eat the egg and toast. When we finally got her on her feet,

Mistress Evelyn seemed to want to twirl around in her nightgown rather than get dressed. I reckoned she felt good being up and about without that corset trap on.

"Catch her before she runs downstairs!" Aunt Lydia hissed. She was highly agitated and had sat down to catch her breath. We got Mistress Evelyn to drink several cups of the sweet cream coffee I made for her, and she seemed nearly sober by the time we put her in her corset.

I could tell she was sobering because she began criticizing everything I did.

"You haven't tied the corset tight enough. . . . Ouch! That's too tight! You have no idea how to tie it correctly? What an idiot!"

"I think I hear Rev calling me," I lied. "I have to go see to him."

"Don't you dare leave yet! Finish helping me dress."

I put her dress over her head, hooked the fasteners hastily, and practically ran out the door.

"You'd better come back and do my hair!"

Rev caught me on the stairs. "Willow, what goes on up there? Isn't Evelyn dressed yet?"

"She . . . she wasn't feeling so well this morning, Rev." We walked back downstairs together.

"Ah, yes. She is so very delicate, my fragile little flower. That's why we must take special care of her. You of all people can understand chronic illness."

"Well, what is it that she has?" I wondered what he would tell me.

"She takes medicine for her pain, poor dear. Her second husband died in a carriage accident—she was with him and suffered some internal injuries. That is why I'm so delighted to have her live at Knotwild, Willow. She will be able to rest and soothe her nervous condition."

We stood at the bottom of the stairs. "I suppose you know best, Rev."

He patted my shoulder and smiled kindly as he turned to go into his study. "Indeed, with God's guidance."

I found some whiskey that Gran used to use in emergencies for folks in need of a painkiller, or as a base to make herbal liniments and tonics. She once had to give it to one of the hands when his ear nearly got chopped off in an accident. It was the only thing that quieted him enough for her to sew the thing back on. I tucked the bottle into the inside pocket of my apron.

"Whatchu got there, gal?" It was Cholly. Never in my life had I seen this man hang around the house so much.

"Nothing." I tried to move past him, but he stood in my way. "*Whatchu* doing up here?" I asked, mimicking him.

"Coming to have our talk."

"I'm too busy with the guests. I'll explain everything after they go."

"*Everything,* you say?"

I ignored his question. "Cholly, I have to go tend to Silvey. Do you mind telling Tiny I need her help up here?"

"Sure can, miss. If you tell me what's that there in your apron pocket."

I was pretty sure he had seen me hide it. There was no excuse I could figure except the truth.

"Silvey is still having chills and aches; Gran used to use it for a cure." I took out the bottle and showed it to him. "I just didn't want Rev or Papa to disapprove."

He had a good laugh at that. Most of his back teeth were missing, so it was like looking down a cavern. "So how come nobody use it on me when I get sick?"

I pushed past him. " 'Cause we wouldn't want to waste it on the likes of you!"

He laughed out loud as I walked away.

I made sure to give Silvey only a small amount in the cup. I kept the bottle downstairs. I realized I could use it to make an herbal tincture for Cato. Just a little with herbs steeped in it would help him bear his pain better. I reckon this was why so many folks got hooked on drinking. Getting rid of physical pain was something Gran knew about, except she treated it mostly with herbs. She said most people's pain settled deep down in their heart, even after the bruises were gone. There were no cures for that.

"This all you got?" Silvey demanded. "Where's the rest?"

"This is all you get," I said without batting an eye. She was in my territory now.

"Fine. I'm feeling right enough to go see to Mistress Evelyn," she said after gulping down the drink. "You dress her?"

"Wait a minute. You feel better just like that?"

"Sure. Sometimes a little drink is all it takes."

I shook my head. "She's dressed. But I left her hair for you to do. I wouldn't know where to start."

Silvey sighed. "And I was having such a nice day. . . ."

I went back downstairs while she dressed. After pouring a bit of the whiskey into a small glass bottle, I took the rest back to Gran's hiding place in the kitchen. How did Silvey know we had whiskey? I hadn't thought of how much was in it before last night. I suddenly wondered if she was going to drink Mistress Evelyn's rum since I hadn't given her much of the whiskey.

After finding a new hiding place for the bottle, I set about clearing Rev and Philippe's breakfast dishes. I had seen them walk down toward the fields as I went into the kitchen. Tiny finally came in.

"Well, you sure got your hands full, huh?" She laughed and took some dishes out of my arms.

"Silvey's sick, so I've been tending to both the gentlemen and the ladies."

"I saw your papa on my way up here, and he tole me you ain't slep last night. Why don't you go take a rest and I'll do the dishes? You don't have to do nothing till they lunch, right?"

Just then Silvey came in, grunted at both of us, and went up the back stairs. We could hear Mistress Evelyn scolding her as soon as she opened the bedroom door.

I was about to speak when the door to the bedroom opened again. Evelyn was listing all of the horrors she had to endure from me. The door closed, and the sound of Aunt Lydia's slow, steady footfalls came down the front stairs.

"Lemme go see if she needs anything. . . ." I excused myself and went into the sitting room.

"Ma'am?"

Madam Lydia turned to me and her face was nearly impossible to read. Her frown lines were the same as Mrs. Rose. "Come here, girl."

I went and stood before her and curtsied, trying to seem friendly.

"I realize you were acting outside of your usual duty this morning; you've certainly never been a lady's maid before. My niece needs a great deal of attention since her . . . accident. I want to express my gratitude for your assistance."

Aunt Lydia untied a little velvet pouch that was hanging around her wrist, just like the one Mrs. Rose gave to Silvey. She reached in and withdrew four shiny coins. She went to drop them in my hand.

"Oh! No, ma'am! I can't take that!" I somehow felt honored by her regard.

She did not withdraw her hand. "I'm sure that this token will help you to remember not to *ever* mention any of this to your master."

My pride sunk deep; she just wanted to pay me for my secrets. She seemed to take my silence as a signal to withdraw two more coins from her purse and drop them into my apron pocket.

I was so stunned that I only nodded.

"Bring me some tea," she said.

I curtsied on my way out.

As I was coming back from giving Lydia her tea, Silvey came down the back stairs. "Her Highness is back in bed," she said. "You're to tell the Reverend that she is simply too weak from all the travel and begs his forgiveness if she does not join him until dinner."

"What? Rev had plans for the day. . . . He was . . ."

"Why are you worried about white folks' business?"

"I'm not! I'm just . . . He'll be disappointed, and I don't like bringing bad news."

"Listen, girl. My aunt gave me a good piece of advice—only know enough about them to keep yourself one step ahead of them. It don't matter what they think or feel, 'less it got something to do with you." She carved off a thick slice of bread and buttered it generously. "Oh, and Mistress say her room is cold and she want more tea," she said between bites.

I pursed my lips, then pointed at the woodpile, the kettle, and the teacups and left.

Poor Rev's face fell considerably when I told him the news. He had been walking with Philippe and I'm sure his company was trying Rev's patience.

"If you please, sir," I said, "I'm feeling a bit tired myself. After I tidy up the bedrooms and prepare your afternoon meal and tea, do you mind if Tiny and Silvey serve you? I'd like to take a rest before I prepare dinner."

"Of course, Willow. I wouldn't want you to take sick again." Rev excused himself, so I was left standing there with Philippe, who was studying me carefully.

I excused myself with a curtsy and went back to the house, made the beds, and emptied the slop jars. Philippe's stank horribly, so I had to cover my face with a rag. The dust made me sneeze, and a good bit of his mess splashed out, which nearly made me bring up my breakfast.

After having to clean all of that up, I knocked softly on Evelyn's door. Silvey called me in.

"Hey!" She waved at me from where she lounged on the settee. A bottle of the Heal-All was open beside her. Mistress Evelyn was sleeping soundly — snoring, in fact.

"I'll need you to help Tiny serve lunch and tea," I said without looking at her. I didn't want to see her like this. I picked up the bottle, stuffed the cork into it, and put it back in Mistress Evelyn's bag. A bottle of pills had spilled out.

"I ain't a serving wench, and I ain't the cook. I'm the lady's maid. That's what I do," she said, pointing her thumb at her chest.

"Well, around here everybody helps out when asked." I realized that I was the only one whispering. "So now I'm telling you that Rev is expecting you. I'll set things up downstairs before I go. And since you're *the lady's maid,* you can service the ladies by taking out their . . . leavings."

Silvey sucked her teeth. "Already did it. I can't stand being in the room with the smell of her piss — all those medicines make her water stink."

"Silvey! Did you give her those pills, too?" I realized why she felt comfortable to speak and act so freely.

"She was all worked up, worried her secrets will get found out." Silvey only lowered her voice a bit. "So I figured it'd help her relax."

I stood over Mistress Evelyn, who was stretched out diagonal on the bed; I lifted up her hand to feel her pulse. It was weak and slow, and she didn't seem to even notice I was touching her.

"C'mon. Let's let her rest, then. I need you to . . . act right . . . so Papa won't find out. He calls it 'drinking the devil' when people are . . ."

"Are what?" Silvey stood up, then lost her balance and had to sit right back down. This time she at least tried to lower her voice. "I ain't drunk! This ain't drunk! You so pure, you don't even know."

I remained silent and helped her get up by anchoring her arm around my shoulder, but she struggled with me. I watched as she attempted to get up three times before she let me help her again. This was the most pathetic thing I'd seen. Papa always used to talk about Cholly Dee drinking, but I'd never once seen him like this, even when he was roaming around Baltimore.

We made it down the back stairs with Silvey only falling on her butt once. I brewed her some strong coffee and gave her some food while I prepared lunch. I made a quick soup from the leftover turkey and made cornmeal bread. While Silvey fell asleep in front of the fire, I went to find Tiny. Hopefully Silvey would be sober enough for her not to notice anything strange, either.

•   •   •

"I'm happy to help, Willow. You didn't even have to fix nothing. I just made up one of my meat pies!" Tiny said as we walked back into the kitchen. She used squirrel meat for her pies, and I didn't think Mistress Evelyn or Aunt Lydia would fancy it. However, when I looked at my timepiece and saw how late it was getting, I thought only of Cato. I hoped to see him in the clear daylight, to look him in the eyes when we spoke. It was enough to drive me mad — to just see his eyes one more time. For a second, I thought of what it would be like to press my lips against his. . . . That would truly be a first kiss to remember, especially if I never saw him again.

"Go 'head and do that pie for dinner, Tiny," I said. If Mistress Evelyn and Madam Lydia didn't like it, they'd just have to starve.

As Tiny and I walked into the kitchen, there was Silvey, reaching for the whiskey bottle I thought I had so carefully hidden.

I snatched it from her hand and poured the whole bottle out the window. Silvey burst into tears. It took everything in me not to slap her.

"Little Luck!" she sobbed.

"What's he got to do with this?" I demanded.

"He's gone!"

"What! Where?"

"He's gone!" She was almost hysterical now. I wanted to shake her, but Tiny put a gentle arm around her.

"Slow down, honey. Tell us what happened."

Silvey hiccupped several times before she was able to say "Telegram."

Tiny turned to me, confused. "What's *telegram?*"

"They're like posted letters, but you get them real quick," I explained. I handed Silvey a glass of water, which she sipped.

"A man on a horse came from town with the message just now. Said it was the first telegram they ever got over there, 'cause they just put in the wires."

"How they get paper to get through a little wire?" Tiny wanted to know.

"Aunt Lydia read it and I heard her tell the Rev. They think he ran here to be with me! I tole him to stay put!" Silvey wailed.

"Well, that's good news, at least," I said, trying to cheer her.

"You stupid fool!" she shouted at me. "How's a deafmute going to find his way out here without getting caught? Or getting eaten by some mountain lion? He don't know where we at!"

"There, there, chile," Tiny coaxed her. "You don't know what miracles can happen."

"He *is* very smart," I said, trying again. "Remember how he found that peach for Mistress? He can find most anything, I'm sure."

"Who knows what could happen to him out there! It's at least a two- or three-day walk — more if he gets lost. Even if no one catches him" — Silvey began to sob again — "Mistress will probably have him whipped or locked in the cellar, or . . ."

"Or sell him," Tiny said, finishing her sentence. I don't think she even knew what she was saying; she was just saying what we were all thinking. Silvey melted into another puddle of tears.

"Oh, but she won't do that! Especially if he was just coming here!" I tried to reason with her.

"She been talking about selling him since she saw this dress in Baltimore she wants to get married in. Her father said he won't pay for a new dress for her third wedding." Silvey wiped her nose on her apron as she explained. "But she's set on having some of those newfangled portraits taken. She always be whispering to her friend how she could sell Luck for the dress and still have plenty left over for shoes!" That plunged her into another deep well of tears.

"But the Reverend won't let her do that!" Tiny said with confidence. She still had faith in the Rev, but I wasn't sure if I did.

"You got to talk to him, Willow."

Their faces were fixed in such a way that I couldn't say no. Silvey's eyes were huge with hopeful tears. Tiny looked like she had faith that I could make things right. I wanted to run from them both, leave them there in the kitchen, run past the house and the barn and the stables and straight past my tree, even over the line into Pennsylvania. I wanted to run straight to Cato's arms. . . . I couldn't look at Silvey or Tiny, afraid they'd know what little courage I had.

Looking at my watch, I said, "I can't . . . right now. But when I come back . . . I'll do it when I come back."

"Come back? From where? Where you be running off to now?" Silvey demanded.

"Now, now," Tiny coaxed. "Willow be the house-keeper 'round here. She got business to tend to. She say she do it later, it'll be done."

"Housekeeper, my eye! I reckon she be off on a frolic in the woods with her beau! Riding horses like she own the place! You ain't white!" Silvey spat.

My jaw dropped, but no words fell out. My heart stopped beating — until I realized she meant Raymond, not Cato.

"Girl, I had about enough of you!" I had never seen Tiny so vexed. "You just a guest here." She removed her arm from around Silvey's shoulder with disdain and grabbed my hand protectively. "And Willow here done everything in her power to comfort you when you was sick and took care of your own mistress. You don't know from nothing how sickly she is her own self, and if she wants to take a break and see Raymond or tend to something else before doing another favor for you, you and me gone do everything we can to help her."

Silvey hung her head. "You're right, Tiny," she finally admitted. "Sorry, Willow. I'm just so worried . . . and scared." She put her hand on her belly and then closed her eyes, squeezing out a few last tears.

I accepted her apology, but Tiny wasn't so satisfied.

"And another thing: if you don't keep outta that liquor, I'm gone have to talk to Ryder, and he be harder on you than your mistress and the Rev combined—'specially if he thought you was abusing his daughter's kindness. Go wash out your mouth and clean up your face."

"Yes, ma'am" was all Silvey could say. She got up and went outside to the pump spigot.

"She a sour one, for sure," Tiny remarked when Silvey was gone. "I seen girls like her before—got venom for anyone who look like they might take they scraps. Comes from living so close up, you know"—she pointed upstairs to indicate Mistress Evelyn—"to those that gots more than they. Lady's maids always be a little high on theyself, but they really just tired of having nothing. Shame, really."

"She's just worried about Little Luck. He's one of those

kinds of young folks that make you want to do right by them. She's rarely apart from him. You don't know what she's been through, Tiny. I see some of it now and can hardly blame her being vexed." But I also knew that I was not putting up with any more of her foolishness.

"And her brother's all she's got, huh? He deaf *and* mute? He need her."

"You know what, Tiny? I'm beginning to think that she needs *him* even more."

"I got here soon as I could!" I called out, climbing down into the riverbed. My spirits fell when I found I was talking to myself. Stupid of me to think he'd still be here. I had to check my feelings. Becoming passionate about someone I'd never see again was foolish.

I looked into my old hiding spot and pulled out my journal. I thumbed through the pages and found a page scattered with Cato's beautiful scrawl:

> *Not to worry — I am safe. Will return tonight, searching for you.*

I sighed with relief . . . and disappointment as I put the copybook back in its place. Goose pimples raised on my arms and the back of my neck. I felt my cheeks burning as my mind conjured up a fantasy of Cato and finding an excuse to have him lie in my arms again. I don't know how long I sat there like that, images running through my head of Cato, his face, the way he talked, all the things he knew. Cato had sparked a flame inside of me, one that I could not deny or ignore, one that I wanted to bring light to every dark corner of my soul.

"Well, now . . . Willow," Rev's voice called out. I nearly jumped out of my skin to see him standing there at the riverbank.

"Rev, what you doing out here?"

"Perhaps I should be asking that of you." The sun was shining, so I couldn't see his eyes through the shadow his hat was making over his face. The tone in his voice was even, but he was clearly agitated.

"Oh, sir, I didn't mean it that way. You know I just come here to think . . . and pray." I remembered what Papa said about acting different around whites when they ran their world with lies and deceit. "I just wanted to take a break, sir. It's been . . . I just wanted some fresh air."

"Yes, I'm sure this has all been quite a bit of excitement for you, to say the least." Rev made a motion like he was planning to climb down to where I was, but I leaped up and came to his level first. I didn't want him to see my hiding spot.

"Is everything OK at the house?" I asked.

"Yes, Silvey and Tiny are doing fine. Evelyn has gotten

up and eaten the soup you made. I had her try your special tea, and it seemed to relieve some of her . . . pain.

"So what'd you come all the way out here for, Rev?"

"Why do you question me, Willow?"

I was struck by the ice in his words. The only thing I could think to do was to curtsy and beg his pardon.

"I . . . I just wondered . . . 'cause you, don't usually come all the way out here. I . . . thought something might be wrong. . . ." I coughed.

Rev quietly studied the ground for a moment.

"I'm thinking about plowing up all this land," he said, motioning all around me with his walking stick. "I need to expand Knotwild's earnings. My future betrothed has extensive needs, so we will be trying out a new crop."

"Yes, Cholly said that. I remember now." I was trying not to seem frightened by the idea of folks working so close to my sacred place.

"Cholly Dee? Oh, yes. He would be the one in charge of things out here. I think that Philippe will start off by managing an office for me in Baltimore, to handle our business in the markets, since we will be exporting more goods."

"Very good, sir." I tried to remain as obedient as I could. "I'm sure you make the best decisions for Knotwild."

"Yes, I try," he said, looking deeply into my eyes. "And you? Are you happy with your decision?"

"I . . ." From the corner of my eye, I swore I saw

something or someone peek out from behind a tree—Cato! What was he doing here now? He said we would meet tonight! I fought to regain my senses.

"Yes, Rev, of course," I said hastily. He looked over his shoulder, in the direction I had seen the figure, but neither of us saw anything stir. How could I convince him that we had to leave?

"I did want to talk to you about something, Willow. What have you done with the cookbook I gave you?"

"I kept it safe, sir. I hid it in my room, with Granmam's things."

"Yes, well, I need to make sure of that. I want you to bring it to me after dinner tonight."

"Of course, sir. Let's return to the house and I can get it for you right now."

"No," he said firmly. "After dinner. I want to have a discussion with you *and* your father."

"Yes, sir."

"I want you to return home now and supervise Tiny making this meat pie for dinner. I know she is very proud of it, but I want you to make sure she uses lamb instead of some other . . . inferior meat. The ladies have delicate palates, so I want you to see to it that the food is not spoiled or burned for dinner tonight. It's your duty to oversee all of this, not Tiny's."

"Rev . . . I . . ." There was no use arguing. His jaw

was set in the way that I knew he would not be open to discussion.

As I turned to leave, all I could do was say a prayer that Cato would have the sense to keep himself hidden from Rev. I nearly lost my senses with fear.

"Willow, are you ill?" Rev's voice was truly concerned as I pretended to faint against him; it made me feel bad to trick him, but it was the only way to keep him from seeing Cato.

"I don't know. . . . I've just been . . . tired." It was the only thing I could think of that wasn't a complete lie. "I'll be fine."

I hesitated again, waiting for Rev to offer to take me back home. He didn't.

"You just need a good rest," he said. "Have Tiny and Silvey do all of the cleaning up tonight. You'll go straight to bed after you, your father, and I have had our talk. Then for the next two days, Lydia, Evelyn, and I will be traveling to visit one of their cousins who lives nearby. You'll only have Philippe to tend to. I will be driving us in the little trap since it isn't too far, and so your father can stay to show Philippe how things work around here. Now, go back home right away. You are clearly not meant to be out in the cold. I'm afraid we are at the end of our Indian summer."

"Yes, of course you're right, sir. But I did want to talk to you about something. . . ."

"Can't it wait?"

"Well, it's about Little Luck, Silvey's brother. . . ."

"I know about it, but it has nothing to do with you nor I. He is the property of Mistress Evelyn's father, so I have no influence in his fate."

"He only ran because he's scared of being without his sister! They're very close, sir. He can't sleep without her."

"Again, I have no say in the matter whatsoever, and neither do you. The best thing for you to do right now is to return to Knotwild and console Silvey."

"But, Rev . . . I'm not sure I can make it back by myself. What if I have another spell?"

"Willow, I'm sure you'll be fine." There was annoyance in his tone again. "Go on, now. I'll be along soon."

I could do nothing but return to the house. I walked slowly, with heavy feet. The forest was at her most beautiful—dressed in yellow and bronze. She flaunted her colors as a breeze shifted and sent leaves dancing as if to some of that wild music I heard coming from the saloons in Baltimore. I was unable to stop to appreciate it. Instead, I held my bonnet close to my face with one hand, clutched my cloak closer to my throat, and quickened my pace.

As I got closer to the house, I saw that someone was walking in my direction; first I thought it was Rachel's husband—she'd asked for me to send down some of Granmam's salve, since one of her little ones cut himself on a nail. Then I saw it was none other than Cholly Dee, clearly ready to collect on this talk he wanted me to have, even though I'd already told him to wait till the guests left. I was surely not yet ready to tell him anything. My mind had been so set on getting Cato mended enough to get himself home, but now I wasn't sure that should be my only goal. I didn't want Cholly questioning me, but still I wondered if there was a way he could help me help Cato.

Cholly Dee boldly walked up to me. "Gal, you 'bout ready to fess up?"

"Cholly, I am most certainly grateful that you assisted me the other night. However, I have no wrongdoings to confess." I was trying to sound as proper as I could.

He smiled. "Oh, you think so? Well, you know, maybe you be right. I had been thinking 'bout what you said before, how it wasn't your fault you didn't know 'bout your mama. I reckoned I would share some of my memory about her, but if you thinks we even up here, then I'll be on my way." Cholly tipped his hat and turned away. I caught his elbow and clutched his arm.

"Wait! I . . . I suppose you're"—I had to spit out the word—"right."

He shook me off of him roughly and had the nerve to say, "Naw, now my feelings hurt."

"Cholly, please. I'll tell you everything," I said. "From the beginning."

"That's more like it," he said. "Go 'head. I'm ready to listen." He sat himself down on a tree stump like it was a throne.

I told him about the day I first saw Cato in the woods, how I went to the auction looking to see if it was the same man I saw, and it wasn't.

"And that's all, really. I've been looking, but I don't see anybody out there anymore. I just go out there to . . . think and pray. I talk to my mama. That's all."

Cholly studied me carefully for a long uncomfortable moment. He broke a sliver of wood off the stump he was sitting on and used it to pick his teeth. "Now, you and I both know well and good that ain't *all.*"

"I've told you a lot, Cholly. Why don't you tell me a little something about my mama and I'll see if I can think of anything more to say."

He laughed. "You bargaining? That's more like it! I'll tell you that your mama was quite sharp with her words as well. Never could get one over on Adlile."

Hearing him say her full name made me sit down in the very spot I had been standing. I repeated it in my head but couldn't seem to get it to come out of my mouth. It was too precious to let go.

"Tell me more, please. What else was she like?"

"That's all."

"What?"

"Gal, you the one who set up the rules. I'm just playing your game."

"Fine. I'll tell you something no one else knows. But then you have to tell me something no one else knows about my mother."

Cholly looked me deep in the eye. "What if the only thing I know is something you might not want to hear?"

I had to think hard on that. "Is it the truth? Will you swear to it?"

"Gal, I swear that I only ever tell you the truth, just 'cause you Adlile's daughter. Can you think of a time when I told you something you found to be a lie?"

He was right—he didn't lie to me, far as I could reckon. I thought of how he had tried to warn me about the bears out by the river. Though I was quite sure that there was a whole heap of truths he wasn't telling me, I hadn't yet found him to be a liar.

"All right, then, Cholly Dee. I'll tell you something nobody knows: I can read."

I thought he'd be impressed or shocked but he just shrugged his shoulders and stood up and stretched. "I already done figured that."

"I can write, too."

He smiled and patted my shoulder. "Good for you! That would have pleased your mama indeed."

"Really? What makes you say so?"

"She could read and write her ownself."

I gasped. "Did Papa and Rev teach her? Did Granmam know?"

He took off his hat and scratched his head. "I don't recall for certain if your granmam knew, but I do remember when I was a boy in our village that Adlile's father was the schoolmaster."

"What?" I didn't think they would have schools in Africa. I didn't think anyone could read or write there — I thought they were savages.

He scoffed. "Her papa taught all the young boys; I reckon it was in his own home. He had traveled and knew languages, like Arabby, I think they called it. We was all followers of *Islam* in our village. He read the big religious books; I 'member that. That's how Adlile learned. It wasn't something she showed off to everybody. It was taboo for her to read in Africa, too, but she was her father's favorite. I reckon it was 'cause she was so bright."

He stopped talking, and I could see that his eyes were lakes of tears just before he wiped his arm over his face.

"Cholly, I never . . ." I reached out to touch him, but he got up and stepped away. I reckoned *Arabby* meant "Arabic." I had read about it in one of Rev's books. It was ancient and mysterious, the book said, and it was spoken throughout northern and sometimes western Africa and even in Europe.

"Nobody knew when she got here, and I don't think she told no one else."

"But my papa had to've known. He could read a little. She would have told him!"

"She didn't know how to read and write in white people's words, just the Arabby. She might've tried to figure out the English, too, but don't know that for certain."

"So you can read and write it, too?"

"Naw, not much no more. I was young. . . . It was too many bad memories."

"Why are they so bad?"

"All my bad memories is of that school," he said. "I can think of nothing else bad about my life back then. My mother and father was loving and kind; I was the eldest son, so I had much respect."

"Then what?" I demanded.

"That's all! I ain't goin' back in my head for them memories!"

"Please, Cholly," I begged. "Please just tell me."

"It was at the school where my fate changed for the worse! We was there when . . ." Cholly sat himself down again — this time like he wasn't sure if he could stand back up. He couldn't hardly take his face out of his hands.

"When?" I felt like a blind dog gnawing on some dry old bone.

"*They* took us! And they killed your mother's father,

right in front of us. They . . . burned his books . . . and . . . chopped him."

"Dear God — you mean . . . his head?"

Cholly Dee nodded with his face still in his hands and sighed deeply. I was in shock.

"My mother? My mother saw this as well?"

"No," he said, sighing deeply, relieved. "No, she was away at that time. I can 'member her telling me she was going for a long visit to see her mother's sister, who lived in another village. I 'member 'cause I told her how much I was gone miss her, and I was sad that whole day for missing her. Her father even scolded me — the only time I ever caught trouble in school, far as I can recall — and it wounded my feelings. It wasn't long after when the men came with guns."

I was relieved to know she had been spared that horror, though it made me nearly weep to think of my mother returning to her home, only to find out what had happened to her father and her friend.

"I never saw her again until she was brought here many years later," Cholly said, composing himself. "It was . . . was like a . . . a terrible miracle to see her and know what she suffered. We was in Baltimore at the market and your papa was . . . We was all close back then. Rev, too. Rev's father, Master Jeffries, had promised to find Ryder a wife to take back with us to Knotwild. It was something Master

Jeffries had tole your grandad Ezra he would do before Ezra died that spring. Ezra wanted his son to get married proper—just like he and his wife, your granmam, did. To have it written down in Rev's big family Bible."

So it wasn't just Papa who liked things so "proper." But that wasn't the story I wanted to hear right now.

"My mother . . . When she first came here, what happened?"

"I tole you I ain't goin' into that, gal." He looked away from me, toward the northwest, where the sun was moving like she was eager to meet the night. It was late afternoon, but the daylight hours were shorter.

"Cholly . . . What did you mean when you said Papa had 'won' my mother?"

"I told you enough. I shouldn't've said nothing." He paused and shook his head.

"Please! Tell me more! Tell me anything about her. I have more secrets I can tell you. . . ." I was prepared to tell him about Mistress Evelyn and her expensive habits, and maybe even about Silvey's drinking if it meant knowing more about my mother. I'd tell him everything . . . except about Cato.

"Gal, ain't you tired of carrying all these secrets? I know I am."

I reached out to him again, and this time he let me rest my hand lightly on his shoulder. "Cholly, don't you see? I need to know! Even hearing about the worst of my mother would help me to navigate my burdens."

"What burdens you got? Spending all your time reading and writing and riding your own damn horse? Waiting on the fancy lady up in the big house? Them burdens?"

"You don't understand. . . ." I began, but suddenly the coins in my apron pocket felt especially heavy, reminding me I had been paid for my silence.

"Or is it the burdens of getting married all proper-like when most gals your age *who look like you* done already been made to have a kid without much consideration to they *feelings* or *desires*."

That riled me up. "Nobody giving consideration to me and who I want to marry so properly! Everybody telling me about my duty and responsibility. Yes, I *do* want to read and write and ride my horse! I *don't* want that to change. I want to care for my family and be useful, but why can't I at least be with the one I love?"

Cholly stared at me. "Just like . . ." I thought I heard him mutter.

"Like my mother was?" I asked. Just then I heard Silvey calling out to me. I turned to see her walking up from the kitchen with a lantern.

". . . she is . . ."

"What?" I nearly broke my neck as I turned back to

Cholly, but he was already walking away into the darkening woods.

"I don't know how you all do down here, but in our kitchen at home, we don't eat no squirrels," Silvey said, out of breath. "Maybe the field folks like it, but Mistress won't eat none of that mess that little woman's cooking up."

I sighed. "You could find something nice to say, Silvey. Back in Baltimore you weren't so . . ."

"Back in Baltimore, things was different," she spat.

"I know that," I said, "but you're making things worse."

We walked the rest of the way back to the house in silence.

Tiny was bustling around the kitchen. There were squirrel carcasses on the table, ready to be skinned and drained.

"Thank you, Tiny, but if you don't mind, I think we'll use lamb this time. You've already made a beautiful crust, I see. Papa says my crust's like sand. Can you show me how you season the meat so well?"

"'Course, Willow; I know gentlefolk have different tastes from yours and mine."

"It's true," I said, glad her feelings weren't hurt. "I'll grind up the lamb."

"Guess I'll mash up the last of those potatoes," Silvey

chimed in, to our surprise. "And I'm sure you'll also need to make some kind of soup to quiet Philippe's appetite."

We were silenced by her consideration.

"What're y'all lookin like that for?" Silvey demanded. "I can be nice, too! Just till Mistress gets up and wants to get dressed for dinner, no mistake."

"Well, what an honor!" Tiny teased. We all laughed, and the weight of the room lifted. It made the work seem less bothersome.

Silvey did a little work but mostly entertained us with stories of the city and the villainous and wondrous things she had witnessed. She told us how she and Mistress traveled to Boston one spring and made the mistake of staying over in New York on the first of May. Every year, that day was reserved for housing leases to change, and everyone who rented had to up and move on the same day. I guessed the lawmakers reckoned it'd be best to get it over all in one day, but it clearly must've been a sight to see! Silvey said she saw a team of oxen dragging a whole house down Broadway. The police said the owner had built the house on land that wasn't his but couldn't bear to build another home from scratch, so he pulled up the house, from the cornerstone to the attic eaves, and caused the most miserable day in the city. The traffic, noise, and the very spectacle was almost impossible to imagine.

"And then this woman wearing a pink-and-purple-and-green-plaid dress, thinking she was so fine, was trying to cross the street and nearly got trampled by a cart carrying a whole family and their belongings. The horses reared up and she got covered in muck! The policeman tried to pull her out of the street, but that family was screaming 'cause she upset all their things, including the piano they was carrying. It sat in the middle of the street for nearly the rest of the day till they could move it, but someone had the mind to start playing in the middle of everything! Oh, I nearly lost my water!"

Tiny laughed so hard, she almost backed into the fire. None of us noticed Philippe standing in the doorway until he cleared his throat. Silvey stood as stiff as a plank.

"Mother wants you. She's been ringing the bell," he said, but did not return to the front rooms.

"Thank you, sir," I said, trying to end the conversation. He looked at me without expression. "Was my fault, sir. I was just boiling water for Mistress's tea. Silvey was waiting on me."

He turned and left without a word.

"That was real clever, Willow." Tiny gave me a nudge. Luckily I had been boiling water in a pot for something else—more eggs for Cato. I wanted to take him some more food tonight. I quickly poured the water into a teapot and Silvey took a tray up, but her hands were shaking. I couldn't tell if it was 'cause she was frightened still, or if maybe it was for need of a drink. I glanced over at Tiny to see if she had noticed it. Our eyes locked and she raised her eyebrows.

"I'm not saying nothing," she declared.

"Me, neither," I agreed.

While the ladies were dressing for dinner (and why, I wondered, did they need to wear different clothes to different meals?) I went down to our cabin. Papa was there, smoking his pipe by the cold fire. I could barely look him in the eye as I spun my thoughts around Cholly's last words.

"You know Rev wants to have a word with us after dinner?" He didn't even say hello.

"Yes, I saw him earlier," I answered. I began to make the herbal tincture for Cato, hoping Papa wouldn't ask me who it was for. "He also said he was taking the ladies to see some of their family for the next day or so. Philippe will be staying on to get an understanding of the farm, he said."

Papa grunted and shifted noisily in his chair. I knew this news was irritating him. It broke my heart a little. His world was changing without his control. Just like mine. I wished he could see it that way.

"Didn't seem to me like Philippe was too interested in farming, though. Rev says he's setting him up to handle business in Baltimore," I told him.

"I know."

While Papa brooded, I continued to fix the tincture, adding herbs to the little bottle of whiskey I'd saved. Then I diluted it with strong tea. I did hope it would ease Cato's pain, but I dreaded him leaving me behind.

"Ain't you supposed to be serving dinner?" Papa said, interrupting my thoughts.

"Yes . . . Are you coming up to eat in the kitchen now, or you want me to save you something?" I remembered what Rev had told me at the river about the cookbook.

"I'll come up in a bit," he answered as I went upstairs to get the book. "I'm going down to check on Samuel. Cholly said he was having a hard time these days with his arthritis."

"All right, Papa," I called from my loft. "I've been meaning to take him some more of that salve on the third shelf in the pantry. It should help ease the swelling."

I heard him leave as I opened Granmam's chest. Where had I put it? Not where I thought — under the blanket she made for my parents' wedding. I searched through the chest twice; I nearly tore up the room searching. The cookbook was not there.

Despite my panic about the book, dinner was easy enough with Tiny and Silvey in the kitchen to help me. I served and tried not to look at any of them, especially Rev. Mistress Evelyn seemed calmer, though she still leaned heavily on

Rev when they entered the dining room, but I'm sure it was 'cause she just liked hanging on him.

"Oh, Jefferson, you are so noble," Mistress Evelyn crooned as Rev escorted her to her seat. "Much like your namesake."

Rev laughed. "My mother was fond of Thomas Jefferson, true, but my father took the name Jefferson Jeffries because he wanted to be more American. Back in the early part of the century, when Great-Grandfather Zacharias had arrived from Switzerland, he was not welcomed because of his heritage. They used to call him a "dirty Swizzer." Great-Grandfather was a self-made man. He worked himself nearly dead building Knotwild from the ground up. He *and* Willow's great-great-grandparents."

I tried to busy myself with cutting equal slices of the meat pie and tried to ignore their eyes on me. I knew the story of my great-great-grandparents well enough. Granmam used to say that where the old master worked himself *nearly dead,* my great-great-grandparents worked building Knotwild *to their graves.*

Mistress Evelyn giggled nervously. "Such talk at the dinner table!"

"Well, it was Willow's grandfather Ezra who built this very table! I don't find it improper to acknowledge his contributions to our comfort," Rev replied.

"Reverend, so many men here in our fine country did

the same as *your* great-grandfather—made civilization out of the wild," Aunt Lydia said. "Which is noble, indeed. I am sure, of course, that he came from excellent European stock."

I think she was trying to politely change the subject away from slavery, but I couldn't help but wonder that if Rev's great-grandfather had made civilization out of the wild, weren't my great-great-grandparents doing the same?

"I don't know about that, dear Aunt Lydia." Rev laughed. "But this great land is built upon redemption, if not anything else, wouldn't you say?"

Aunt Lydia fanned herself so hard that she blew out one of the candles. "Well! I've never heard it put so . . . ungracefully." She acted like Rev had just picked his nose and wiped it on the word *America.* I thought what he was telling them was quite graceful.

"I'm sure that Jeff means that we all have a chance to be forgiven here, to start over," Mistress Evelyn said. "It's true that this country has given many people a chance to take advantage of that."

Everyone turned and looked at her, surprised. It was the clearest and nicest thing I'd ever heard her say. Rev caught her eye, and he reached out and squeezed her hand tenderly. I wondered if she was just talking about her husband who left her for Texas. Either way, it seemed to be what brought them together.

Mistress Evelyn giggled nervously and dabbed the corner of her eye while Philippe rolled his eyes. I took the awkward moment to start clearing their soup plates to serve the meat pie. They all seemed relieved to have something to distract them. I waited until Rev took his first bite. He caught my eye and nodded.

"Very good, Willow," he said. "Delicious."

I curtsied and took the dishes down to the kitchen. Silvey and Tiny were talking closely. They stopped as soon as I walked in.

"What?" I demanded. I was vexed about the cookbook. I knew the only person who could have—would have—taken it was Silvey or Papa. And although Papa was in a strange mood when we spoke, I thought he would've confronted me with it. I couldn't figure why Silvey would take it, but she was the only one up in my room without me.

Tiny got up and motioned for me to come with her. She opened up the cupboard door slowly. Inside, tucked in blankets and sleeping soundly, was Little Luck.

"He listened to the coach driver getting directions before we left," Silvey whispered.

"Listened? He's deaf!" I nearly raised my voice.

"Shhh! He reads lips pretty good. 'Course, he got lost, but I think he might've jumped on somebody's coach and rode most of the way."

"How'd you figure all this out?"

"We understand each other. We been together since he was born, and we figured out how to make hand signals. He taught himself to read my lips when I talked. He had to stay useful so Mistress wouldn't have an excuse to sell him or mistreat him . . . too much."

"It's nothing but a miracle!" Tiny exclaimed. "Willow, you should've seen them waving they hands about and even making pictures in the ashes!"

"I never saw you all doing that," I said.

"We don't do it much 'round folks we don't know or trust."

Her words stung. "Well, we gotta hide him somewhere — *not* in the house!" I said, knowing they would be wanting their next course upstairs soon, and Papa could come in any minute. "Tiny, you got to go find Cholly. But don't tell him it's for me, 'cause he may not come. Stay clear of Papa. Silvey, we gotta wake this boy up."

Less than five minutes later, Papa, Tiny, and Cholly all showed up in the kitchen at the same time.

"What's he doing here?" Papa wanted to know.

Silvey started trembling next to me. I stood in fear until I realized Papa meant Cholly Dee.

"Oh! I had this here sack of rice . . . to send down to the quarters. None a us could carry it down, so . . ."

"Fine," Papa interrupted. "Where's my dinner?"

"On the hearth," I told him, and he went to get it. I locked eyes with Cholly, silently begging him to go along. His expression was blank.

"Cholly," I said slowly, "this is real heavy and you gotta be careful not to rip the sack."

"I thinks I can handle all that, *Miz* Willow," he said, mocking my tone.

"I'll go, too," Silvey said. She started to head toward the door.

"That don't make no sense," Papa said from the kitchen table. "Why you need to go all the way down there with him when your job's up here?"

"Well, she's never seen the rest of the quarters, Papa. She didn't get a proper tour," I said, hoping he wouldn't notice the tremble in my voice.

"What kind of proper tour she getting now, in the dark?"

Silvey looked at me with panic in her eyes. Tiny stepped forward.

"I was just taking her down to meet the folks and see Rachel's twins."

I didn't think Tiny could lie like that, but I was grateful! "She got time before her mistress will need her, Papa. They haven't even rung for dessert yet."

Just then, of course, the bell rang.

I looked down just as Cholly picked up the sack of "rice." He paused for a moment, and I could tell he knew it wasn't rice.

"Well, whoever's coming, let's go," he said quickly. "I'll get 'er back before she's missed, Ryder."

"You better, Cholly Dee. I don't want to have to come looking," Papa said, and returned to eating his meal.

Cholly shook his head as they left.

I organized the fruit compote desserts on a tray. The glass made quite a noise, as my hands were clumsy.

"You better be careful, Willow," Papa said, scolding.

"Yes, Papa," I said, nearly breathless as I went up to serve.

Finally dinner was over and they were all sitting in the parlor talking. I cleared the dishes and started scraping the food into the pig's bucket. Papa had gone outside to smoke his pipe, so I used the time to finally boil eggs for Cato and gather up some more leftovers into a bundle. I couldn't help but think of him, even though the world was spinning all around me like a hurricane.

"He's safe," Silvey said, running in. "That Cholly Dee was real nice. He gave him his bed, even."

"I'm so relieved," I said, almost hugging her. Then I remembered the cookbook. "For Little Luck, that is."

"Cholly tole me to tell you not to worry; he keeping this secret for free. What'd he mean by that?"

"I—I don't know," I stammered. "Nothing, I'm sure. He says stupid things all the time."

Silvey eyed me carefully. I was trying to get up the courage to ask her if she took the book, but Papa came in.

"What are you girls in here whispering about?" he asked. "Now that my Willow finally has a companion her age, I'm 'fraid it'll lead her to mischief."

"Don't be silly, Papa!" I said, and laughed nervously.

Papa sat down. "Well, then, Silvey, tell me 'bout yourself. How long you been with your mistress?"

Silvey cleared her throat twice. "I been with her family since I was born," she said. "Her father said she could keep me when I was 'round twelve or eleven. Don't know for sure."

"You got people?"

"Yes, sir" was all she said.

"Well," Papa said, leaning forward, "where are they? How many you got?"

Silvey cleared her throat again. "My aunt stay in Annapolis with Mistress Evelyn's family. And I . . . I got a brother."

"Oh, yes," Papa said sympathetically. "Willow told me about his . . . ailments. The Reverend said something about him running off. How kind it was of your master to allow you two to live together. Did your brother disobey him often?"

"He didn't! He ain't like that!" Silvey was getting upset. "He just . . ."

The bell rang. I knew it was probably Mistress Evelyn, so I told Silvey to go. She nearly ran from the room.

"Papa! That was cruel," I said when she was gone. "She's been sick with worry about Little Luck. He only wants to be close to his sister."

"Now you know what I mean, about making sacrifices so we can stick together as a family. It's everything, and most people like us don't have the luxury."

"Don't you think I know that? Don't you think I'm sacrificing enough?" Both of us were surprised that I raised my voice at him. "I'm sorry. . . ." I was quick to apologize when I saw Papa's face, but then I realized that his look was because Rev was standing in the doorway.

"Oh . . . Rev . . . I . . ." There was nothing I could say.

"Willow, the ladies are getting ready to retire," he said coldly. "Please tend to their rooms and prepare their beds. Your father and I will meet you in my study."

"Yes, sir." I curtsied again, then gathered wood and coal and went up the back stairs to the guest room.

I could hear that the ladies were still talking downstairs,

so I opened the door without knocking. Silvey was taking a hearty swig of Mistress Evelyn's medicinal rum. She wiped her mouth and looked sheepish.

"I'm not saying I'm surprised," I said, pushing past her to start the fire. I knelt down and shoveled the ashes out of the hearth, then arranged the wood on the grate.

"You don't know what it's like!" she hissed. "I got problems you don't got!"

"And that's gonna help you solve them?" I asked, nodding toward the bottle.

"It helps. . . ."

"If it helped you so much, you'd already have a plan to take care of this mess with your brother instead of waiting for me to fix it." I lit a bundle of straw with a candle.

"I don't need nothing from you!"

"Well, then, why'd you take my things?"

"I don't want nothing from you!" she repeated, crying.

Her tears seemed real. While she calmed herself, I stirred up the coals until they turned red. I didn't know what to believe. I put a few of the hot coals into the brass bed warmer and slid it under the covers of the bed so the sheets wouldn't be too cold for the delicate ladies. It made me think of Cato, who was probably right now shivering in the piercing wind.

Silvey wiped her tears on her sleeve as she poured her

mistress's medicine into a glass. I watched her water it down with more rum and slip some drops of the laudanum in. She stirred it with her finger.

"There. Now she'll sleep all night," Silvey said.

"You didn't take anything? You promise?" I asked, hearing the ladies making their way up the stairs.

Silvey went to the door to let them in. Without looking at me she said, "I don't have it."

After I finished starting the fire in Philippe's room and warming his bed, I went back downstairs to find Papa and Rev. I could think of nothing but what I was going to say to Rev when he asked for the cookbook back. I knew it was a crime for him to be found out by anyone about my reading, and with Philippe creeping about . . .

Just as I was about to knock on the door to the study, I could hear Rev and Papa arguing. I paused to listen.

"Ryder, as her father, I'll let you make the decision, but I don't think you should force her. We can find someone else, perhaps next year."

"You gonna hem and haw over it just 'cause Willow likes pretty stories 'bout falling in love? She just scared of the responsibility. That's why we gotta make her do this now, I tell you. Merriend ain't that far away. She'll be able to see her child often enough."

"You know as well as I what things are like over there. *You* wouldn't even want to have to go work there. I'd hate to think . . ."

Papa cut in. "Tell Rawlins he can have the first if it's a girl. If not, then *I* will go work for him myself . . . till Willow has another child, a boy. Willow's a good girl; she'll do what we tell her. Thank God she's not like Lily in that way."

"Ryder, perhaps you should tell her about her mother."

"No! Willow can never know, Jeff. It would break her heart! *Adlile* made her choice."

Rev said, "Sometimes I think we didn't give her much of a choice. . . ."

"None of that matters now, Jeff! I just want Willow taken care of, married proper, and marked in the big family Bible — as your kin, like you promised. This Raymond ain't much to look at, but he's real smart, and that's what Willow needs — someone more clever than she is. You can't just find that at auction."

"I have Evelyn to think of now. Philippe will be my heir if Evelyn and I don't have children of our own."

"Jeff, you can't tell me you really want that fool handling our affairs! I've seen him after that girl Silvey."

"Ryder! Careful how you speak about my future son! I know he seems . . . uninterested and perhaps a bit of a *cad* . . . but his mother says he has a good head for figures and a good heart. He might help us double Knotwild's worth. And these are *my* affairs, not yours."

"You used to say something different. You used to say this place was ours—your family's and mine. You said we had to stick together. That's what I'm trying to do, Jeff. Why can't you see that?"

"At what cost, Ryder? Are you saying you don't care if your daughter becomes as unhappy as your wife? Don't lose Willow the way you lost Lily."

The foul silence in the room seeped out from under the cracks of the door. I heard a floorboard creak, and I jumped. My hand had been frozen in midair, about to knock. From the corner of my eye, I saw Philippe watching me from the sitting room. To my surprise, Papa opened the door suddenly. He looked at me for only a moment, but I think he saw Philippe, 'cause he said nothing, just pushed past me and walked away.

"Come in, Willow." Rev sighed. He was sitting at his desk. I closed the door behind me.

"Shall I bring up more wood for the fire, sir?" It was the only thing I could think to say.

"No, it's fine. I won't be in here long. We'll be leaving early in the morning. I'm hoping Evelyn won't be too agitated by the ride. Since we won't be riding over planked roads, I want you to see to it that there are extra pillows and blankets in the buggy."

"Yes, sir." I kept my head down and studied my hands. "She seems real delicate, sir."

"My little glass hummingbird . . . I wish she didn't have to take so much medicine."

For a moment, I thought about agreeing with him.

"Please make sure Philippe is comfortable in my absence. They will all leave by the coach from Taneytown the day after we return."

"Yes, sir." I turned to leave.

"Willow, the cookbook?"

"Oh, about that, sir." I chose my words carefully.

"What is it?" He tapped on the desk with his reading glasses.

"Well, uh, seeing how delicate Mistress Evelyn is, I was thinking . . ."

"Willow, do you have the book or not?"

"Oh! Yes, sir!" I lied. "I was just . . . *hoping* . . . you might let me . . . hold the book till you get back."

He raised an eyebrow.

"I just was feeling so bad about messing up that chocolate dessert for the mistress and wanted to make up for it. I saw a nice recipe in there for a chocolate cake I thought I might be able to have done when you all got back. You know . . . a surprise for the mistress. Hopefully she'll see that we're all . . . uh . . . real happy . . . she's coming here to live."

Rev looked me in the eye and got up, then walked around the desk to stand in front of me and patted my shoulder.

"Willow, I'm touched. You're a clever and sensitive girl. Thank you for thinking of Evelyn and wanting her to love Knotwild as much as we do." He sighed as though the weight of the world were his alone. "I wish . . ." Rev began, but then turned to sit in his big high-backed chair by the fire, the one where I used to sit at his knee to listen to the accounts of his travels, the souls he'd saved, and most memorably, where he and Papa taught me to read the Bible.

"I pray that you will find some contentment in your marriage, Willow. It is not the ideal situation for you, I know. Your father wants you to start your married life as soon as possible; he thinks it will be for the best. There's some stipulations we have to follow for the . . . transaction. Do you understand what that means?"

"You mean there's conditions to the agreement between you and Rawlins."

Rev's face showed he was impressed.

"Yes, exactly. I'll let your father explain the details. . . . I'm sorry . . . I can't . . ." He looked into the fire like it was going to make everything clear. "It's just . . . I wanted you to know. We all make sacrifices, Willow."

What sacrifice was he making that was equal to mine? There was a tricky word that I once saw in one of Rev's books to describe someone who said one thing but did another — *hypocrite.* I wanted to write that word down on fine parchment paper with a quill pen and indigo ink and leave it like a sign on Rev's desk. I wanted to paint the walls with the word.

"Your mother made a sacrifice for you, and you have made one for your father. It won't be the last, I'm afraid."

"I'm not afraid," I said. "I'm sure my mother made sacrifices 'cause she loved me. Every mother does, I'm sure of it. I might make the same decisions for my own child someday."

I waited for him to say something else or dismiss me, but he just kept looking at the fire.

"If that'll be all, Rev . . ."

The clock struck nine times before he nodded wearily.

"Yes, thank you, Willow. Good night."

I couldn't bear to go back to our cabin to face Papa just yet. I knew he'd still be boiling mad, so I wandered down to the quarters, where all the field hands lived. In three hours I'd see Cato again. The bell signaling lights-out had long since been rung, but there was still smoke curling out of several chimneys and the faint glow of candlelight in many windows. A candle was still lit in Cholly's cabin, but the curtains were drawn. I knocked three times.

"Who's there?" he demanded from behind the closed door.

"Willow."

The door cracked open, and Cholly peered out. "You alone?"

"Yes."

"Nobody follow you?"

I looked around, but I hadn't honestly thought about being watched.

He opened the door and yanked me inside. "For a girl who likes sneaking around all the time, you sure don't know the first thing about not getting caught."

I pulled my arm away as I walked in. Little Luck was sitting up in the bed, smiling to see me. I went to him and hugged him heartily. I kissed his cheek and pulled his ear. I was so glad he was safe.

"What are we to do with him?" I said.

"We? I thought *you* all had it figured," Cholly said, placing himself in the rocking chair by the fireplace. I had never been here before. It was simple but surprisingly clean. Besides the rocking chair, there was only a table, a stool, which was taken up by a sleepy one-eared cat, and a straw-filled mattress. The curtains were just old frayed blankets, nailed up for privacy. There was a marked difference from my home, which was not only the larger space but also offered more comfort. We had proper beds, made of cedar, so our mattresses were off the floor. And our mattresses were filled with feather and wool. We had proper bed linens, too, either passed down from the big house or made by Granmam. I knew that Cholly Dee was a man who lived on his own and not to expect many niceties. Even Tiny's cabin had some comforts, like properly sewn curtains and handmade braided rugs, but it was smaller than this, and she also only had a straw mattress on the floor and one chair.

Cholly said nothing, just sat grunting and shaking his head. Little Luck sweetly wrapped his arms around me and gave me another big squeeze. I couldn't help but laugh when he winked at me as though he already knew everything would turn out right.

There was a knock at the door.

Cholly bolted upright and in one step had his left hand on the door, and I noticed his right hand rested on a large knife tied to his waist. Little Luck hid under the blanket.

"Who's there?" he demanded.

"It's just me: Tiny! I brought food for the little boy," she said rather loudly.

Cholly opened the door to let her in. "How y'all gone keep him a secret I surely don't know."

He shook his head and moaned when the door was barely closed and Silvey pushed her way in. After her, though, he pushed the one-eared cat off the stool and sat by the window, keeping watch through a hole in the curtain.

Tiny, Silvey, and I fussed over Little Luck as he and Silvey held each other tightly.

After a while I finally said, "We do need a plan, you know. There's got to be a way to sneak him back home. . . ."

Luck shook his head wildly. He pointed between himself and Silvey over and over again. Silvey started to cry. "He won't go nowhere without me," she explained.

"Why?" I demanded.

Silvey and Little Luck made several hand gestures between themselves. Luck seemed very upset with Silvey. He got up and went to the fireplace and waved at me to come with him.

"Stop it, Luck," Silvey said. I could tell she both did and didn't want something to be revealed. Luck, on the other hand, was not torn about their *predicament.*

He scattered some ash from the fire onto the hearth and crudely drew two men. Next to one he drew the letter *F.* I was surprised that he knew the alphabet. "You can read?" I whispered, almost afraid to know the answer.

Luck shook his head and pointed to the letter, drawing a question mark after it.

"Who is this?" I asked, confused. I could think of no one whose name began with an *F.*

Luck stared at me desperately and drew the *F* again, so

it was deeper and clearer in the ash. Then he drew a large X over the picture of one of the men. He looked at Silvey, his eyes pleading.

"What does this mean?" I asked. "Who is *F*? Why is he crossed out?"

Silvey took a deep breath and sighed. We all waited. Finally, Luck rapped his knuckles on the floor to get her attention.

"Philippe," she said through clenched teeth. "It's Philippe. He's trying to protect me from Philippe."

Tiny, Cholly, and I looked at one another.

Silvey hung her head. Tears fell onto her apron. "But Philippe got to have his way. . . . Already did. . . ." Her voice sounded like she had run out of hiding places.

"Listen, gal," Cholly said, standing up. "I'll take a walk outta here if you need to speak plain to the womenfolk. I think I understand enough already. . . ."

I didn't understand.

"She don't have to say nothing." Tiny gently took Silvey in her arms, and Silvey broke down into sobbing. Cholly began to pace the floor. I was still not getting it. I looked at Luck and raised my eyebrows and shoulders.

He shook his head. He drew another figure in the ash — a woman, I could tell by the dress — but he had drawn a circle in the middle of the dress. My confusion was clear, because he then drew an arrow between the circle and the man. Silvey and Philippe . . .

"You're pregnant?" I nearly shouted. The F was for father. "What about your beau, the sailor, in Baltimore?"

Silvey's cries grew louder.

I sucked in my breath. "You don't know which is the father?"

"No, you damn fool!"

I felt as though she had slapped me in the face. I knew Silvey was less . . . innocent than I was, but I hadn't expected this.

"I don't think *I'm* the one who's the fool here!" I stung her back.

"You two better hush!" Cholly hissed. "Both of you is foolish, pitiful girls! Y'all don't know what kind of trouble you getting all us into! And I mean *all* of us."

We were silent for a moment until Tiny spoke up. "It's a cruel, hard life. Us colored womenfolks got it the worst. Mens just take, take, take. Even if you a free woman, you gots to belong to some man."

Cholly snorted loudly. "Men slaves don't got it much better. They study how to take away a body's dignity."

"At least you don't be made to bear they children," Tiny said quietly but clearly. "And then see them sold away."

"Philippe ain't like that!" Silvey spoke up. "He tole me

today if the Reverend sets him up in Baltimore, he'd have me and Little Luck with him. He say lots of fashionable men have they . . . um . . . favorite women with them in the city, and nobody sees wrong by it."

With that, Luck knocked on the floor again three times. Silvey pretended to ignore him, and he did it again. He yanked on my sleeve and pointed to his drawing of Philippe, crossing him out again and again, shaking his head.

Silvey made a face at him and gestured to him to stop it, or else.

"Did he really say that," I asked, "or do you want to *believe* he'll do that?"

"Stop!" she hissed back at me and Little Luck. "There ain't nothing more I gotta tell nobody!"

"You don't know if it's his baby," Cholly Dee said, midstride. "But if it don't look like him, he ain't gonna be so keen to set you all up so nice, huh?"

Silvey began to cry again into Tiny's lap.

"Silvey, how could you!" I scolded; I couldn't help it.

Cholly cut his eyes at me as if he wished he could shake me. "Sound to me like she didn't have the luxury of having a choice." He grunted loudly and walked outside, slamming the door behind him.

"Save judgment for the Lord," Tiny said, scolding me as well. I looked into the fire, ashamed. I guess for her, the plan with Philippe in Baltimore seemed perfect — she'd have her family with her and still be able to be with the sailor she loved, even if only in secret. I reckoned, in a way, I knew what she was trying to do.

I went over and touched her shoulder. She shrugged me off. After a moment, I tried again, and this time she let my hand rest on her arm.

"There, now," Tiny coaxed. "You need some friends, both of you. You all might just be the only hope each other has."

Little Luck came over and sat down next to us, pointing at himself, too. Silvey laughed.

"He came out here 'cause he think he protecting me, even though Philippe bullies him. Little Luck's the one who always keep me from drinking too much, the one who takes care of me when I'm wretched. What we gonna do now?"

All their eyes looked to me for an answer. Responsibility, I reckoned, was quite close to agony. But then I thought, *Perhaps it's love that's the agony; responsibility just comes along with it.* Somehow the solution was right in front of me, but I couldn't see it clearly.

"Right now we all need some rest," I said. "I'll have a plan by tomorrow."

When everyone else was finally asleep, I put on my mother's dress and Clarissa's wool cape, bonnet, and shoes, then I crept out of the house. The wind had picked up and there were clouds rolling in from the west, but there was a full, clear moon, so it was easy to see Cato's figure sitting by the riverside.

"Cato!" I cried out despite myself. He turned to me and reached out his hand — I nearly ran into his arms. He said nothing, just held me tightly while I sobbed into his neck.

Next thing I knew, softly at first, he simply brushed his lips against my forehead as he rocked me gently. His kisses were tender, and I was hungry for them. As clouds dimmed the moon's light, I lifted my face, and he kissed my tears, one by one. Unable to stand it any longer, in the darkness I searched for his lips with my own. When our lips touched, it was like a fire started within us and we could not stop it for fear of growing cold and dark again. At that moment, there was nothing in the world I wanted more than him. He was sweet and his caress was familiar, but it also had a new kind of power I had never felt before; it sent ripples down my spine. I pushed off his hat and lost my hands in his overgrown halo of tight curls. He held my other hand as we kissed over and over again, not once letting go.

"Willow . . ." he said, finally catching his breath, pressing his forehead to mine. "Please say you'll leave with me. I can't stand to think of leaving you here. I know you are loyal to your father, and to this place . . . but couldn't you please be loyal to me?"

Before I could answer him, there was a *crack! boom!* We jumped into each other's arms more closely—if that were possible. Lightning split open the sky, and for a moment, it was like daylight. We could see each other clearly, and, again, we were swept up into kissing.

I regained my senses when the world returned to quiet and dark. "Cato, you have to leave tomorrow night."

He shook his head. "Listen to me, Willow. I can't stay another night. If you won't come with me, I'm here to say good-bye."

Thunder and lightning struck again, and I wrenched myself from his embrace and stood up quickly. The wind picked up; it was going to rain any second.

"No, you can't! Please!"

"Come back to my shelter with me," he said, shouting over the wind and the first beating drops of rain. "We can talk in there till the storm is over!"

"No, I should go," I said.

"Please?" he asked, holding out his hand to me. "There's things I have to tell you before I go."

There was no strength in me to deny him. I nodded and helped him stand. He draped his arm around me and we walked into Pennsylvania together, past my mama's grave, past Mason and Dixon's marker, and found his little home, his tree, just as the storm hit. Cato made a little tent with the blanket I had brought him and some big sticks, but the only way we could both fit inside was to be half lying down and entwined.

By the time the storm passed, our legs were drenched with rain and we were exhausted with loving.

"Say you'll come with me tonight," Cato whispered in my ear. The way his lips tickled my skin I thought I might swoon, but I was already lying down.

"It's more than just me," I whispered back.

"Your father? I thought he wouldn't leave!"

"No, not him. Two others, a brother and sister who need safety—that's why we can't leave tonight. Can you take them to your town, your Haven, where all the children are born free?"

"Yes, Willow . . . of course, but I must know . . . will you be my wife?"

I was struck silent. I knew at once it was what I wanted. But I thought of my father, of leaving him forever. My heart was lifted and broken at the same time. I swallowed the lump that was growing in my throat.

I told Cato everything about Little Luck and Silvey. I even told him what Tiny said about women being owned by men, even when they were free. It made me cry again. When I was out of tears, we held each other in the silence of the night, only broken by the echo of the rain as its last drops fell from the trees.

"She's right," Cato said finally. "If we're to have equality between the races, and the classes, why not have equality between the genders? I want you as my wife, Willow, because you're the woman I love. You're just as thirsty for knowledge as I am, and I respect your convictions. But if you feel as though marriage would mean chains for you, then I won't be the one to enslave you. I don't want to be the master of anyone. I'd rather not have you at all than to know that you feel owned by me!"

I loved hearing the words he strung together as though each were a pearl. I kissed his face again and again.

It nearly broke Cato's heart to have to send Willow back again into her dangerous world. Even just for the day. His instincts had told him to leave last night, but he had put it off for her. Cato was also conflicted about telling Willow how he'd found Knotwild and how he knew her Rev Jeff. He'd meant to tell her last night before he left, but now that she had agreed to come with him, he wasn't sure it made much sense for her to know.

As he watched Willow leave at first light, he realized his energy had almost completely returned. The swelling in his ankle was almost gone, though he still couldn't put his full weight on it without the crutch he'd fashioned from a branch. He needed to rest a few hours to prepare for the journey ahead.

Cato drifted in and out of sleep, dreaming of his home and its comforts, wondering what his father would say when he returned. Cato wiped his face roughly, realizing all at once how much his father had provided for him and his sisters, how grateful he was. Atlantus would surely have to respect him after all of this, and he knew Atlantus and his sisters would respect and love Willow for her tenacity and her wit.

Cato stretched and decided to hobble around a bit to get the life back into his body after a night so lovely yet cramped in the cold, tiny space of his tree. He felt as though his body had aged considerably since he'd set off. He'd talk to Willow about heading to Canada in the spring. He imagined them in a covered wagon, heading toward the golden sunset.

Cato continued to walk and fantasized about Willow and himself as pioneers, carving their way through the wilderness. He started heading back to the river to wash his face and to gather Willow's journal to take with them. He stepped over the Mason-Dixon Line. *Last time I ever step in a slave state again,* he thought.

Suddenly, Cato realized that the lightness he felt wasn't just because of Willow—he didn't have his gun. He had put it and his papers in his rucksack when he'd brought Willow to his hideout last night. *No reason to take chances,* he thought. *Better to have it with me.* He turned around and headed back. Cato noticed something in the grass — a button carved in the shape of a shell. He smiled broadly; it belonged to Willow. He bent to get it when his ears pricked at a sound. Cato stood and turned around, thinking it was Willow, but all he saw was the butt of a rifle as it crashed down upon his head.

It was a mournful walk back to Knotwild at first light, leaving Cato and returning to face the choices now before me.

"Are you sure you want this," he'd asked, caressing my hand.

"Yes," I'd told him, looking into his eyes. All night we'd talked about how I would get proper schooling when I got to his town. I wanted to read every book he'd read and learn to read maps as well as he could. Cato wanted us to go West someday. It pained me to think of being so far from my father, but Pennsylvania might as well be Texas as far as Papa was concerned.

Cato had stroked my cheek gently with his hand. The softness of the frosty light gave us another chance to see each other clearly as we said good-bye. I was deeply in love.

As I walked past Mama's grave, I noticed one of the buttons had broken off my dress. It made me shudder.

Granmam always said everything happened for a reason. I stood there at Mama's grave for a moment, to say good-bye. I whispered a quiet prayer that she would watch over us all.

Just as I got back to the house, Papa was already walking up to ring the bell; I waved but he did not wave back, though I was sure he saw me. Fear struck at my heart. We had planned for Silvey to sleep in my bed last night to make it look as though she were me; had he found her? I had to start breakfast; I knew I had to hurry before Rev and the ladies would be wanting to leave, so I had no time to find out.

To my relief, Silvey finally came up to the kitchen not long after the first bell was rung and told me that Papa had not called for me or come up to the loft at all. I could see she was still tired, so I poured her some strong tea. I'd heard her retching in the outhouse when I went to the root cellar for potatoes. She must've been feeling terrible from not drinking as much as her usual, plus being pregnant. Her hands shook a bit as she tried to sip the hot brew. Remembering how much she and her brother loved sweets, I dropped two precious lumps of sugar into her drink. She twitched her mouth into a half smile but refused when I tried to get her to eat some toast before going up to her mistress.

"I just want to get her packed up and gone!" she said.

I understood that. I'd feel better once they were on the road.

"So, what's this plan you got figured that had you out all night?" she asked as I was preparing Lydia's and Evelyn's tea and eggs.

"Shush!" I scolded her. "I'll tell you after they go. Just see if you can save a few drops of that laudanum."

The look on her face told me that she didn't know what I was talking about.

"The opium—that tincture she love so much. See if you can swipe just a bit of it, for just in case," I whispered.

"She holds on to that closer than her diamonds," Silvey whispered back, helping me plate the eggs. "What you need it for?"

"Like I said—just in case. Just see if you can do it." I winked as I sent her up with the tray, and I began setting the breakfast table. Rev came in and sat down, but we had little to say to each other outside of the usual pleasantries. I brought him his porridge and tea and returned to the kitchen.

Papa was in there, standing by the fire, eating his porridge. He only grunted before setting his bowl, still half full, on the table and walking out as Silvey came down with the dishes.

Something wasn't right. Papa never once in my life ignored me.

"I got it!" Silvey was very pleased with herself. She set the tray down and showed me a teacup with the brownish liquid in the bottom.

"You got a lot! Won't she know?"

"No, I poured some tea into the bottle. Plus, her doctor always gives her more. The old lady's on her way down. You gotta help me finish dressing Mistress and bring down her bags so they can go quick."

"Why I *gotta* help you? Aren't I helping you enough? I got my own work to do!"

"Promise I'll come back and help you when it's all done," Silvey said, her hands in prayer. "Please?"

"After I see if Rev wants anything from me. Philippe will be wanting breakfast, too."

She smiled, nodded, and went back up the stairs.

Aunt Lydia was sitting at the table with Rev when I walked in. I waited quietly by the buffet.

"Reverend, although it is a generous offer, I hope that you will take into consideration that our Philippe is still quite young, only nineteen, and hasn't had enough . . . example . . . in gentlemanly ways. Evelyn's father and I had hoped that your influence would refine him."

They hadn't noticed me, so I stayed quiet and listened.

"Refined? I'm not so sure I'm the one . . ." Rev chuckled.

"He needs to calm some of his, shall we say . . .
passions . . . and . . . preoccupations. I'm afraid that throwing him into the jaws of the business world of Baltimore
this spring would be too soon for him. He is excellent with
figures and such—please do not misinterpret what I'm saying. I just think if he were to stay here for a few years . . .
perhaps find a nice country wife, get married before setting
up in the city, since he will be inheriting Knotwild one
day . . ."

"Dear Aunt Lydia," Rev said in a condescending tone,
"I truly appreciate your concern, but I think a man can be
made strong only by facing the demons that haunt him. As
far as I see it, Philippe has never had much responsibility
because of how his mother and grandfather spoil him,
so he needs it now more than ever. I think he'll be fine.
Besides, I've been invited to speak at a few churches in
London this coming summer, so Evelyn and I will be traveling most of the year. I'll need him in Baltimore. Ryder
will manage things here as usual."

She cleared her throat. "Far be it for me to judge, but
Evelyn's father did mention his *concern* about your practices
in handling your slaves, and being here, I must say that I
am inclined to agree. He worries that you are too trusting
of them, too lenient. . . ."

"His fears and yours are unfounded, madam," Rev

replied curtly. "I have written to Mr. Wickoff explaining my philosophy. If *he* wants Philippe to inherit Knotwild, he will have to prove himself to *my* satisfaction."

"Reverend, I mean no offense," Lydia protested. "And I appreciate your candor, but—"

Just then Rev saw me standing there, listening. "What is it Willow?"

"I . . . I just came to see if you and Madam need anything."

"No, unless you want something, Lydia?" Rev said. Lydia shook her head no.

"I suppose we should be heading out now," Rev continued. "It's a two-hour trip south in the buggy, and I want to get there in enough time to enjoy the day. And I know how Evelyn hates the roads, so I want to make sure that we can drive at a leisurely pace and stop as often as she needs."

"You are so thoughtful, Reverend," Madam Lydia said. "Girl, go see what you can do to help Mistress Evelyn along."

"Yes, ma'am." I curtsied and went down through the kitchen. As I climbed the back stairs, I heard voices in the hall. It was Philippe and Silvey. I couldn't make out what they were saying, but when I got to the top of the stairs, I saw he held her tight by the wrist.

"The Reverend and Madam Lydia sent me up to help get Mistress Evelyn ready," I said. Philippe released Silvey so she and I could enter Mistress Evelyn's room. He stood there in the hall in his dressing gown with a scowl on his face as I closed the door behind me.

Evelyn was at her dressing table, drinking her medicine. The room smelled strong of it.

"What did my dear sweet Philippe want, Silvey?" she asked.

"Just wanting to know when you was ready to leave . . . so he could say good-bye," Silvey lied.

"Oh, he dotes on his mother so!" Mistress Evelyn said. "Yes, I do believe I am ready. Did you pack all of my medicines?" She stood up, but I had to reach out to steady her. "I'd hate to be ill on the road. Silvey, do give me another drop of my tincture. Then I'll be sure to sleep most of the journey."

Silvey squeezed another two drops into the teacup and winked at me when Mistress Evelyn wasn't looking. We finished putting her things together, but Mistress Evelyn complained the whole time about having to give herself her own medicine for two days.

"Maybe you should come to nurse me, Silvey. In case I get ill. I always get so confused. . . . Yes, I do think you should come, too."

Silvey looked at me in a panic.

I thought quickly and said, "Mistress, the buggy only has room for you, Madam Lydia, and Rev. Plus, with all your things . . ."

"So? We'll just take a larger carriage."

"There is no other carriage but the big coach, and that'll call for a driver and footman. Rev was taking real pleasure in driving you himself, he said."

"Oh, how silly! But I suppose if that would please him . . ."

"Yes, he said he was looking forward to it, ma'am. And the big carriage bumps around a lot. I put extra cushions and blankets in the buggy for you, too."

She sighed, powdering her face again. "I suppose I can do it myself, and my cousin *is* studying to be a doctor." She drank the last of her tea.

"You," she said, pointing at me. "Take my bags down. Silvey, where's my perfume? Spray me."

I went down with the bags, grateful to get away. Papa had the buggy and two horses waiting at the front of the house. He took the bags and loaded them up without speaking or looking at me.

"Papa?" I wasn't sure what I wanted to say; I just wanted him to look at me, but he didn't look up at all.

Rev came out, and Papa went to speak to him. Madam Lydia and Mistress Evelyn came out soon after, followed by Philippe, who was still not dressed and still scowling. Mistress Evelyn reeked of some terrible musk, but it did cover the smell of rum.

"Well, then, we're off," Rev said once they were all in the buggy. "Philippe, with Ryder as your guide, I expect that you will be quite versed in everything there is to know about Knotwild by the time I get back. He knows this place better than I do, I often think. And I trust Willow to take care of your needs."

Philippe smirked and said, "I'm sure she will, Reverend." Then he kissed his mother and aunt good-bye.

Rev flashed me a quick look as they drove off, but I could read nothing in his expression. I waved good-bye, knowing I would never see him again.

Just as they turned the bend, Philippe said, "Hitch me up a horse."

Papa looked confused. "I thought we'd start down by the silos, sir. You want to have a look at the fields first?"

"No, I'm going to Taneytown. And I've been invited for dinner at Merriend, so I'll be out late into the night," Philippe answered matter-of-factly. "Silvey, help me with my riding boots."

"But 'scuse me, *suh*. . . . Rev said . . ." Papa took off his hat and looked at the ground the same way I'd seen him do at Merriend.

"I don't care what he said. I'm the master here now!

You'll do what I say and keep your mouth shut about it when they get back."

He went back up, with Silvey trailing after him. She looked as though she dreaded every step.

Papa stalked off in the direction of the stables. I wanted to try to rescue Silvey, but I caught sight of Cholly Dee going down into the root cellar. He motioned for me to follow.

"Tell me how you gone get them two outta here," he said, lighting a candle.

"We're leaving tonight," I told him. "I've got someone who got a way to take us to a safe place in Pennsylvania."

"Who *we?*" he asked, his brow raising his hat a bit. "What *us?*"

"Silvey, Little Luck, and me."

"What? Oh, no! *You* ain't goin' nowhere! What you need to leave for? You got it good here! Just stay where you safe."

"You sound just like my father," I spat. "I'm not marrying Raymond and giving my children to Rawlins! I'm not!"

Hot tears ran down my cheeks. I wiped them away quickly, trying to look brave and defiant.

"I guess I do sound like Ryder. Listen, Willow, I promised your mama to keep you out of trouble and watch over you always."

"Why would my mother make you promise that? I'm

not your responsibility! I'm nobody's child now! I don't want to leave Papa, but I . . . I . . ." The tears flowed over my chin. "I want to be free! I want to make my own decisions about what to do with myself! I used to think I could have that here, but I know it's not true. Don't stand in my way, Cholly."

He stood there quietly for a moment, then shook his head and sighed.

"I ain't standing in your way. But I'm goin' with you."

I was shocked. "Why?"

"I promised your mama. I don't break no promises."

"Why did she want *you* to promise? Why?"

"I promised; that's all you need to know. Now, tell me how you planning all this to work."

As I thought about it, it would be good to have another strong man with us. Cato would need help walking, and I wasn't sure how much Silvey could take in her condition.

"Silvey! I have to go help her now. Philippe's got her up in his room. I'll come find you after."

"Girl, I hope you know what you're doing. This could go real wrong real quick."

"I have a good plan," I said, climbing the stairs. "It can't go wrong."

I was too late to help Silvey. By the time I got back to the house, Philippe was leaving. He got on the horse Papa had waiting, and he headed toward Taneytown. I looked in his room and found Silvey crying, crumpled in the corner with her lip split open, bleeding.

"What happened?"

"He . . . he . . ." She sniffed. "I tole him I wasn't feeling well . . . being pregnant and all, and he just haul off and slap me. Said he would tell his mama to sell Luck and me both if I didn't do what he say!"

I had one of Tiny's handkerchiefs and I dabbed at her mouth. She winced and turned away.

"Sure could use a drink now." She laughed quietly.

"You don't need it, Silvey. You're strong without it. We're going to get away from here tonight! He'll never be able to treat you this way again!"

"How you so sure this gone work? I been thinking. Nobody gonna want a lady's maid all big with a fatherless child, and a deaf-mute boy. How we gonna eat? How we gonna live?"

"Listen, I know it's hard to believe, but there's a place up in Pennsylvania they call Haven. It's a town where only free blacks live."

She laughed again but it hurt her lip too much. "There ain't no such place! Where they get money?"

"People work for themselves or for others. They work together. We can really be free!"

"So now you coming, too? How we getting there?

How you know where to go? Lord, why'd I think I could trust you?"

"There you go again! You want to stay here, then stay. It's fine by me. But I'm going tonight. There's someone waiting in the woods to take me. Cholly says he's coming, too. We can do it!"

She shook her head. "Where you get all this hope from? When we met in Baltimore, you ain't have quite so much spark."

"I'm helping you because you need me." It was my turn to laugh. "I've always had hope—I was too much of a slave to let it show. And I could always see you were good people. Just because I wore a white woman's clothes, you judged me?"

"It's the way you be talking. It ain't like me, but proper. It makes me mad 'cause I ain't got no learning and I know you does."

"What?" I tried to sound as if I didn't know what she was talking about.

"Don't play. You talk like you got learnin'. I could tell. . . ." She stood up and brushed herself off. "And so could Philippe. That's why he made me take this. . . ."

She reached under her apron and pulled out the cookbook. I grabbed it out of her hands and had to hold myself back from hitting her with it.

"I'm sorry!" she pleaded, seeing the fury in my eyes.

"He made me do it, but I stole it back! He wanted some kind of proof that your Rev had taught you how to read. He was gonna use it 'gainst him. He's afraid somebody will find out about Mistress Evelyn's divorce or their debts and it'll keep Rev from marrying her. Old lady Lydia been helping them, but she can't hardly take no more."

"But Rev loves her! He would help them, no matter what."

"I don't know what you been doin' out here, but lemme tell you: love don't do nothing for nobody."

"But what about your sailor in Baltimore? What about George?"

She scoffed. "What's that kind of love gone do for gals like us? It ain't making money, that's for sure. Otherwise, love would've bought all our freedom a long time ago."

Silvey's words stayed with me as the rest of the morning meandered by, as slow as molasses in January. I cleaned up the house, even made a few meals and baked some corn-bread to set by for the trip, but also so Papa wouldn't be hungry once I was gone. I went through the house memorizing everything, especially in Rev's study room, looking at books that I'd spent days, weeks, months staring at, ciphering the words, letter by letter. I dared to sit in Rev's chair. It smelled of him. I opened a drawer and found *Romeo and Juliet* atop a stack of fresh blank paper. As I thumbed though the book to find the last lines I'd read, I found two lines that were marked in the second act:

> *And art thou chang'd? Pronounce this sentence then:*
> *Women may fall, when there's no strength in men.*

Compelled to continue reading, I was startled by the big clock striking twelve times; I dropped the book and lost the page. I put the book away with shaking hands, although I was tempted to take it with me.

I was struck by how painful it all was, thinking this would be the last time I sat in this room.

I couldn't help myself when I saw the ink and big plumed quill.

Rev Jeff,

    It break my heart to leave this only place I've known. You have been kind to me and it will never be forgotton. When you said I could be free it scairt me to my bones. Perhaps you knew I would not leave my father and thats why you could make such offers. Or perhaps you only worried you might get found out. But you and Papa do me no justice by keeping so many secrets. By specting me to keep your secrets from each

other. I suppose I am wrong for expecting more from
my station, but you let me, didnt you? I did not mean
for this to become bitter. I only wished to tell you a
heartfelt goodbye. And to say this: some women are not
ready to fall just because their men lose strength. I will
not lose my strength, because I know how loved I have
been by men like my papa and you. Even if we cant all
be strong at the same time or for the same reasons, I love
you both the same.

I signed the letter, folded it, and put it in his drawer under the book. Then I went down to our cabin to put things into order. I went through my belongings and picked a few items to carry with me, then sewed the money Madam Lydia gave me into my underclothes. Who knew what I would need in my new life? What does one carry to freedom? Memories mostly, stale and fresh alike.

I took some of my great-grandmother's and grand-mother's things: a tuft of hair tied in a bit of muslin with a ribbon, a hand-sewn bonnet, also Granmam's shawl. On top of that I packed food, water, and all the herbs and tinctures I could carry. I wrapped the bottles in my own christening dress so they would stay quiet. I put in extra underclothes and wool stockings for Silvey, and one of my old coats for Little Luck; it would be quite cold walking at night.

When I was finished cleaning the cabin, my clock locket said it was only four thirty. I took my bag down to Cholly's. We were meeting Cato at midnight so we could travel as far into Pennsylvania as we could by morning.

Knotwild was strangely quiet. Usually there'd be children running around, playing some game, but I saw none. The women often took turns staying back while everyone else was in the fields, especially since Old Samuel was weak. Two or more would watch the little ones and prepare food and tend the gardens, but I heard no voices. I went to Cholly's cabin. It was quiet. I knocked and looked in. Silvey was there taking a nap with Little Luck, who was hiding under the blanket with the one-eared cat.

"Where's everyone?"

"Something your papa brought in from the woods," Silvey said, yawning. "Cholly said we should stay here, and he went to go find out."

"I'll go down and see. We're leaving at midnight, so you two get as much rest as you can so we can walk all night."

Silvey promptly lay back down and closed her eyes. Little Luck and the cat played with a bit of string.

As I left them with the bags, I wondered what it could

be. . . . Had Papa shot a deer? He'd be real proud if he'd gotten a big buck. Rev used to have the head of one that he and Papa hunted themselves when they was just boys. It hung in his bedroom until one day it just fell and cracked. Rev used to say it was Granmam's doing, since she thought it watched her when she was in the room. I thought so, too, and was glad when it was gone.

Maybe Papa got one of those bears that was around the river! Rev could sell the fur for some good money, maybe throw us all a real fancy Christmas party. I stopped myself from thinking of a future I didn't belong to.

I walked down the wooded path that led from the cabins to the fields. Passing the church on the way, the late-afternoon light was glittering through the windows; I stopped and sighed a deep good-bye.

Farther down the path, Tiny sat on a fallen tree with her hands covering her face, rocking back and forth.

"Tiny?" I touched her shoulder, but she just fell to pieces, crying.

"What is it? What happened?"

"Your pa—" she sobbed.

"Is he hurt?"

She shook her head furiously.

Folks were walking up toward us from the fields. As they passed, all looked disturbed. Rachel stopped and helped me get Tiny on her feet and walking.

"Your papa's found a fugitive," she said. "Caught him out in the woods, by the river, trying to get over into Pennsyl—"

I dropped Tiny's arm and ran down the path, past the rest of the field hands and excited children. I ran until I saw Papa dragging Cato behind him with a rope tied around his arms.

"No! No! Papa, wait! He's not a fugitive!" I cried. Cato's hands were tied, and he was bleeding all down his face. Papa ignored my pleading. I pulled at his arm and tried to block his way. He walked as though I were a ghost, pushing past me carelessly.

Cholly caught up with me, pulled me back, and whispered in my ear. "C'mon, gal. Let's see what he plan to do."

"Cato!" I moaned.

"Shush, now! Keep your head up. Is he the one you been saying would help us?"

I could barely nod—I felt faint and my lungs were closing up on me, but Cholly held me up.

"You got to keep your wits about you! C'mon, now!"

Cholly shook me, and I tried my best to get air in my lungs. "Yes," I muttered. "But he's free! He got papers! Papa can't keep him. . . ." We'd reached the clearing at the center of the cabins. Papa dropped the rope, and Cato fell over like a sack of flour. I heard Cato moaning. Papa stood up on the stump.

"Y'all know what I feel about fugitives. This one here's gonna get sold way down deep south. He so conniving it'd be dangerous to keep him up this far north. Can't trust one like this nohow! Look how he stole some white man's coat! And he been lurking around Rev's land, stealing from right from under our noses!"

"Papa! You're wrong! He's stolen nothing!" I cried, on my knees before him.

Papa's gaze finally settled on me. I wished it hadn't — it was the coldest stare I'd ever seen. He stepped down off the stump and walked straight at me, with that stare burning through me like an icicle dagger.

"Papa, please!" I begged.

"Ryder —" Cholly called out. Papa ignored us both; he grabbed my hand and dropped something in it. Then he slapped me. My ears were buzzing as I fell over, stunned.

It took me a while to regain my senses. Everything was spinning and then dark. I finally heard Cholly calling my name.

"C'mon, gal! Git up!"

Something felt familiar in the palm of my hand. I opened my eyes. It was the button from my dress.

"Cato!" I called, realizing that Papa must have followed me last night or somehow seen us this morning. "Oh, God! Cato! Where is he? He'll kill him!"

"Ryder took him to the icehouse. He sent somebody over to Merriend to get Boss H."

I looked around; everyone was staring at me. Tiny was at my side.

"He chained him up, Willow," she told me. "How you know him? How?"

"He . . . He's . . ." I couldn't explain. I could only think of how to get him away from here, as quick as I could. "Where's Papa now?"

"He went up to your place, Willow," Tiny said. She and Cholly passed a serious look between them. "He throwing all your things out the door."

Indeed, Papa was making a hasty pile outside our cabin. What truly struck at my heart was that he was throwing away my grandmother's things as well. That was when I knew the height of rage shadowing my father's good senses. There was nothing I could say except to beg Papa to listen to me, but my throat grew coarse as the air in my chest grew thin. I wheezed and moaned on my knees in the yard, but he paid no attention.

"Ryder, you need to stop. Look at your daughter!" Cholly tried to reason but it was no use.

Tiny cried just as much as I did, if not more. She held my hand and rocked back and forth on her heels. She'd even tried standing in the doorway to get my father to stop and think for a moment, but he just pushed past her and continued putting out all the things I ever made—and even the linens and mattress.

Finally he'd managed to discard everything that held a trace of my spirit.

"But, Papa—Cato is freeborn! He has papers! Check his coat—he showed me himself!" There was no use pretending I didn't know him.

"I checked his pockets when I caught him *trespassing,* and they were empty. He prolly paid somebody to write some mess up for him. You can't trust a fugitive! How many times have I said it?"

I thought for a moment—if he didn't have the papers on him, they were back at the tree.

"I know where they are, Papa! I only have to go get them and show you!"

"Naw, gal. You got but one decision to make. You either with me, and you forsake this fugitive, or you ain't."

I couldn't answer. Back when Rev had asked me to choose between freedom and Knotwild, I knew I couldn't leave my father. This time around . . .

"You wanna forsake all the things me and Rev given you?" Papa demanded when I hesitated. "You willing to sneak about and *defile yourself* with the likes of *him*?"

Papa grabbed my arm and yanked me away from Cholly. He pushed me into Rev's house and up the trapdoor to the attic, then clicked the latch as he left.

Cato recalled being struck, even being tied up and dragged by a rope tightly knotted around his arms, cutting off his breath . . . but he couldn't figure how he'd ended up in chains and half frozen. It took a while for his eyes to focus on the figure pacing back and forth in the dark room, cradling a gun in his arms like a baby. There was a lantern on the floor near Cato; its fire was his only warmth. There were several huge blocks of ice stacked in more of the straw he lay upon. Hanging from the walls were all the sharp, gleaming tools for cutting and toting ice. Cato's lip was split from being gagged, and where he was hit on his head throbbed in time with his heartbeat. Never had he been so afraid — not even when he was alone in the woods. Vaguely he remembered hearing Willow's voice, but it could've been a dream. Would he ever see her again? Would he ever see his family again? He mustered all the strength in his spirit to keep himself from panic.

The man saw Cato was awake, and he stopped pacing and stared at him. To Cato's surprise, his eyes were green. They glowed catlike in the flickering light as he leaned close to Cato's face.

"You come down a road you had no business being on, boy. You done violated the only things in the world I held sacred—my land and my daughter! Well, you're gonna learn a lesson here tonight."

Cato couldn't hold back the moan that rose up from his heart. Willow's father . . . No wonder this man looked so crazed; if he'd seen them parting this morning . . . his papers . . . his gun . . . all back at the tree . . . all useless to him now.

I sat there for hours in the stiff, stale air, next to a small window that lifted no higher than the width of my hand. I put my face to it so I could get some breeze.

I was left alone to torture myself, wondering how everything had gone so terribly wrong. I thought I'd been so careful, but it wasn't enough. I remembered seeing the fishermen in Baltimore, how when they were casting their huge nets from such tiny boats, they'd end up dragging in whatever came up with the fish. I once saw them pull up a broken guitar, a slimy shoe, and a heap of rusted silverware. I felt like I had cast a net and got caught up in it myself.

Rawlins, Boss H, and Philippe would be here soon, and they would sell Cato . . . or worse. I didn't even know the terrors that awaited him. It was all my fault.

•   •   •

Outside the little attic window, the light grew dim. The window faced the west, so I could see the deep-orange sun slipping behind the mountains, but that was all. I couldn't tell what was happening outside, if anyone had arrived. I heard nothing except the lonely calls of the birds settling for the night. I was sitting propped up on an old crate that Rev's things were in. Searching through it, I found a few books and some letters from Rev's first wife, Clarissa, but no quill and just half a bottle of dried-up ink. Serves me right, I guess, but it was in my nature to want to write to Mama, to pour out my heart. I spoke aloud instead.

"Mama, Granmam, Great-Granmam — if any of you all can hear me, if any of you still care and haven't yet forsaken me, please, *please* guide me now. If it is right for me, if it is your will for me to stay here at Knotwild, to marry Raymond and forget about Cato, please help me to accept that fate and forgive my father."

It took me forever to get those words out. It broke my heart most to say *forget about Cato*. Could I ever truly do that? How could I even stay here without . . . What was the word? *Remorse*. I covered my face with my hands, trying to hide the bitterness I felt in my heart for Papa.

What Cholly said about my mother . . . I remembered the look in his eyes when he talked about her. Not with remorse, like my father. Although it also brought Cholly pain to speak of her, there was always a lightness in his voice; *he loved her.* How did I not see this before? Maybe because I hadn't had the feelings yet myself. But I knew love now; I knew how powerful and dangerous it was. Could it be that my mother loved him, too?

I tried to distract myself by reading what I could of Clarissa's letters in the near dark. Mostly they were about the house, and how Gran, whom she called "Mammy," was taking good care of her needs while she was with child.

> *But, my darling husband, I'm sorry to report that the new wench you bought in Baltimore to be Ryder's wife is causing more harm than good. Lily is quite sullen and often sneaks away from the house. I see that she will not be suitable for a lady's maid. Mammy says Ryder is driven mad when Lily speaks to Cholly Dee.*

My mouth was agape; I searched through the box for more about my mother. There was another letter, dated a few months later.

> *How wonderful it was to have you home, my love. These last two weeks without you have been too long. Your daughter continues to grow and amaze me each day. Mammy told me yesterday that Lily is with child. I think it might be best to sell her after she weans the*

babe. She has been such a chore to train! She is a pure African, and I have not the wits to make her submit to my needs, and you are soft with the whip. I went for a walk yesterday and overheard her telling some of the field hands they should all desert Knotwild. I told Mammy right away, and she said she'd handle it herself. But if it were not for her condition, I might think Lily dangerous.

Suddenly I heard noise below me, then the click of the latch, and the door opened and down slid the ladder. I braced myself, thinking it would be Papa. A few moments passed but no one came up. Plucking up my courage, I crawled over and peered down into the dark shadows. I couldn't see anyone and it frightened me, wondering who could have unlatched the door. Philippe? Rawlins? The fear gripped me and I shrank back against the window again until Little Luck's face appeared, holding up a small candle.

I cried out with joy and surprise. "How did you—?" I was about to question him, but he put his finger to his mouth and hurriedly motioned for me to come down. This time I did not hesitate.

Little Luck and I went quietly down to the kitchen. I had him snuff the light so no one would see us. I knew the house by heart and could guide us out easily. As I pulled him toward the cabins, Luck shook his head and yanked my arm so I would follow him into the woods, heading toward the river.

Cholly and Silvey were already waiting at my tree.

"Let's go," Cholly said, and turned north. Everyone followed him, except for me. I was fixed to the spot.

"I can't."

They all turned and looked back at me.

"You don't got a choice. They got him, Willow. There ain't no way to save him."

"I'll make a way, Cholly. I know where his papers are. I'm taking them back — they'll have to let him go!"

"You don't understand, girl. Ryder already gave him up. He got him chained up in the icehouse. He watching Cato with a gun, and your groom-to-be is right outside the door, keeping watch till Boss H come back with Philippe. Once they get here, which could be anytime now, it's over. *They* don't *have* to do nothing 'bout no papers. They *got* him. If they don't kill him tonight, they gonna sell him tomorrow. It's done. Best we can do is take the time we got to run. We ain't got a choice."

"Cholly, I thought they can't come after you once you're over the Mason-Dixon Line."

"Says who?"

"Says the federal government."

"Gal, don't you know those laws keep changing?"

Silvey chimed in. "Well, if you all want to stand around arguing on this damn imaginary line and see if Boss H and Philippe are going to wait for the *government* to stop them from killing us and dragging our dead bodies back to Maryland, then you go right ahead. I ain't never heard of no white man getting in trouble for getting his rightful Negroes back."

"Well, if I can get there before Boss H and Philippe and show Cato's papers to Papa, I think he'll let him go."

"Those some mighty high stakes," Cholly said. "What you betting with?"

"Myself. I'll stay if Papa lets him go. Or at least holds him until Rev gets back. Rev won't sell him if he has papers. Papa just wants our family line to continue. I'll do that. I'll give him an heir. But I can't let Cato be sold. . . ."

"Well, what about us?" Silvey demanded. "You the only one who know where we supposed to be going! You just leaving us?"

"Cato said he has a map in his bag. I'll take you to it."

"None of us read maps, Willow!"

"I'll show you, Silvey. But I won't leave Cato like this. . . ."

I took them to Cato's hideout and showed them the directions.

"Cato said he walked directly south for about a day or so. There's a Quaker farm there—they have two turtle-doves painted above the barn door." Cholly had brought a lantern, so I was able to show them the symbols for North, South, East, and West. Cato had made the map himself; the two turtledoves were drawn to show the farm.

"Show the farmer the map and tell him Cato sent you," I told them. "But if something don't look right, just keep going east. Ask about towns called Columbia or Lancaster. Near there is a black settlement called Haven. . . ."

Cholly grabbed my hand as it began to shake.

"We'll wait for you," he said. "We'll get to this barn and we'll wait for you there."

"I told you. I'm not coming, Cholly. I'm giving up my freedom for his."

"Don't do that, Willow. He'll not be able to live with himself. I should know. . . ."

"Tell me the truth now, Cholly Dee." I clung to his hand so he couldn't let go. "Are you my father?"

"Willow, girl, if I was, we'd be long gone by now," he said. "Your mama was faithful to her vows . . . but we couldn't stop loving each other. You don't know what it was like when your mama came to Knotwild. For me, I was getting a part of my life back, and for her, too. We had to be with each other, even just to talk. Your papa never understood that. He didn't like us to talk about Africa. He was jealous. . . . She chose your papa so he'd leave me alone."

I let go of his hand.

"I tried to get her to run with me, but she took her promises serious. She didn't want to split you from your father after losing her family. But then she found out they was planning to sell her. . . ."

"She knew?"

"Yes. Your father knew, too."

"He did? But he tried to stop them, didn't he?"

Cholly shook his head and stared at the ground.

"But when did she get so sick?"

"She didn't get sick, Willow."

"What do you mean?"

"Only your father and the Reverend can say what really happened."

Silvey interrupted. "I'm real sorry, but us and my fatherless child will be dead if we don't leave right now."

"She's right, Cholly. They need you. You've kept your promise to my mother — promise me you'll look after these two now."

Cholly nodded but kept his eyes fixed on the stars. "We'll wait for you," he repeated.

"Willow, far as I see it, you a fool for going back there," Silvey said. "I respect you, though. Be brave, girl."

"Thanks, Silvey. You be brave, too." I hugged her and Luck. I even let Cholly grab me for a quick embrace, and we all parted ways with tears as silent as the moon.

Ryder continued to pace the floor. "This place belong to me as much as it belong to the man whose name is scrawled on the deed," he said. "It been mine since before I was born, passed down from my grandmother to my father, and now its responsibility belongs to me. Willow needs to have a boy child so it can be passed down to him. My family's bones feed this soil; their flesh bled into every piece of lumber that made every building. My grandmother sanded and nailed up these very walls. She had to work just as hard as — harder than — any man. She had to do terrible, wretched things . . . but she always said it was worth it just to have all our people together, to see her children's children. She herself was ripped away from her own mother. . . . But if you think I'm just gonna let some runaway darkie ruin all we built . . . Hell no! God Almighty himself would have to tear me from it!"

Ryder continued pacing, muttering wildly to himself.

"This is all Adlile's fault! But there was something about her . . . drove myself mad with desire to make her mine. I knew how she felt about Cholly . . . and how he felt about her. Something in me couldn't let him have her! I thought she'd love me when she saw what a better life I could give her — a chance to be a lady's maid, to have some of the comforts of serving the master rather than slaving in the fields."

Ryder kicked at one of the blocks of ice repeatedly. Cato feared he would be next.

"I'm stronger, smarter than Cholly! I've got better breeding, and I can read and write figures — who is he but a heathen? We couldn't even get him to accept the Bible! At least Lily did that — she loved to hear me read the Scriptures, and then she'd ask to look at the text with me. I even showed her the alphabet — she picked it up so quick! Like Willow . . ."

The ice chips were flying around and hit Cato's body like shards of glass. He could do nothing but turn his face away.

"Rev's wife, Clarissa, was a fine, respectable lady. I'd hoped Lily would look up to her, to want to refine herself. I thought I could have what she and Jeff had — they were happy. I thought we could be like them! But then Lily went and tried to run off when she was still pregnant, saying she didn't want her child growing up a slave, so me and Mama had to keep her locked in the house. Then when she gave birth and the baby was strong, Rev said we had to sell Lily.

I protested, but I knew he was right. I couldn't let her run with my child!"

By now, Ryder was sobbing. It was like he was back in the past, reeling at his own sins.

—————

I snuck up to Tiny's cabin and climbed in her window. She was sitting by the fire, sewing furiously, as if it could make all of her pain go away.

"I was wondering when you'd be coming back," she said when she heard me land on her floor with a thud. She didn't even look up from her stitches.

"Cato . . ." I whispered.

"Don't fret too much. Ryder ain't kilt him," she said quietly. "Least, we didn't hear no gun go off."

I sighed with relief.

"But your papa done sent for Raymond to come help him guard till *they* get here."

I sat next to her by the fire.

"The Almighty knows, I know what it's like to want to keep a little something to yourself, something that is yours only in the world." Tiny wiped away a tear and sighed. "But you ain't been the same since you got back from the city, and now I come to find out all this. . . ." She waved her hand in front of her face, fanning away her tears. "You got some telling to do!"

She was right. Tiny had taken up for me so many times, and I had treated her as though she didn't even know me. I suppose I never thought that she'd want to hear my sorrows when they compared so weak against hers.

So I told her the story, from beginning to end. How I first saw Cato waving me to freedom, everything about Baltimore and Rev's offer, all the way up to early this morning, when I left Cato in the woods.

"If only my father didn't insist on me being married. . . . Why must it matter so much?" I said.

Tiny only stared into the fire. After a long moment, she looked back at me, her head resting on her hand as she rocked in her chair. "You don't even know how hard it is, Willow. You don't even know what it's like in the rest of the world. You know why I stay here? Why I'll never run from this place? 'Cause it's the only place where I was never forced to do nothing with my body I didn't want to do. I been nothing but a pitcher of water to men — black and white alike — something to fill up and then empty back out again."

She got up and paced the floor. "Maybe your papa wants you married 'cause that's the only shred of respectability he could give you in this world. None of us ever had that. You think Rachel got papers on her man? No! Ain't nobody get papers when they a slave, 'cept maybe a bill of sale! Nobody 'round here but you. And what I wouldn't give for that! I'm just property, Willow. My children, too. All I'm meant to do is make money for my master."

"You're more than that, Tiny!"

"You and me know that, but nobody else cares if I'm more than that. My kin will never know me. They ain't got no ways to find me, 'cause my name ain't written nowhere. But you, Willow, you in Rev's book."

"But that'll be all I have if I stay here. Not that it don't mean a lot, Tiny, but Cato's given me a chance to have a life that belongs to me."

"But then you'll belong to Cato! If you his wife, that always gone be true."

"Cato doesn't think like that." I thought suddenly of Silvey. I had judged her too harshly! What else could women cling to except for the brittle words of men?

Tiny sat down again. "Willow, I don't want nothing but your happiness, but you got to admit that the laws of men is the same even for white women. They got they society to worry about. We all got prices to pay; we all some man's property. I want you to be free, Willow, and I ain't standing in the way if you all gone run. But I ain't leaving. I'm tired and I'm fearful of what I don't know. It's that simple. I hope you won't judge me harsh for that."

"Tiny!" I went over and hugged her. "You mean the world to me. I want your happiness, too. You'll be safe and content here at Knotwild as long as Rev's alive."

"I'll help you as much as I can, Willow, though I can't say there's much I can do, 'cept maybe take care of your papa while you're gone."

"Just knowing you're with me in spirit helps. I've got to get in to see Cato, see how bad he's hurt. I got his freedom papers—when Papa sees them, he can't deny it. We have to . . ."

"I'll get in to see Cato," she said. "Ryder'll never let you in. I'll see how hurt he is. You figure out how to talk to your papa without him locking you up in that attic again."

We embraced before she left, and I hastily pushed the few things I would need into Cato's bag. Tiny had taken all of my things and neatly folded and piled them on top of my mattress, which she'd also dragged into her cabin. I wondered if I would ever have any other friend in the world like her.

———————————

There was someone at the door, banging. Cato thought the sound was in his head; it vibrated as though it were. Most of what Ryder had said was a mystery to Cato; sometimes he was confused about where he even was— back in the woods or with a man crazed with loss. But he did know this: Willow was also in danger if she wasn't already chained somewhere like him. Or worse. He writhed in the metal cuffs trapping his ankles and wrists. His healing ankle was burning hot and swollen, chafing against the chains.

Ryder wiped up his face and went to the door. Cato could only hear whispers, a woman's voice. Ryder was shaking his head, but finally he cracked open the door and a woman's face peered in at Cato. Somehow she pushed her way in.

"Now, Ryder, I'm telling you! You can't sell this boy if he's gonna be all busted up! Just let me clean him up a bit and give him some water!"

Though Cato couldn't be sure, he thought the woman winked at him. He moaned with agony and grinded his teeth when she touched his head. It was all he could do to keep from passing out. She gently cleaned his wounds and dressed them with a salve that smelled like Willow. Next, she washed the dried blood that had caked on his face and eyes and even gathered some ice chips into a handkerchief and put it on his swollen ankle. It made Cato's skin cringe and his teeth chatter.

Ryder went to stand outside for a moment, and the woman, said, "I'm Tiny. Willow sent me; tole me what to do. She say she comin' for you! Gone get you outta here soon!"

She removed the gag from his mouth and told him not to talk. His throat was so parched, he doubted that he could utter a word. She held his head so he could drink some water, and then she had him drink some bitter remedy he was sure Willow had concocted.

"She wanted you to know she's safe."

Cato managed to nod toward the door where Ryder stood outside. "Danger," he tried to say, but hardly a murmur came out.

"Don't worry none!" Tiny assured him.

Cato moaned and tried to shake his head, but it was too painful. It was all so confusing. He could hardly keep his eyes open, even when she put the gag back in his mouth and left.

I snuck through the woods to get around being seen. The night's cloak was sparkling with stars. The stable door was cracked open, but no one was inside. Careful as I was not to be seen, Mayapple made a ruckus as soon as she smelled me. I'd been neglecting her of late, and she was clearly scolding me by stamping her hooves and making noises from deep in her throat.

"Shh!" I said, saddling her up as quickly as I could. She stamped around so much it was hard to fasten all the buckles in the dark.

"Well, look what I found here."

The familiar voice made me jump, but I tried to hide it.

"Hey there, Raymond!" I tried to speak as my usual

self, but my voice was a butterfly in the wind. It was dark, but he carried a short candle that illuminated his face.

"Surprised you here; your papa said you was doing somthin' up in the house, so you couldn't come down. Said you was scairt of the fugitive 'cause he was a Wild Man living in the forest!" He laughed.

I laughed, too, nervously.

"So, then, what you doing out here, Willow?"

Smiling, I said, "Can you keep a secret? Just between you and me?" I even reached out and touched his arm, drawing him into the stall with me. Mayapple wasn't happy about that; her muscles twitched and she snorted. I rested my hand on her neck to steady her. I could tell Raymond was excited at the prospect of sharing something with me. Carefully I took the candle away from him and set it on the water barrel.

"The new lady's maid from Baltimore gave me some rum. I came out here to try it. . . ." I pulled the flask with the powerful mix of laudanum, rum, and sleeping herbs out of my apron pocket.

"Rum? Willow, that ain't like you; you a good girl. I know I came on mighty strong, but I just wanted you to like me the same."

My heart softened. Maybe he really wasn't so bad.

"Give me that flask," he said. "I won't let you do it."

"You're right, Raymond. I'm sorry," I said, handing it

over to him. "I reckon I never tried to get to know who you really are."

"Who I am? I ain't nothing but the wits God gave me." He laughed bitterly. "This scar reminds me of that every day."

"How?"

"You owe me a kiss for not telling your papa about this," he said, ignoring my question and pulling me toward him. I tried to think only of Cato—and how I had to save him—and not show my discomfort in Raymond's arms.

"Tell me about your scar, Raymond," I said, stalling for time.

"I don't ever talk about that day . . ." he said quietly. Then, to my surprise, he drank down what must've been half the flask.

"I thought you were against drinking!"

"I'm against womenfolk drinking, not men," he said, after knocking back the rest. I was surprised he didn't gag at the taste of the tonic.

"I only had moonshine once before," he said, hiccupping. "Some mess somebody cooked up in the mountains . . . tasted terrible—this here is much better!"

I didn't know what to say—I'd only wanted him to take a few sips; that should have put him to sleep for a few hours. I'd meant to use the rest of it while we were on the run. But Raymond didn't seem affected.

"Where's my kiss?" he demanded. There was nothing for me to do but to kiss him, full on the mouth. I couldn't have him let Papa know I was here yet.

"That's nice . . ." he said softly. "I ain't kissed a girl before. . . . Sometimes I used to never think I would 'cause I was so . . ." He slurred out a few more words before his mouth fell slack. I could barely hold him up as he sank to the floor in an opium trance.

I covered him up with a blanket, finished fastening Mayapple's harness, and led her quietly out into the woods.

When you a slave, they try to push you to the limits of your dignity, but if you was able to stand up after, you'd won. They only respect how much you want to thrive, not how willing you is to die. Not that you trying to win they respect, but even if they kill you, it'd better be while you standing on your own two feet.

Cato was half remembering something his father had always said. He only woke when cold water was splashed on his face. He shuddered and gasped but felt that it strangely brought him back to life. He'd been lost in the darkness of the past.

Ryder stood over Cato in the flickering lamplight. Cato tried not to flinch when Ryder reached down at him, but to his surprise, Ryder pulled the gag out of his mouth.

"How long you been out in the woods?" Ryder asked.

Cato tried to talk, but his throat was dry and sore, so Ryder gave him water.

"Almost two months."

"That's a long time," Ryder said as he sat back on his heels and nodded toward Cato's ankle. "Looks like it hurts."

Cato stayed silent, unsure of what to make of Ryder's sudden change.

"I just went to check in on our Willow," Ryder said. "But she ain't where I left her. I'm not sure how she got out, but she done left us both. Ain't that something? Women. Can't trust 'em." He spat.

"I'm glad," Cato said sincerely. "I'm glad she's gone. She needs to be free."

Ryder looked strange, his mouth twitched as he studied Cato's face. "Maybe you *is* free, like she said, but you ain't got no papers to prove it one way or 'nother. Either way, I think you been putting too many ideas in Willow's head. She free enough here at Knotwild, with her loving family. What would she do in the world without me and Rev? We'll get her back, mark my words. . . . We'll find her."

"You don't know the first thing about love. You only wanted to own Willow just as you are owned," Cato told him boldly. He knew his fate was his own now that Willow was gone. Ryder would either kill him or sell him, he was certain. Reverend Jeffries wasn't on the plantation, or else Cato would've tried to bargain for his life. No, there was none of that now.

"You think *you* know something about love?" Ryder laughed. "Boy, what are you? Maybe sixteen, seventeen? All you got to know about love is that Willow left your ass here and took herself to freedom without you. Just like her mother! Womenfolk is like that — showing you affections one minute and running to someone else the next. That's why I wanted Willow married to someone who would . . ."

"Control her?"

"Shut up, boy. Why you think God made us the stronger sex? Women's minds and bodies are weak. They need us to put them right."

"Ain't that the same thing *masters* say about *us*? How they justify slavery?"

Ryder was quiet for a moment, but the silence didn't last long. Two white men came bursting through the door, drunk and looking ready to make trouble.

I walked Mayapple into the woods and tied her reins to a tree. My plan was to put Cato on her back and send him north, hoping May would stay calm enough to take him someplace safe. I knew Papa wouldn't let Cato go unless I stayed, and the only way to get Cato into Pennsylvania would be to send him with the next best thing if I couldn't be with him. May wasn't happy to be left alone in the woods; she snorted as I walked away, and I could hear her tail swishing in dismay.

"I'll be back," I called. "Promise! Just stay here till I need you, hear me?"

Well, damn, Ryder, you already busted him up!" the white man in plain farmer clothes said. "Sir, I was right! A bet's a bet!" He held out his hand to the other, clearly a gentleman.

"I didn't believe it, Hendricks! I never would have believed I'd see a darkie capture and chain up one of his own!" the gentleman said, stumbling a bit as he pulled out several coins.

Cato didn't see the expression on Ryder's face change, but his eyes shifted to a dark corner of the room.

"Mr. Philippe, I tole you these darkies over here is *trained* good for the Reverend, but they ain't got the same respect for other white mens. You gonna have to make sure they respects you the same, else they'll be turning on you real quick."

"Then I'm so lucky to have the esteemed overseer of

Merriend Farm to educate me," the gentleman Philippe said. "I'm glad that your master was still laid up with the gout and sent you to deliver the news."

"Well, I have to say, sir, that I was quite glad to find you in the saloon! After riding at full speed, I needed a refreshment! And to find you with such a pretty lass in your lap!" Hendricks slurred most of his words.

"Yes, dear Amy? Was that her name? She was delightful! But it was necessary that you found me, and that we could then share a drink and get to know each other." Philippe swayed a bit and steadied himself against the wall.

Hendricks laughed. "That was more than just one drink! And then the round we had after I fell off my horse!"

Philippe fell over with laughter while Hendricks tenderly petted his own arm, which hung limply across his chest in a makeshift sling. They guffawed, hooted, and snorted until they seemed to remember that there were two other people in the small room with them, one of whom was chained to the floor.

"Damn, it's cold in here!" Hendricks said as if he had not noticed the blocks of ice all around him. "I reckon it's warmer outside!"

"Quite right," Philippe said. "Let's go in the house to warm ourselves by the fire with a drink. Ryder, take him outside, strip him down, and tie him up."

"Yes, suh," Ryder mumbled, his eyes still locked with the darkness.

"Oh, and tell your daughter and Silvey to come to the house to serve us."

The two men stumbled outside, laughing.

Ryder did not look Cato in the eyes, simply went and got the rope hanging on the wall. He was careful to tie Cato up before unlocking the chains, anticipating Cato's idea to try to overpower him.

"Ryder, please—you don't have to do this!" Cato pleaded. "I was freeborn in Pennsylvania! Let me go! I have papers! You could say I ran off, and I could hide until after they've gone. . . ."

"And then what? They'd be talking about selling me next! I ain't risking what I've got for you."

"Then leave with me! We'll find Willow together— I'm freeborn! I swear! Your master, Reverend Jeffries—he even knows that I'm free!"

Ryder ignored him and continued unlocking the chains. He pushed Cato up to his feet, but Cato fought him all the way. Ryder grabbed the gun and pointed it at Cato. "I could kill you now, just for stealing my daughter's virtue, not to mention your crooked lies."

"I'm no liar and I stole nothing! Willow and I love each other! We want to marry!"

"Shut up and move!" Ryder yelled.

Cato had no choice but to limp slowly.

"You think I don't know about love?" Ryder said with his gun at Cato's back. "I loved my wife with all my heart and wished I only had time to show her I loved her even more — that I was the right choice for her! Willow is all I have left . . . !" Ryder pushed Cato out the door.

———————

I crept back to the stables and saw that Raymond was still there, undisturbed and snoring. As I left, I saw Boss H and Philippe leaving the icehouse; the air squeezed out of my lungs, and my heart stopped for a moment as I was stricken with fear they'd see me.

As they stumbled along, I heard Philippe say that he had a flask of whiskey in his bags that they could share. I didn't understand how they could want more when they could already barely stand.

I stayed hidden and gathered my wits about me, thinking of what to do next. I felt around in Cato's bag for his papers to show Papa, when my fingers touched cold metal. A gun, and it was loaded; I should have known Cato wouldn't have traveled alone and unarmed. Papa had taught me how to shoot so we could hunt together. I reckon I remembered enough.

Just as I laid my hand on Cato's papers, he and Papa

emerged from the icehouse. At a distance, I followed them to the front of the house. I noticed that Papa was holding a gun. He untied Cato's hands and ordered him to take off his coat and shirt.

"Papa! Stop!" I called out, trying not to draw the attention of the men in the house. "Papa, I have Cato's papers! Now you have to let him go!"

"Willow?" Papa looked at me like I was a ghost. "You came back to tell me what *I* got to do? I don't have to do nothing! Don't think you coming back here will change my mind."

"But this proves it's against the law to keep him! You can't deny this! Papa, if you let Cato go free, I promise I'll stay here with you and Raymond. I'll do whatever it takes to take care of you and Knotwild properly."

"Willow! Don't say that! Run now!" Cato moaned. "Don't stay for me!"

"Shut up, both of you!" Papa shouted.

"What's going on out here?" Philippe hollered as he stepped out onto the porch with Boss H right behind him. "Why haven't you stripped him down? Where's Silvey?"

Papa and I were both silent, not sure which of us was supposed to answer which question.

"Answer me!" he yelled again.

Papa pushed the gun into the back of Cato's head to get him to take off his coat and shirt.

"Sir, beg your pardon, but Silvey ain't been feeling well. She's sleep," I told him. I was holding Cato's bag and trying to hide his papers at the same time. I wasn't sure what they would do if they saw he had papers—but my gut told me it just might make things worse.

"I'm getting tired of Silvey's laziness," Philippe mumbled. "Hendricks, get me your horsewhip."

I was frozen with fear. The look on Cato's face nearly sent me running to the woods, screaming, but I was locked to the spot.

While Boss H followed his orders, Philippe went up to the house and came back with two lanterns.

"Papa, *please*!" I begged again before they returned, but Papa continued to hold the gun at Cato's head and began to tie him to the bell post. A low, mournful tone escaped from the bell when Papa wrapped the rope around Cato's wrists. Cato did not make it easy for him.

"You can't let them do this! I promise I'll stay here with you, Papa!" My cries fell on deaf ears.

"Gimme that whip!" Philippe slurred. "I'm gonna show you how it's done!"

"It ain't proper for a gentleman to whip a slave, sir! It's beneath your station!" Boss H told him. "I'll do it."

Hendricks tried to work the whip, but he had difficulty since one of his arms was hurt and the other one was drunk. Philippe laughed through it, but it was agony for the rest of us. I don't think Hendricks hurt Cato too bad, but I couldn't tell, since he had turned his face away from me.

"You know what'd be even better?" Philippe finally said, sitting on the ground. "Ryder, you do it. And take that gun from him, Hendricks. I'm not keen on darkies with guns."

Hendricks gave his own gun to Philippe and took the one from my father. Papa dropped his hands and his head when Hendricks handed him the whip.

"I can't . . ." Papa said quietly.

"What?" Philippe demanded. "You damn well can, and I better see you cut some skin!"

"It ain't my place, sir. . . . Rev would want us to leave him alone till he gets back here . . . 'case the boy got papers or something. . . ."

"Papers? I thought he was a fugitive! You already opened up a big chunk of his head, but now you won't whip him?" Philippe said.

"See, he trying to undermine your authority! I told you he's tricky!" Hendricks waved the gun in my father's face.

"I wanted to make sure he didn't get away . . ." Papa began.

"He does have papers!" I shouted, unable to stop myself. I reached into the bag to pull them out. "I found his bag. . . ."

Philippe looked at me as if he had forgotten I was even there. "Oh! Then that makes this even more interesting! Yes, then. Hand them over." He read over the papers quickly, crumpled them into a ball, and threw them aside. "I've seen better forgeries in Baltimore!"

"They're real!" I said defiantly.

"And how would you know what they say?" He raised his eyebrow, pointing his gun at my face. "We'll have a conversation about that later, just you and I. But for now, Ryder — get on with it. I want to see a slave beating a free darkie. What entertainment!"

Papa hesitated.

"If you don't do it, I'll shoot her," Philippe said coldly.

All I could do was stare at the gun in my face as I heard the whip crack once, twice, three times. Each time I heard the whip, I wished that he would pull the trigger, just to release me from this nightmare.

Philippe lowered his gun as he watched my father. I looked toward Cato, and he was watching me. He still looked as proud and brave as the first day I saw him. His eyes told me he had not given up, and neither should I.

Hendricks lowered his gun for a moment in contemplation. "Where'd Raymond get to? He usually comes running whenever I'm around. . . ."

In that moment, when Philippe's attention was on Boss H and Boss H was looking for Raymond, from the corner of my eye I saw Papa strike the whip not at Cato's back, but at the bell pole, not far above Cato's head. I wondered why Papa tied Cato there. Papa had talked so often about replacing that post—how it was cracked and brittle with age and might snap at any strong wind—but for some reason, he never did.

Cato shivered from cold and pain. Part of him wished he might black out again. The worst part to Cato was the humiliation of it all. He kept his eyes turned away from Willow's face so she wouldn't see the fear and embarrassment there. But he couldn't look away when he heard the men talking about her father whipping him, and then Willow telling them that he had papers . . . but he knew it meant nothing to these men. He winced, remembering what his father had said to him before he began his journey, about paper being only made of thin wood. Then he heard his father's voice replacing his angry memories: *Even if they kill you, it'd better be while you standing on your own two feet.*

It made Cato straighten his knees a bit, despite the pain, despite everything. He remembered that he was Atlantus's son, and that made him very proud.

Now he turned to look at Willow. He wanted her to know that nothing could break either of their spirits, nothing could break their bond. One of the men was pointing a gun in Willow's face. Cato's feelings surged as Willow caught his eye, just as he heard the whip crack for a fourth time, heard the splitting of the dry wood above his head. The bell wobbled and he pushed it away from himself instinctively.

As Hendricks raised his arms to protect himself, his gun went off. The bell landed with a clanging thunk on his head, and he crumpled under it.

Philippe howled; Hendricks's gun had shot him in the backside. He fell, waving his gun at all of us.

"You all stay right where you are!" Philippe writhed in pain. "Where's my Silvey? Silvey! I need you!" he cried out.

"You'll never lay your hands on her again!" Willow shouted at him. She reached into Cato's bag and did the very thing Cato had feared most.

Philippe saw me draw the gun from the bag and we both paused.

"*Willow!*" Papa and Cato both shouted my name at the same time, throwing my concentration. Next thing I knew, they were both running in my direction. Cato lunged at Philippe, and Papa jumped between me and Philippe's gun just as it went off. Cato caught Philippe's arm, knocking him out with a quick elbow to the head.

But it was too late. Papa lay there before me, shot straight through his left arm, his blood darkening his shirt. I knelt by him, afraid to move him. "Papa! I'm so sorry. . . . You shouldn't have done that!" I wept. I began to tear off the ruffled hem of my mama's dress to bandage him.

"Don't fret, Mite. It ain't that bad," Papa said softly. "I'd jump in front of another bullet if I had the chance to save you."

"No, Papa! I'll patch you up! You'll come with us!"

"Girl, you all got to get going," he told me as I clung to him. "You don't have time for me."

Cato came and put his arms around me. "He's right, Willow. We have to leave right now if we're ever to have a chance."

"No!" I shouted at Cato, pushing him away. "You go! I'm staying here! I can't leave you like this, Papa!"

He patted my hand as if I were still a small girl. "Stop this, Willow. You know you want to go. You want to be free. I know it, too. I was a fool, thinking I could keep you and your mama, just 'cause I wanted you. I'm not asking you to stay, Mite."

This was my last chance, "Papa, can you please just tell me, what happened to my mother?"

Papa sighed deep. "Rev had decided to sell Adlile. Clarissa was afraid she would keep causing trouble . . . so

I agreed. I thought maybe a few months at another plantation would show her how good she had it here, and Rev would let me buy her back. . . ."

Tears welled up and spilled over his cheeks as he continued. "Me and Rev took her to Taneytown to auction. I remember she was so quiet the whole ride. We didn't tell her what was going to happen, but maybe she knew. It was breaking my heart, but Rev kept saying it was for the best, to keep harmony at Knotwild. Willow, I had to protect you!"

"Papa . . . how could you?" My tears mixed with the blood on his shirt.

"I couldn't! I didn't . . ." he sobbed. "When Rev went to sign the papers for her sale, I begged her to repent, to see she was better off with us. She agreed with me, said she wanted to be a family . . . so I untied her, but I told her if she ran, I'd kill her if she ever tried to take you. I went in to tell Jeff to tear up the papers, but when we came back, she was gone."

"She left me?"

"I know now I didn't give her much choice. She knew you'd be safe with me, but she couldn't be sure for herself if she got sold."

"What did Rev say? Did he know?"

"Yes, he knew."

My head was spinning. My mother might still be *alive*?

"What do you want to do, Willow?" Cato asked gently as he squeezed my shoulders tight.

"There is no choice," Papa said, and kissed my hand.

Cato and I stood, he leaned on me as he put his shirt and coat back on, careful of his wounds. I paused again before we walked away from my father, from Knotwild. I could hear Mayapple's whinny, waiting for us in the distance.

"Don't worry about me. I'm made of good stock!" Papa said, and I almost believed he would be just fine. I held back my tears as we turned away.

"Willow," I heard Papa call as we walked into the woods, "don't forget to write!"

Epilogue

May 12, 1851
Near Barrie, Ontario

Dearest Papa,

    We are Canadians now! It is a hard life but a good life because it is all *ours. We spend most of our evening hours reading, writing, and talking by the fire; so many of our days are spent chopping wood. Our home is simple and close to the town — we are welcomed wherever we go. Mayapple is well. She carried us across the border as though she were the one getting freed! Cholly Dee,*

Silvey, and her brother are safe and live nearby with
baby Agnes, named for Silvey and Little Luck's mother.
The wee thing resembles her father, Philippe, but we
don't hold it against her. I'm sure Mistress Evelyn
would faint to hear it! Although you never met him,
Little Luck is most industrious and provides well for
his sister and niece, with the help of Cholly Dee, whose
mood changed considerably with freedom. He is actually
likable now.

For months we were all the most welcomed dinner
guests of the town, since we had such a fascinating story
to tell. Perhaps one day I will tell it to you in person.

My penmanship has improved and it has proven
useful and lucrative—I am paid to write letters
for those who cannot write themselves. Cato has been
working for the town, drawing maps and planning
future development.

We are also quite busy organizing and funding
others who have "freed themselves," as we say. Cato is
studying the new Fugitive Slave Law, and we've decided
that his father's whole settlement from Pennsylvania
is going to move up here. Yes, all of them—the
preparations have already begun. In the months since the
law was passed to allow slavers to recapture their lost
human property over the Mason-Dixon Line, their town,
Haven, has been raided again and again. This law has

tightened the noose of slavery all the more. I fear it will never end.

With God's help we will perhaps create a new settlement farther west. As my friend Mary Shadd says, "Why stay where we are not wanted?" She is freeborn colored from West Chester, Pennsylvania, and now she's up here writing a book: "A Plea for Emigration," she thinks she'll call it—to encourage more of us to pack up and head north to build anew. Canada offers the only safety for us these days.

Often I wonder if my mother made it this far. . . . Everywhere we go, I ask if anyone knows her. Mary told me a peculiar story once of a woman in her American town who made a daring escape from slavers trying to recapture her after she had already "freed herself" twice. She scaled the fences and walls of the town, Mary said, just to stay free!

I like to think of my mama so daring.

Papa, I do not know if you will ever read this letter. I think of you every day, praying that Tiny cooks your porridge right and that you sleep well. I pray for Rev and everyone at Knotwild. I pray that you will tell them that only the weather is cold here, not the hearts of the citizens. . . . There is a place where we can all live free. . . . Although it is not perfect, it is beautiful. But without you, Papa . . .

"Is that to your father?" Cato asked as I stared into the fire, trying to find the right words to ask my father to join us here in Canada.

He kissed my cheek when I nodded, then went back to reading his law books. To ask my father to leave Knotwild was impossible, I knew. But still, I began this letter every Sunday night, and never finished. I had a dream a month ago that Papa, Rev, Tiny, Rachel and her family, and everyone from Knotwild was planning to come, just like Cato's family.

"I don't know why you do that to yourself," Cato said, seeing me stare into the fire again. "He's a part of Knotwild. He'd rather burn down the old house walls before leave. You know that."

"What else can I do, Cato? Just forget him? Even Cholly thinks maybe there's a chance. . . ."

"Ryder is a slave! In every sense of the word. He was so enslaved that he was willing to enslave others just to have a sense of control."

"Cato, he's my father. And you don't know what it's like to be owned all your life. Especially by family—you don't know what that does to you inside. It ate him up, ate his heart right up. You'll never really understand."

He stood up, and the chair made a horrible screech as he shoved it away to pace in front of the hearth. "Willow, you've asked me to forgive him, but I don't know if I can. I really don't. Not like you."

"I know," I said, coughing deeply. I had asthma regularly now, but Cato was always happy to follow my directions for making Granmam's tea and tinctures. We often joked that we could make a good bit of money selling them at market.

The journey to our cozy Canadian "shanty" lasted almost two cold months, stopping here and there, dependent on strangers for shelter, then another six weeks before we felt safe enough to call one place home. There were times I didn't think we'd make it. We ran for our lives, and it tested our love. We couldn't stay in Haven for more than a few days for fear of being caught. Although I don't think Rev and Papa sent anyone after me or Cholly, we did see a listing in a newspaper that there were slave catchers looking for two young people that nearly matched Silvey's and Little Luck's descriptions. We weren't surprised that Mistress Evelyn and Philippe would be looking to exchange their hides into cash. Whatever excuses Papa gave about what all had happened must've been grand — but I'm sure Rev would've found the letter I left him. He would've known I left on my own, but I've spent many hours pondering if he and Papa would ever be able to reconcile.

I went over to Cato and looked at his profile — the

scars were still there. He still walked with a painful limp. I touched him and waited until he looked into my eyes.

"I don't really think I've forgiven him completely either, especially about my mother. I think maybe if he were here, I'd hate the sight of him. But I'm trying," I said, drawing him into my arms.

"And I'm just asking you to try to keep a *little* space open in your heart for him. 'Cause, Cato, my love, an open heart is the only thing that can keep us free."

Acknowledgments

I couldn't have written this book without the open arms, doors, and hearts of my loving family, friends, colleagues, and students who stayed faithful, understanding, and supportive throughout the last five years.

So many people have given *Willow* their time and energy, perhaps without even knowing, and I am deeply grateful to you all. I would especially like to thank my parents and sister for their unconditional love. I could do nothing without my BFF dream team: Heidi, Margot and Christa, Sienna and Bri, Lakiska, Leyla, Farrah, Ebony, and "The Claires." Hugs to the Mahogany Mavens for reading, rereading, and then asking for more. Thanks also goes to Christina, who, in the homestretch, always made me feel important and beautiful. Also, a big shout-out to all my favorite people and places in West Cape May, New Jersey. RIP, Higher Grounds Cafe!

I'd like to give special thanks to the keen ears and wise heart of E. B. Lewis for listening to so many pages and for always enthusiastically validating my talent and my creative process. This project might not have happened without him!

Finally, my deep appreciation goes to my editor, Katie Cunningham, for always encouraging me to trust my own writing.